"We're going to make love again."

Pepper didn't deny it.

"It's going to happen, whether we want it to or not," Cole continued, "so we might as well agree to explore this out-of-control attraction we have."

"You mean we'll…"

"We'll be lovers," he finished.

Cole heard her breath catch. He touched a finger to her lips. They were moist and soft.

"So, it's a deal?"

"With one stipulation," Pepper said when Cole took his finger away. "Whatever happens on this island stays on this island. When we get back to San Francisco, we go back to our previous relationship."

He leaned forward, unable to resist taking a taste of her lips. "Accepted."

He wasn't going to try to convince her otherwise right now. Not with words. Not when he could use much more persuasive—and pleasurable—means.

"Now, partner, let's find someplace more private," he murmured.

Blaze™

Dear Reader,

How much would you like to escape and have an ISLAND FLING—especially in these months when it looks as if winter will never give up and go away? That's part of the premise that my editor and I discussed when she asked me to participate in this wonderful 24 HOURS: ISLAND FLING miniseries.

So I started thinking and brainstorming with Jo Leigh and Kimberly Raye, the other authors in the series, and we came up with a name—Escapade Island. And that name became the inspiration for my story *When She Was Bad...*

Her aunt Irene's latest *escapade*—stealing a priceless Monet—is the reason ex-debutante Pepper Rossi comes to the island. Her goal is to rescue her aunt and return the Monet to its owners. Only, her plan is derailed by sexy ex-CIA agent Cole Buchanan. Not only is he her biggest rival at work, but he's also the one man who can melt her insides simply by being in the same space with her. And of course, there's one final complication to the premise. The whole story has to take place in 24 hours!

I hope you'll enjoy your stay on Escapade Island and that you'll have fun finding out just how much trouble Pepper and Cole can get themselves into in a single day. (I hope you'll enjoy Aunt Irene's story, too! I had so much fun writing it.) For an excerpt —the prologue—please visit my Web site: www.carasummers.com. You'll also find news about contests and upcoming releases.

Happy reading,

Cara Summers

WHEN SHE WAS BAD...

Cara Summers

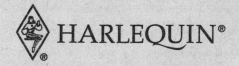

HARLEQUIN®

TORONTO • NEW YORK • LONDON
AMSTERDAM • PARIS • SYDNEY • HAMBURG
STOCKHOLM • ATHENS • TOKYO • MILAN • MADRID
PRAGUE • WARSAW • BUDAPEST • AUCKLAND

To my fellow Blaze writer, Jo Leigh.
When it comes to real-life romance heroines, you are my
inspiration. Congratulations and happiness always!

And special thanks to my cousins-in-law, Ron Sims
and Gary Wilkie, for your inspiration, too.

ISBN 0-373-79243-3

WHEN SHE WAS BAD...

Copyright © 2006 by Carolyn Hanlon.

This edition published by arrangement with Harlequin Books S.A.

www.eHarlequin.com

Printed in U.S.A.

Prologue

IT WAS THE PERFECT night for a burglary.

Pepper Rossi tried to push the paranoid thought away, but it continued to nag her as she peered through the French doors. The small balcony outside the Atwells' penthouse suite was bathed in shadows. The moon, which had been bright and full an hour before during the preview party, was now trapped behind a batch of paralyzed clouds. In Pepper's mind, the whole scene provided an excellent setting for a little second-story work.

Her aunt Irene, the most immediate cause of her paranoia, was the queen of second-story work. As the star of a local reality show—*Are You Safe?*—Irene Rossi broke into the homes of prominent San Franciscans on a weekly basis. And Irene also had a motive for stealing the priceless Monet that Pepper was currently babysitting while the Atwells and their guests were attending a gala performance of the symphony.

But Irene wouldn't actually go so far as to steal a Monet, would she?

A little voice in the back of Pepper's mind shouted, *Yes!*

Don't panic, Pepper lectured herself as she stepped back from the first set of French doors and moved to check the next. So what if the queasy feeling in her stomach was warning her that disaster was imminent? She'd had these premonitions before, and they hadn't *always* panned out.

Just because her aunt had attended the Atwells' preview party for the upcoming charity auction on Sunday night didn't mean that she'd come to case the place. After all, most of the movers and shakers in San Francisco had been invited for a private viewing of the Monet that would be auctioned to benefit the new children's wing at the hospital. The guest list had included Pepper's father who was running for mayor in the fall election, and he'd brought his sister Irene as his guest. Simple as that.

At the next set of French doors, Pepper tested the lock and peered out. Nothing. But she couldn't quite stop worrying about her aunt. Over the years, Irene had been the only one of her Rossi relatives who'd kept in touch with her. There'd been birthday cards, surprise presents and letters, and she'd gotten pretty close to her aunt. That meant she was privy to all the details surrounding Irene's forty-year star-crossed romance with ex-mobster Butch Castellano.

Pepper was aware that during his time in prison, Butch had become a legitimate businessman and was now running a resort in the Caribbean, that he had a weakness for French Impressionist paintings, and that he'd reneged on his promise to allow Irene to join him after his release from prison. Butch's excuse for breaking up with Irene was that he still didn't think he was good enough for her.

She also knew that Irene had taken his excuse literally and was determined to prove that she was bad enough for him.

Would she do something as drastic as steal a priceless Monet? Pepper sent up a little prayer that her aunt wouldn't be so foolish.

Fighting off another wave of queasiness, she dashed into the bedroom. The Monet was still there resting on its easel. Feeling a little better, she crossed to the French doors and checked the lock. It held. She was not going to blow this job. This was her big chance to prove to her brothers that she was a competent PI. And she was. Hadn't she received the highest grade in the PI training class she'd taken?

The problem was that being a PI in a test-taking situation had turned out to be radically different than being a PI in the real world. She'd always been able to ace tests, but so far her career at Rossi Investigations, her brothers' fledgling security firm, could best be described as hit and miss.

And she could lay the blame for that solidly at the feet of Cole Buchanan. Fisting her hands on her hips, Pepper marched out of the bedroom. Cole was ruining everything. Why on earth had he moved to San Francisco and joined Rossi Investigations at the same time that she had? It wasn't fair. Every time she thought about it she wanted to kick something.

Since she'd paid a week's salary for the high-heeled red shoes she was wearing, she resisted the urge.

Instead, she imagined Cole as a rag doll and mentally stuck a pin into his arm. First off, he affected her in a way that no other man ever had. She was certain that she lost brain cells whenever he was near her, starting with the first time they'd ever met at one of her father's weekly family dinners. She'd just arrived in San Francisco and had been anxious to make a good impression on the family she'd just found out she had and was just beginning to know. Everyone who attended Peter Rossi's Sunday dinners was required to bring a dish they'd prepared, and she'd been holding hers, a pasta salad in a newly purchased glass bowl, when Cole Buchanan had walked into the kitchen.

That's when it had happened. It was just as if the man had put a spell on her. The very instant her eyes had met his, her mind had quite simply gone blank. All she'd been aware of was the strangest sensation—an electric jolt that had hit her right smack in her center and radiated through her whole system.

The next thing she'd known, the pasta was lying at her feet with little bits of shattered glass sparkling through it. And that had been just the beginning of the disaster. When she'd knelt to clean up the mess, she'd gotten a shard of glass in her hand. Before she could even react, Cole had lifted her up, settled her on a counter and begun to administer first aid.

If simply looking at him had jolted her system, having him hold her hand had nearly destroyed it. Close up, the man's effect on her had increased to the point that she'd been tempted to kiss him—a man she hadn't even met!

Even now, she could recall that moment when his face had been so close to hers that she could see the color of his eyes, a fascinating mixture of gray and green. And she remembered exactly how his breath had felt on her lips, how that whisper of heat had sent flashes of fire along her nerve endings. And she also vividly remembered the hot coil of desire that had grown inside of her. All she would have had to do was lean a little bit forward and she could have tasted him. The desire to do that had bordered on desperation.

And it still did. Mentally, she plunged a second pin into the rag doll's other arm. Then she forced herself to recheck the French doors in the living room of the suite. Each time she was near Cole Buchanan, the strength of her desire to kiss the man had only increased. It had grown into an obsession. And she couldn't seem to get away from him.

Every time she did some field work, her brothers invariably sent Cole to check on her. The only reason he wasn't here tonight was because Evan Atwell had assured her brothers that he was confident she could handle the Monet babysitting job by herself.

And that was another thing that she could blame Cole for. He'd ruined her romantic life. Evan was such a nice man, and thanks to Cole she'd had to break off her relationship with him. She and Evan had dated for almost three months, but she couldn't in all conscience continue to see him when she felt the way she did about Cole. Even if she was determined never to act on her feelings.

Mentally, she considered a spot for a third pin and decided on a leg and stabbed it in.

Cole Buchanan was the last man on earth she should be attracted to. They were literally as different as night and day. Plus, he just happened to be her biggest nightmare come true. Cole was her brother Luke's best friend from college and her brothers had hired him right after they'd hired her. She'd moved to San Francisco determined to prove to her newly discovered family that she could fit in and the person she had to compete against was a costume and mask short of being a super hero.

He was an ex–CIA agent, and she was an ex–Philadelphia debutante. He was good with guns; her hand shook whenever she picked one up. Oh, she was great at the shooting range, but she didn't think she would ever have the nerve to actually point her weapon at a real person. Cole was trained in hand-to-hand combat; she was enrolled in a karate class. The list went on and on.

It simply wasn't fair. Not only had he ruined her romantic life, but he also stood in the way of her goal of becoming a partner in her brothers' firm. How could they possibly consider her for the position when they could have him?

But in spite of the fact that she was about to stick another pin in him, if Cole Buchanan walked in right now, she'd want to kiss him.

The sudden ringing of her cell phone had her jumping. She grabbed it out of her blazer, dropped it and managed to catch it before it hit the floor. Her heart sank when she saw it was Luke, her oldest brother.

"Is everything okay?" he asked.

"Everything's fine." Except she was mentally obsessing about Cole Buchanan instead of keeping her mind on the Monet. Just to make sure, she ran back into the bedroom to check. The painting was still there on its easel.

"You sure you can handle this alone?" he asked.

She stiffened. "Evan thought that I could."

"Yeah, I know." This comment was followed by an almost inaudible sigh. Pepper knew the tone of that sigh. She'd heard it often enough. It was the same kind of sigh her grandmother had made whenever she'd failed to live up to the responsibility of being a Pendleton.

Thanks to her parents' messy divorce when she was less than a year old, she'd grown up in Philadelphia in her grandmother Pendleton's house, and she'd never so much as seen or talked to her brothers until eight months ago. She wouldn't have even known they existed if her aunt Irene hadn't told her in the letters they'd exchanged. When she'd pressed her grandmother, she'd learned her father had signed her away in the divorce settlement, agreeing not to contact her until her twenty-fifth birthday. He'd kept the boys; her mother had kept her.

According to her grandmother, the Rossis simply hadn't wanted her, and she was better off for it. She'd never fit in with them because she was a Pendleton. Her aunt Irene had claimed that her father had only agreed to the settlement because her mother had asked her father to on her death bed. Pepper suspected that the truth was somewhere in between.

"It's intermission, and I'm just checking in," Luke was saying. What he didn't say—and what she already knew— was that this was a high-profile job for Rossi Investigations. If they screwed up—if *she* screwed up—the news would be in all the papers, and that was not the kind of PR her brothers needed. "There are quite a few French doors in that suite. Not the best set-up when you're guarding a priceless painting."

Pepper lifted her chin. "I am perfectly capable of handling this job."

"Okay, okay," Luke said. "Wait a minute…" For a moment, Pepper could only hear muffled voices. Then Luke said, "Dad wants to know if Irene is there with you."

Pepper felt her stomach sink. "Isn't she with you?"

"She must be around," Luke said. "Dad just hasn't seen her for a while, and intermission is about over. The Stravinsky piece gave her a headache, and he thought she might have headed back to keep you company. You've got me on speed dial, right?"

"You're number one," Pepper assured him, but she was already running toward the balcony doors in the bedroom. All of her earlier paranoia returned in a rush. One glance through the glass panes told her it was too dark to see a thing on the balcony. The clouds still blocked the full moon.

"Better still, call Cole if you need backup."

Pepper frowned. "Why?"

"He's closer." Luke chuckled. "The Stravinsky gave him a headache too, and he left to take a walk."

A suspicion formed in Pepper's mind. Whirling, she raced from the bedroom and headed down the short corridor to the double doors of the suite. The symphony hall was only five blocks away from the hotel. Cole wouldn't come back here to check on her, would he? One glance through the peephole confirmed that he had. Cole Buchanan stood leaning against the wall in the hallway, not ten feet away.

A flood of emotions streamed through her. Resentment, jealousy, anxiety—all of those she'd learned to deal with on a daily basis. But there didn't seem to be anything she could do to block her body's instant response to him. Her pulse was racing, her body melting, as desire tightened hot and hard inside of her. Even worse, she could feel her brain cells coming unglued. She couldn't even get a clear picture of that rag doll anymore.

She certainly tried to analyze her reaction to him. She couldn't deny that he was handsome—if you liked the James-Bond-on-a-scruffy-day type. She evidently did.

But it wasn't just his looks that drew her in. She'd decided that it must have something to do with his size. Whenever she was around him, he seemed to take up more than his fair share of space. Even now, she was aware of those broad shoulders, that long subtly muscled body. He had his arms crossed and her eyes were drawn to his wide-palmed hands and those strong, lean fingers. A tremor moved through her. Every time she saw those hands or pictured them in her mind, she thought about what they might feel like on her skin. Her knees melted.

Dragging herself away from the peephole, she leaned against the wall for a moment. Would those hands move in that slow, easy way he walked—as if they had all the time in the world and intended to take it? Another tremor moved through her. She was getting very, very good at creating this fantasy, and it was getting easier and easier to slip into it.

COLE BUCHANAN DRAGGED himself out of the little fantasy he'd been weaving in his mind and began to pace the hallway. Where Pepper Rossi was concerned, he'd lived on fantasy alone since before he'd even met her. His fascination with her had started the first time Luke Rossi had shown him a picture of her over six months ago. He'd made excuses for himself at the time, blaming the instant attraction on the fact that he was drawn to the whole Rossi family. He'd grown up in the foster care system, and despite that he'd lived with a lot of families, he'd never run into one like the Rossis. Luke had invited him home for that first Thanksgiving twelve years ago, and just like that, they'd welcomed him as if he'd been born a Rossi.

But any thought that his interest in Pepper had more to do with her family than any real connection between them had vanished the first moment he'd laid eyes on her. His lips curved at the memory. He'd watched her walk into one of Peter Rossi's Sunday gatherings, and he hadn't hesitated to follow her into the kitchen to be alone with her. She'd looked into his eyes and he'd felt as if he'd been sucker-punched in the gut. For a moment, his mind had been wiped clean as a slate.

No woman had ever affected him that way. And when she'd dropped that bowl of pasta, he'd had his first inkling that the chemistry between them was operating both ways.

That suspicion had been confirmed while he'd finessed the sliver of glass out of the palm of her hand. She'd begun to tremble. He'd never made a woman tremble before by simply holding her hand. And the pulse at her throat had hammered so frantically that he'd almost kissed her right then and there.

Not only hadn't they been introduced, but she'd come with a date, Evan Atwell, who might have walked in on them at any moment. And that might not have been enough to stop him. Not even the idea that she was his best friend's sister, and that making a move on her might jeopardize his relationship with the only real family he'd ever known, would have kept him from kissing her.

What had stopped him cold was the sudden fear that if he tasted her even once, he might not be able to stop himself from having her. Right there in Peter Rossi's kitchen.

No other woman had ever tempted him that way. Only Pepper.

Turning, Cole glanced at the door to the penthouse suite. That had been his primary reason for deciding to bide his time. If there was one thing he'd learned in life, it was that a man didn't take a flying leap into unknown territory without checking it out and figuring all the angles first. Knowledge was key. So he'd spent some time learning about Pepper Rossi. It hadn't been hard since her brothers had directed him to keep an eye on her.

On the outside, everything about her was militarily neat yet feminine, from the cap of dark hair she wore in a spiky cut to the business suits she favored at the office. The only thing that jarred the image a bit were the ankle-breaking shoes she always wore. Tonight, she'd been wearing strappy red sandals.

He'd never seen her in casual attire—not even at the family dinners her father hosted every Sunday. And he'd never seen her relax or laugh. Even around her family, she always seemed to be "on," as if she was afraid that she would do something wrong. As if she was constantly keeping herself in check.

He'd known about her long separation from her brothers and father and about her close relationship with her aunt Irene.

He'd even flown to Chicago and done some investigating into her past as a Pendleton. On the surface, it would seem she'd lived in the lap of luxury for twenty-four years. But there'd been a down side. Pepper's grandmother, Eleanor Pendleton, was one cold fish, and according to what he'd discovered, she ran her house with the sternness and discipline of a five-star general. Despite that Pepper had graduated first in her class in both high school and college, Eleanor Pendleton had seldom been pleased with her granddaughter.

But the most interesting thing he'd learned about her was that she didn't have much self-confidence, and she often coped with a difficult situation by pretending in her mind that she was someone else. She'd admitted as much to him the day she'd rescued a pet parakeet and then been afraid to climb down from the roof. When she'd finally screwed up the courage to drop into his arms, she confessed that she'd been imagining herself as a trapeze artist.

That was the day that it had finally clicked for him. She'd coped with her move to San Francisco by playing different roles—the good daughter, the perfect sister, the top-notch investigator. That realization had made him even more curious about discovering the real Pepper Rossi.

Cole shoved his hands into his pockets, and once more studied the door to the suite. He had no doubt that she'd spotted him through the peephole by now. If he'd been in there babysitting that Monet, he'd have checked the peephole regularly. She probably thought that Luke or Matt had sent him to back her up. But they hadn't. And he hadn't come back to play guardian angel either. Far from it. The one and only reason he'd come back to the suite was because he wanted Pepper Rossi, and good idea or not, he'd decided to act on his desire.

For six long months, he'd bided his time and it had been pure torture. Just seeing her, being in the same room with her, had been like taking a slow walk over hot, burning coals. He could do nothing to put out the fire, but neither could he escape it.

One kiss. That's what he'd promised himself all during the first part of the symphony. One kiss and at least he'd know if what he'd been fantasizing about for months would be as potent in reality. Of course, it wouldn't hurt to check and see if the Monet was secure. But he wasn't a man who lied to himself. The main reason he'd come back was that he wanted Pepper Rossi. Now.

PEPPER DREW IN A DEEP breath and let it out. Scraping up what strength she had left, she pushed herself away from the wall and moved back into the living room of the suite. This was not the time to indulge in the fantasies that had been plaguing her for six months. She had to concentrate. She had a Monet to guard and a somewhat eccentric aunt who might arrive at any moment to steal it.

Pepper drew in a deep breath and let it out. If her aunt tried to steal the painting, she would handle it the way she'd handled every other challenge in her life. She'd just pretend she was someone else, someone much more competent than Pepper Rossi.

In the six months since she'd joined her brothers' security firm, she'd researched as many fictional female detectives as she could find—Nancy Drew, Kinsey Millhone, V.I. Warshawski.

Her personal favorite detective was Nora Charles, the better half of the *Thin Man* couple. But for tonight, she thought that she'd better opt for Veronica Mars, a TV teen super sleuth, who was always so smart and unflappable— even when family matters intruded.

The one person she couldn't be was herself. Her track record on being Pepper Rossi was not good. At the top of the list was her absolute failure as a daughter; otherwise, her father wouldn't have let her mother and grandmother have her as part of a divorce settlement.

Chin up, Pepper drew in a deep breath and strode once more toward the bedroom. The moment she stepped through the doorway, her premonition of imminent disaster was confirmed in spades. The soft scrape of metal against metal was the first clue, and a moment later, the French doors opened and Irene Rossi strolled into the room.

No alarm sounded.

Pepper stepped directly into her aunt's path and tried to remember who she'd decided to be. Mrs. Thin Man would be pouring a martini right now.

"Aunt Irene." Pepper tried a smile. "How nice to see you. How about a drink?"

Irene shot her a straight, no-nonsense look. "You're a smart girl. You know I didn't come for a drink. I came for the Monet."

Okay, Mrs. Thin Man was out. Raising both hands, palms out, Pepper tried to channel the always reasonable Veronica Mars. "That's not a good idea."

"It's the best one I can come up with. I've waited forty years for Butch Castellano to get out of the slammer." Irene fisted both hands on her hips and tapped one foot. "And now he's decided to live the rest of his life on some isolated island without me? Ha! Not going to happen!"

Pepper searched for the right words, but all she came up with was, "No man is worth committing a felony for."

Irene laughed and patted Pepper's arm. "You haven't met the right man yet. I knew the first time I looked at Butch that he was the only man for me. But I let my own fears and other people's good intentions talk me out of it. I intend to remedy that mistake. Besides, I'm not stealing the painting. I'm only borrowing it for a few days so that I can make my point. I'm going to give it to Butch for Valentine's Day. Deep down he has a romantic streak. That's probably why he's still hung up on some foolish idea that he's not good enough for me. But don't worry. He'd never keep the Monet."

"How can you be so certain?"

"He hasn't done anything illegal in over thirty-five years. He made all his money in the stock market. He's a genius."

Pepper's heart swelled a little at the pride in her aunt's voice. Every time Irene talked about Butch, her face glowed, her voice softened. But there was a part of Pepper that worried her aunt was headed for disappointment. What if Butch had told her the simple truth—that he just didn't want her anymore?

"I don't want you to worry about the painting," Irene

said. "In forty-eight hours, you can recover the Monet and return it to its owner. You'll be a hero, your brothers will thank you, and I'll be living happily ever after in paradise."

Pepper thought frantically. Her aunt's scenario would probably make a good movie—if Brad Pitt and Julia Roberts starred in it. But things rarely worked out that neatly in real life. "What if Butch doesn't get your point?"

Irene's eyes narrowed. "He'll get it. Believe me."

"You could end up in jail."

"Nah. I've got a backup plan."

Pepper wished that she had one. Pulling her gun would be a waste of time. Her aunt would laugh. Pepper had lamented to her aunt on more than one occasion about what a ninny she was when it came to the idea of actually shooting her firearm at a real person. Desperate, she tried a bluff. "I'm not here alone. Cole is here."

"No, he isn't. I checked all the rooms through the French doors. There are way too many of them, by the way. Your brothers never should have allowed the Atwells to hold their preview party here. They're practically begging to have the painting stolen."

"I'm serious, Aunt Irene. Cole is outside in the hallway. He could come in at any minute."

"I'll just have to hurry, won't I?" Irene scooted around her and lifted the painting off the easel.

Before Pepper could think of another tack to take with her aunt, the doorbell of the suite chimed. Her stomach took a lurch deep into the queasy zone. "That's Cole."

"Go out there and distract him."

"And just how do you expect me to do that? He's here to check up on me. Nobody trusts me to be able to safeguard this painting, and Cole will be in here like a shot."

Irene sent her an exasperated look. "There's an age-old way for a woman to distract a man. And it works every time. Just kiss him. I only need five minutes."

"Five minutes? Aunt Irene—"

"You want to kiss him, don't you?"

She opened her mouth to answer—to argue, to agree, she wasn't quite sure—but her aunt was already at the French doors.

The doorbell chimed again.

"Go," Irene turned back. "Time is crucial here. I'm not the only one who's trying to steal this Monet. I ran into another guy on the roof. At least if *I* take the painting, the Atwells will get it back."

"Another guy? Who?" Pepper asked.

"I didn't ask. I shot him with a tranquilizer."

"A tranquilizer?"

"I carry them with me when I do my show—in case I run into unfriendly dogs."

The doorbell chimed for the third time, and Pepper knew she had to make a decision. Short of shooting her aunt, Pepper didn't see any way of stopping her.

"Hurry," Irene said. "I need time to climb back up to the roof."

Turning, Pepper hurried out of the bedroom, slamming the door behind her, and raced for the double doors. One quick glance through the peephole told her that Cole was indeed the person ringing the doorbell. The moment that she let him into the suite, he would want to check on the Monet. And Irene's advice was repeating itself in her mind over and over and over. *Just kiss him. Just kiss him. Just kiss him.*

Releasing the bolt, she opened the door.

Cole let his gaze take in the suite. "Everything okay?"

"Fine." To her horror, she didn't sound fine. Her voice had come out in a squeak. She sounded like Minnie Mouse.

Cole frowned. "What is it?"

When he moved past her in the direction of the bedroom, Pepper tried her best to block out the chant in her head and said the first thing that came into her head. "It's you."

He kept walking.

Later, she would try to analyze what made her do it. It wasn't just desperation to save her aunt. It was something more.

She shot after him and grabbed his arm, pulling until he turned to face her. "You're what's wrong with me. I'm tired of the way you make me feel when you walk into a room."

Cole gave her an intent look. "And just how do I make you feel?"

Pepper's heart pounded. Her mind raced. She was almost sure she was going to hyperventilate. "It all started in Peter's kitchen. Now every time you walk into a room, I can't think of anything but kissing you. I want it to stop. So maybe we ought to just kiss and get it over with."

She saw a flicker of surprise in his eyes, but it couldn't hold a candle to her own. She'd had no idea those words were going to come out of her mouth. Now she had no idea how to take them back.

IF PEPPER ROSSI had slapped him across the face, Cole Buchanan would not have been more surprised. He'd known she was smart. Was she intuitive too? Had she spotted him through the peephole and read his mind?

The more rational side of his mind told him, no, she was up to something. But his body paid no attention to his brain. He was already stepping closer so that their bodies were nearly touching.

A shiver moved through her, but it wasn't fear he saw in her eyes. It was a mix of desire and nerves, almost exactly what he was feeling. But still he hesitated. This was what he'd come for, but the rational side of his brain reminded him that nothing that came this easily could be trusted.

"Don't you want to kiss me?" Pepper didn't wait for his answer. Instead, she closed the little distance that was left between them, placed her hands on his shoulders and rose onto her tiptoes. It was her scent that hit him first, something that reminded him of hot tropical nights. Her wide, amber-colored eyes were the next thing that registered in the rational part of his mind. When he dropped his gaze to her mouth, his rational mind began to shut down. Her lips were parted, moist, waiting...

But what little was left of his brain was still suspicious. The Pepper he'd come to know in the last few months was wary of him. This woman was... Suddenly it clicked. She was playing a role.

"Who are you pretending to be?" he asked.

"What?" Her eyes widened and became wary.

Bingo. "You're pretending to be someone else, and I want to know who I'm kissing."

She met his eyes steadily. "I was going for Angelina Jolie. I figured she might be your type."

The corners of his mouth curved. He reached out

and gently rubbed his thumb over her bottom lip. So lush. "Not even close. I've never had a fantasy about kissing *her*. What if I told you I came back here just to kiss you? That I've been dreaming of kissing you since you dropped that bowl of pasta?"

Her breath hitched and surprise now mixed with the desire he saw in her eyes. Satisfied, he framed her face with his hands. In some part of his mind, he registered that her skin was even softer and her hair even silkier than he'd dreamed. But all of his attention was on her mouth.

Leaning down, he brushed his lips against hers. It wasn't a kiss, just the barest pressure of his mouth to hers, yet his blood began to pound in his head.

When he drew back, she moistened her lips with her tongue as if she hadn't gotten enough of his taste. Heat shot through him. He wanted more of her too. Unable to resist, he sampled her lower lip with his tongue, then drew it into his mouth and nipped it. Pleasure clouded her eyes and her pulse quickened beneath his thumb at her temple.

Hunger for her rose with a speed that shocked him. He was just going to kiss her, he reminded himself. They were here on a job. But he only had to press his mouth to hers again for his intention to change. One more taste was all it took, and without another thought, he plunged them both deeper.

He wasn't a man who particularly liked surprises, but this seemed to be his night for them. He'd thought he'd known what she would taste like, but her flavor was more sinfully sweet than he'd anticipated. The deeper he probed, the darker and richer it grew. Her response was unexpected too. Her nails dug into his shoulders, and her mouth was as greedy, as avid, as his. He'd sensed the passion held in check beneath that pressed and polished exterior, but this was more. She was more than he'd anticipated. He only had to cup her bottom with his hands and she scooted up, wrapping her arms and legs around him.

What astonished him most was his response to her. He'd never been so aware of a woman before—the press of that small, strong body against his and the husky sound of her voice when she said his name triggered explosions of pleasure that went far beyond any fantasy he'd been able to conjure up. His blood had burned before but never quite like this. And control—he never lost it—never. But he could feel it slipping as surely as he could feel the synapses disconnecting in his brain. When she arched against him and began to rub against his hardness, something inside him snapped.

One thought streamed through him. He wanted her and he could have her. Now. The certainty of that, the power of it, shot through him and he moved toward the bedroom. Once he had her pressed against the door, his hands began to move of their own accord, unfastening her slacks and his own. When he'd finally dragged hers off, some dim corner of his mind cleared enough to remember the Monet, the job.

"The painting," he murmured as he lifted her again. "We'll finish this in the bedroom where the Monet is."

He lifted her again and opened the door. But he didn't step over the threshold. Even in the darkness of the room's interior, he could see that the easel was empty and the door to the balcony stood open.

As his blood cooled and his mind cleared, Cole was pretty sure of one thing. He was holding the thief's accomplice in his arms.

1

PEPPER SCANNED Escapade Island's small airport, but the miracle she'd been praying for didn't occur. There was no sign of Irene or the Monet. As per usual, her plan to become Pepper Rossi, super sleuth, was not going well.

This time she couldn't in all conscience lay the blame at Cole Buchanan's feet. If she'd been distracted during the past few days because she couldn't pry him loose from her thoughts, she had no one to blame but herself. She'd started what had happened in the penthouse suite. She'd acted, as usual, on impulse and gotten in way over her head. Acting without thinking things through was a flaw that her grandmother Pendleton had initially pointed out to her when she was about four. And Pepper knew the accompanying lecture by heart. Trouble was, she mostly ignored it, so she'd been a constant disappointment to her grandmother. The end result was that she'd left Chicago. Moving to San Francisco was a golden opportunity to start fresh and to finally fit in with a family. But now the same thing was threatening to happen with the Rossis. She was screwing up, and she couldn't seem to fit in with them either.

And kissing Cole Buchanan hadn't been her only impulsive act two nights ago. She'd also helped her aunt steal a priceless Monet. And now she'd lost track of both.

"Please, God." She repeated the prayer that she'd been sending up on a regular basis during the commuter flight to Escapade Island. "I promise, if you'll just let me find Irene and recover the Monet, I'll never do another impulsive thing in my life. Really."

Quickening her pace, she threaded her way through her fellow deplaning passengers, trying to ignore the headache that pounded at full throttle behind her eyes. Tailing people had been one of her strengths in the PI course she'd taken. Still, she'd lost Irene in the crowd at the Miami airport. She hadn't panicked because she figured that her aunt would eventually board the connecting flight to Escapade Island. But it was a tall man, speaking with a French accent, wearing a beret and sporting a goatee, who'd taken the final empty seat just before takeoff.

Pepper skidded to a stop and barely missed crashing into the couple in front of her. They'd stopped to embrace. She wasn't sure if it was the clinch or the fact that they were wearing long trench coats, but several other people had slowed down or stopped to watch them. This close, she could see that they were older than they'd seemed at a distance—in their seventies, she figured. Well, more power to them, she thought as she dodged to her left and sped around the small crowd that was gathering.

She had to figure out why Irene had missed the flight. Her first thought was that her aunt had spotted her in the Miami airport and changed her plans. But that didn't make sense. First of all, Pepper had disguised herself in a blond wig and jeans. Irene had never seen her in either. Ladies never wore jeans. Grandmother Pendleton had drilled that into her at a very early age. And jeans had been forbidden at the exclusive boarding school she'd been sent to for high school. It had been part of her grandmother's attempt to turn her into a lady like her mother, but it hadn't exactly paid off.

Pepper wished that she could remember her mother. All she really had to go on were the stories that her grandmother had told her of how perfectly her mother had always acted in any situation. So far, she hadn't had the courage to pump her brothers or her father about her mother. She would—once she felt more comfortable around them…once she fit in.

Glancing up, Pepper caught her reflection in the glass wall that ran the length of the airport. Except for the strappy red high-heeled sandals, she barely recognized herself. The thin gold hoops at her ears had been a last-minute addition to the disguise. According to her grandmother, a true lady wore studs. The Jackie O sunglasses and a small black duffel she'd slung over her shoulder completed the outfit. She barely recognized herself, so there was no way that Irene had "made" her.

But even if she had, her aunt wouldn't have changed her plans. In the letters that her aunt had sent her over the years, Pepper had come to know her pretty well. And she'd come to admire the fact that once Irene had a goal, she went after it full throttle. That was how Irene had gotten her own TV show. And when the ratings had dropped during the first season, Irene had broken into the mayor's mansion to prove that even the "best" security system had its flaws. If Irene was hell-bent on giving the Monet to Butch Castellano on Valentine's Day, which was tomorrow, she'd let nothing and no one stand in her way.

Pepper was holding on to that thought. On the bright side, Evan Atwell's mother had decided not to report the theft to the authorities. That would have meant canceling the charity auction, and she didn't want to do that until she had to. Too much time and planning had gone into it, she'd claimed. Instead, Althea Atwell was going to give Rossi Investigations until Sunday, the day of the charity auction, to recover the painting. She wanted the Monet back, and she expected the team at RI to get it. There'd been the threat of a law suit if they weren't able to produce the Monet by Sunday. But even without a lawsuit, if the news was made public that the painting had been stolen while Rossi Investigations was on the job, the bad publicity might ruin her brothers' fledgling business.

Luke and Matt hadn't spoken one word of reproach to her, but they'd been clearly disappointed. They'd encouraged her to take a few days off. The subtext was that they didn't want her help, and she could hardly blame them.

She hadn't told anyone—neither the police nor her brothers—about Irene's involvement. If Luke and Matt had known about it, they would have stopped her aunt from flying to Escapade Island to give the painting to Butch. As much as Pepper loved her brothers, she hadn't been able to betray her aunt. But she hadn't told Irene she was following her to the island either. She wasn't as sold on Butch Castellano's born-again honesty as her aunt was, and one way or another she was going to make sure that the painting got back to San Francisco by Sunday night. And then—she shot a glance heavenward—she was definitely going to mend her impulsive ways.

Striding into the main room of the airport, Pepper glanced at her watch again and for the first time the date registered. Her stomach plummeted, and her headache accelerated into the chaotic rhythm of kettle drums.

Today was Friday the thirteenth.

No wonder she'd lost her aunt. If her luck went the way it usually did, Irene's disappearance was just the first thing that would go wrong today. In her experience, bad luck always came in threes.

When someone plowed into her from behind, Pepper stumbled and felt herself grabbed and steadied.

"Sorry, ma'am. You all right?"

Turning, she found herself looking up into the eyes of a tall man wearing a cowboy hat. "Yes. I'm fine."

"Glad to hear it." Then he touched the brim of his hat. "My lady's getting away from me." Stepping around her, he lengthened his stride, and Pepper caught a glimpse of a woman beating a fast path to the exit sign.

It occurred to her then that almost everyone on the flight had been part of a couple, including the trench coat couple who'd stopped traffic. Hardly surprising, she thought. On the Internet, Escapade Island advertised itself as the perfect vacation spot for lovers, and tomorrow *was* Valentine's Day. The flight attendants on the plane from Miami had been really into the spirit of the holiday. There'd been streamers and plump little cupids decorating the cabin, and they'd even passed out chocolate hearts wrapped in red and pink foil.

As usual, she was without a current lover. In fact, she'd been without one for some time. Of course, she'd nearly managed to catapult herself out of the celibate state when she'd kissed Cole two nights ago.

But she wasn't going to think about that—much—until she'd recovered the Monet.

Before that, her last serious and intimate relationship with a man had been in college, and it had ended when Bobby Caswell had graduated a year ahead of her and gone back home to marry his high school sweetheart. She'd thought she'd been in love. And Bobby had definitely been in love—with another woman.

Naturally, she'd been a little man shy after that. In Philadelphia, she'd gone out with a string of eligible bachelors that her grandmother had selected, but she'd never quite clicked with any of them. Those relationships had rarely lasted beyond the first date. And even though she'd gone out with Evan Atwell for almost six months, their relationship had never progressed beyond the platonic stage.

Of course, she'd broken things off with him at the three-month stage, but for some reason he'd still wanted to "date" her. She thought it had something to do with the fact that his mother had approved of her, and he wanted some time to break the news to her. And truth be told, continuing to date Evan had given her a shield against Cole. As long as she was officially dating Evan, she hadn't had to face what she was going to do about what she felt for him.

It didn't take a super sleuth to recognize a pattern in her history with men. It was the history of her life. She never measured up.

As a result, she was sex starved.

That was the only explanation she could see for the way she'd responded so...explosively to Cole Buchanan's kiss. In the past day and a half, she'd given it some careful thought—even though she'd vowed not to think about it—and she'd figured it out. Cole had wanted her. It was only natural that she'd be attracted to that. And she'd wanted him. She'd known that from that very first moment in her father's kitchen. So the explosion had occurred. She'd aced her chemistry classes, so she should have foreseen it and been more prepared. She would be if he ever kissed her again.

Pepper frowned as she dashed around yet another strolling couple. Dammit, she was thinking about that kiss again. In the last day and a half, she hadn't been able to get it out of her mind. Nor could she stop fantasizing about what might have happened if Cole hadn't discovered that the Monet was gone.

Grimly, she pushed those fantasies out of her mind. Reality check. Number one, the Monet was missing. Two, her aunt was missing. Three, she had to recover both of them. Kissing Cole Buchanan was not on her current to-do list.

Not that the opportunity for another kiss was going to present itself anytime soon. She hadn't even seen Cole since that night. He hadn't been at the office yesterday, hadn't tried to contact her.

Obviously, the experience hadn't been memorable for Cole at all. Perhaps that flood of desire was a common occurrence for him. He was probably used to getting swept away like that. Or maybe the experience hadn't been mutual. Perhaps *he* hadn't been swept away.

Damn. She stepped out of the stream of passengers and steadied herself against a nearby wall. Just thinking about that kiss was all it took for the sensations to come streaming back. She pressed the heel of her hand against her heart to still the hammering, and she drew in a deep breath as heat flooded her body and melted her bones. No man had ever made her feel so wanton, so weak, so…incredible.

And she wanted so much to feel that way again—to see

where those sensations would lead. Pressing her hand to her stomach, she concentrated on breathing. Thank heavens she'd gotten away from San Francisco. If she'd run into Cole again, she wasn't sure she could keep her impulsive side—that part of her she'd learned she must control—in check.

Stop thinking about it. Pepper drew in another deep breath, stiffened her spine, and pushed herself away from the wall. Information. That's what she needed. Knowledge was power. Irene had missed the flight, so she'd be on the next one to the island. If nothing else, her aunt was resourceful. Plus, she'd committed grand larceny for an old boyfriend, so she would hardly let a missed flight get in the way of giving the Monet to him.

Striding through an archway, Pepper scanned the main room of the airport. It was high-ceilinged and open to the air on one side. Here and there cement planters bulged with huge red flowers and smaller orange and pink ones. Pepper was abruptly and completely charmed. She didn't think she'd seen either species of flower before, and she was sure she hadn't experienced the scent—something between the exotic aroma of gardenia and the innocence of lily of the valley.

Of course, she'd never seen anything like this island before either. The bird's-eye view from the plane had looked like a carefully constructed movie set. A blue lagoon snaked through the forest of palm trees that covered almost half of the island. From what she could see, the hotel offered rooms with balconies that overlooked the ocean, as well as separate little thatched-roof bungalows along stretches of white sand beaches.

But it was the surrounding sea itself that fascinated her.

She turned to the open side of the room and took another look at the water now. She'd seen the Pacific, but even on the sunniest day, it had never been this shade of turquoise. While she waited for Irene to arrive on the next plane, she might walk over and check it out.

Information, she reminded herself. Scanning the room again, she saw uniformed agents standing behind a counter, checking in luggage and handing out boarding passes to departing visitors. There were lines, and she didn't have time for them. Finally, she spotted what she was looking for. Beneath a large round clock stood a young tall man wearing white shorts and a blue flowered shirt. The counter in front of him sported a banner that read, Welcome to Escapade Island…Where Pleasure Is Limitless.

Crossing her fingers, Pepper sent up another silent prayer as she strode toward the counter. *Please let me find Aunt Irene and get the Monet back to the Atwells. And let that happen today. Please.* Her experience was that the more specific she made her prayers, the more likely they were to be answered in a timely fashion.

When she reached the counter, she noted that the tall man standing behind it had a pleasant face and a smoothly shaved head. His name tag read Gari and when he glanced up from the book he was reading, he beamed a smile at her.

"Welcome to Escapade Island, miss. My name is Garibaldi, but I go by Gari." He ran a head over his head, and his grin widened. "My friend Reynaldo said that if I didn't nickname myself, I might get stuck with Baldy, so I went with Gari. How do you like our island?"

"It's lovely." Charmed by the young man's enthusiasm, Pepper found herself smiling back. His voice had a musical lilt to it and a slight accent that she couldn't quite place. British? Because the counter was a bit high, she placed her hands on it and raised herself even higher up on her tiptoes. "Are you from the island?"

"No, I'm a transplant from Miami. My friend Reynaldo was hired to run the specialty gift shop in the hotel, and I came with him. Now, I'm hooked. I mean, why leave paradise?" He waved a hand, and although she hadn't thought it possible, his smile brightened.

Pepper found her gaze moving back to the sea. "It reminds me of a movie set."

"Oh, it's real all right." Reaching beneath the counter, he handed her a small booklet. "Originally, this island was home to one of the largest sugar plantations in the area. This little book gives the history of the island and of some of the people who lived here."

"Thanks." Tearing her gaze away from the sea, Pepper took the book and tucked it in her duffel.

"Now tell me what I can do to make your stay a more pleasant one."

"My aunt. She missed the plane from Miami."

"Not to worry." Gari beamed a smile at her. "There'll be another plane tomorrow."

"Tomorrow? You're joking."

"No, ma'am. There's only one flight a day from the mainland."

"That's...I...she has to get here today."

Gari chuckled. "No problem. Here on the island, tomorrow is as good as today."

"No. Tomorrow is very definitely a problem." Even as her mind raced, Pepper's heart sank. *Friday the Thirteenth, Part II.* That had to be it. "I need to get back to Miami. I have to find my aunt."

"Today's flight back to the mainland is booked. And there are several people ahead of you on standby."

"But my aunt…she can't wait until tomorrow."

"Now, don't you worry, miss. Whatever is worrying you will wait. You'll see. Time has a different flavor here on the island, and what seemed so important on the mainland will soon matter very little on Escapade Island. Take one walk on the beach and you'll see what I mean."

Pepper's gaze shifted to the sea again. The strength of her desire to take off her sandals and walk on that white, white sand surprised her. She couldn't ever recall being drawn to a beach before. Certainly not in Philadelphia where she'd grown up, and not in San Francisco either. She'd always had way too many things to do. Pleasing her grandmother and now proving herself to her brothers and her father had taken all of her time and concentration. Especially with the amount of time she had to spend on damage control when she screwed up.

She didn't have time now either, she reminded herself. She had a Monet to recover. If she had an inner beach bunny struggling to emerge, it would have to wait its turn. Right now, she'd better channel Veronica Mars, girl super sleuth, again. Turning back to Gari, she upped the wattage on her own smile. "That sounds delightful, but—"

"It does sound delightful."

Pepper jumped. Even before she whirled around, she recognized the voice. Sure enough, Cole Buchanan was standing behind her. Panic erupted. She thought of running. But she had no doubt that if she bolted, he'd catch her. And this was an island. How far could she run?

"Good decision," he said as though reading her mind, his hand closing around her upper arm.

Just that one touch had ribbons of heat unfurling up her arm. Fighting the sudden melting sensation that threatened to paralyze her, Pepper searched her mind for something to say. No use pretending that he'd made a mistake. Clearly, he'd seen through her disguise.

So…what did you say to a man you'd nearly made love to after one kiss? That you definitely would have made love to him if a Monet hadn't been snatched from right under your nose? That you still wanted to make love to him? The adrenaline coursing through her veins wasn't just panic, she realized. She still wanted to jump the man. Pushing down the feelings now churning in her stomach, she smiled at him and said the first thing that came into her mind, "Of all the gin joints in all the world…"

Gari chuckled. "*Casablanca,* right? You have to meet my friend Reynaldo. He's a movie buff, too."

Cole's lips didn't so much as twitch.

"I gather you two know each other," Gari said.

"Yes." Cole and Pepper spoke in unison.

"That's wonderful," Gari said. "No lady this lovely should be alone on Escapade Island, especially this weekend. We're celebrating Valentine's Day in a big way." Pulling out two tickets from beneath the counter, he handed them to Cole. "Those are good for two free drinks at the poolside café. Come down as soon as you get settled. I work the one to nine o'clock shift." He winked at Cole. "Valentine's Day was invented for lovers, and this is not a lady who should be alone."

"She won't be," Cole said.

Pepper's mind was racing. What was Cole doing on Escapade Island? One thing she knew for sure—the answer wasn't going to be good. It took some effort, but she kept her eyes on his—at least what she could see of them behind amber-colored sunglasses.

Cole still didn't return her smile. "Shall we go?" Without waiting for a reply, he drew her toward the exit.

Friday the thirteenth had struck its third blow, Pepper decided. Didn't that mean that her luck had to change?

COLE HAD TO HAND IT to her. For one minute, he'd been sure she was going to cut and run, but she hadn't. Neither had she caused a scene in front of the beaming Gari, and she hadn't protested when he'd drawn her out of the airport and helped her into the little convertible he'd rented from the island agency. Pepper Rossi had class. That was one of the things that had drawn him to her in the first place.

Damned if he didn't admire her guts too. The line from *Casablanca* had nearly made him laugh. But his reaction to seeing her again wasn't a laughing matter. Even in the blond wig and the low-slung jeans, he'd picked her out of the crowd of deplaning passengers. Of course, he'd been looking for her, and her petite build was one clue, the ankle-breaking shoes another. Plus, she was one of the few passengers who hadn't been part of a couple.

But even before the rational side of his brain had picked up on all those details, his body had responded to her, heating the way it always did. Blindfolded, he'd know when she walked into a room, and from the very first, he'd never been able to completely control the effect that she had on him.

Even now and even despite that she'd helped someone steal that Monet right out from under his nose, he still wanted her. And he had a hunch that her partner in crime was none other than her boyfriend, Evan Atwell. The jealousy that he'd always felt whenever he'd seen Pepper in Evan's company had sharpened, slicing through him like a knife, when he'd figured it out.

He'd spent some time puzzling through it, but so far it was the only theory that fit all the pieces. Oh, he didn't have all the details pinned down quite yet, but greed was a prime motive, and collecting the insurance at the same time that you sold the Monet to a private collector who didn't care much about the law was one way to have your cake and eat it too.

Once you looked at it, the evidence was all there. Evan had insisted that Pepper handle the security arrangements for the Monet by herself. Then there was the fact that she'd made a move on him the moment he'd walked into the suite. Whatever his intentions had been when he'd come there from the symphony, she'd initiated the kiss. But what had nailed the theory for him was his discovery that both Pepper and Evan Atwell had booked airline tickets to an island owned by a French Impressionist collector immediately following the theft.

He flicked her a brief glance. She might look innocent, but there wasn't a doubt in his mind that she was guilty as sin. Pepper Rossi had a reputation for getting herself in trouble, but this was the deepest hole she'd dug yet. And she'd done it for another man.

But, somehow, knowing that didn't seem to diminish the fact that he still wanted her. Desperately. In the day and a half since he'd last seen her, his desire for her had only grown. He'd had a taste, and similar to Adam's experience with the apple, he wanted more. And he'd have it just as soon as he straightened the mess she'd gotten herself into.

She wanted him too. Whatever her motives for kissing

him in the penthouse suite, she hadn't faked her response. And she wanted him right now. The moment she'd turned to face him in the airport, he'd seen the pulse beating at her throat. He knew that pulse. For six months, he'd seen it quicken every time he was near her, and watching her respond to him like that, knowing that at least something of what he was feeling was reciprocated, had made it almost impossible for him to bide his time and keep his distance. It was going to make it pure hell to resist her now.

Easing the car to a stop, Cole turned to study her as he waited for an old man to lead a cow across the road. The disguise was a good one. He'd never seen her wear anything but the most conservative suits and jewelry to the office. He suppressed the urge to reach out and trace the gold hoop in her ear.

With any woman other than Pepper Rossi, he would have been able to develop a strategy. He was good at that. It had been his ticket for survival in the foster care system. With each new family, he'd studied them, learning as much as he could, and then he'd developed a strategy for fitting in. Role-playing had been key. But he hadn't yet figured out a strategy for dealing with Pepper Rossi. From the moment he'd first laid eyes on her, he hadn't been sure of his moves. The last time a woman had made him this wary, he'd been fourteen and she'd been sixteen. But even then, he hadn't taken long to figure it out.

Six months hadn't helped him figure out how to handle Pepper, partly due to the fact that he could never quite predict what she would do. Like that kiss.

When the cow finally made it to the other side of the road, he eased the car into gear and drove forward. One thing he did know, in a battle, forewarned was forearmed.

He was not going to let what he felt for Pepper Rossi interfere with recovering the Monet. The Rossis had done so much for him over the years—

"Why are you here?" she asked.

He shot her a brief glance as he turned the car onto the narrow road that wound along the coast. She was looking straight ahead, blond hair blowing in the wind, chin lifted, hands clasped tightly in her lap. He'd seen her sit the same way at meetings with her brothers and at family dinners with her father. She was wound up tight as usual. Not good, because that too was one of the things that drew him to her. Because he badly wanted to see what would happen when she came unwound. Now that he'd had a sample, he was going to have more.

"I'm here to save your pretty little ass."

2

IRENE CAME AWAKE SLOWLY, her mind surfacing and then drifting under again. The dreamy sensation was so pleasant that she postponed opening her eyes. Far away, she heard the thrum of a motor and there was a scent she couldn't quite place—something spicy and…male. It had been a long time since she'd woken up with a man in her bed.

A sudden thump jarred every bone in her body. She opened her eyes and looked around. Bits and pieces of reality floated like bubbles into her mind. The first one popped. She wasn't in bed at all. She was on a plane, and she could see a forest of palm trees and a long one-story building through the small window to her right. Beyond that she saw a stretch of turquoise-blue sea, bright enough to make her blink. Beautiful.

"Are you feeling better?"

Irene jerked around to face the man who'd spoken. Her first impression was that she was looking at one of the seven dwarves. Did that make her Snow White? Good Lord, she hoped not. She shook her head a little to clear it, but her impression of the man next to her didn't change. The dwarf had blue eyes, thinning white hair and a beard, a weathered looking face and he was radiating joviality.

"I'm Happy Johansson."

Perfect name for a dwarf, she thought as she shook his hand. "I'm Irene. And you should think about toning down that cologne."

"You think?" A few extra lines appeared on her seatmate's forehead.

As Irene glanced around the plane, another of the bubbles in her head burst. The last thing she recalled was being in the Miami airport. She'd bought a book and then slipped into the bar to grab a beer… After that, everything was hazy. Obviously, she'd gotten on the commuter flight to Escapade Island, but the details of that were very vague. She could only seem to conjure up bits and pieces. Had she been in a wheelchair? That couldn't be right. She'd never been in a wheelchair in her life.

"It isn't really a cologne," the man next to her was saying. "It's the pheromone extract they sent us with the welcome letter."

"What welcome letter?" she asked.

"I got mine right after I booked the weekend. And I used the exact amount that they suggested. I could use all the help I can get. Look around. There's going to be a lot of competition."

"Competition?" Irene scanned the people in the row across the aisle. The two men looked tanned and buff and a good thirty years her junior. The bronze-skinned Amazon in the aisle seat ahead of them was wearing khaki shorts, an animal print tank, and a gold snake bracelet on her upper arm. Sheena, queen of the jungle, Irene thought.

Happy nodded. "I figure at my age I have to try harder."

No shit, Irene thought. Just then, another of the bubbles in her head popped. She'd been in the Miami airport to change planes on the way to Butch's island. She was going to give the Monet to him as a Valentine's Day present, and if that didn't bring him to his senses, she was just going to have to jump him. Feeling much better, she glanced around the plane again. Why were the details of boarding the plane so fuzzy?

"Have you been to Camp E.D.E.N. before?"

"Camp E.D.E.N." Irene tried the word out but it didn't scare up a memory. "No, I've never even heard of it."

Butch had named his island Escapade. They'd chosen the name together just before he'd been released from prison. She recalled how thrilled he'd been. She'd read and reread that letter he'd sent telling her how much he'd valued her friendship over the years, how much he wanted it to continue. Butch wasn't a man who'd had a way with words, so she'd treasured each little thing he'd said in it— and in the next letter too when he'd told her how proud he was of what she'd made of her life during his time in prison. Then had come the letter telling her that he didn't want her to join him on the island until the resort was finished. He wanted to surprise her. So she'd gone along with that—until she'd gotten the final "Dear Jane" letter a month ago. Now, in retrospect she saw that all the earlier letters were just preludes to the one that would tell her he thought it was best that they cancel their plans to get together, that he didn't want to see her, didn't want her to come and join him on the island as they'd planned. They had to face the simple fact that they were just too different and that he wasn't and never would be good enough for her.

Even now, Irene got furious just thinking about it. Butch Castellano had dumped her. It had been bad enough when her parents had gotten him to agree to dump her forty years ago. Maybe they had been wrong for each other then. After all, he'd been climbing the ladder in a crime family, and she'd been about to go to college. In the end, she'd agreed to the separation, which had extended to forty years when he'd been sent to an upstate New York prison. But they'd kept in touch over the years, and he'd gone straight. Every cent that he'd earned to build his resort had come from legitimate sources. And her feelings for Butch had never diminished; in fact, they'd grown. They'd made plans, and she'd waited for him.

And now he'd dumped her. Dumped her after forty years. A sudden thought occurred to her. Had he changed the name of the island as one final message to her that their lifelong relationship was indeed over?

As the plane taxied to a stop, Irene considered that possibility. He'd certainly changed his mind about her and about the life they'd planned to have together. She pressed her fingers to her temple and tried to will away the panic that was threatening to erupt.

Happy took her hand. "It's my first experience with a sex camp, too. And I'm ripe for the picking."

Snatching her hand away, Irene stared at him. "Sex camp?" Panic threatened again. Butch might have decided she was too good for him, but he would not be building a sex camp on his island. "This is the first I've heard about a sex camp. What are you talking about?"

"Oh, it's nothing to be worried about. The woman who runs the place is a bit overwhelming at first, but I understand that the whole purpose of the camp is to allow you to explore your inner sex god or goddess. Discovery and experimentation are the key words. And you don't have to participate in the group sex if you feel uncomfortable."

"Group sex?" This definitely wasn't Butch's island, Irene decided. "I'm not going to any sex camp. I'm going to the Escapade Resort."

Happy leaned closer. "What's in a name? 'A rose by any other name would smell as sweet.'"

Irene put both hands on his chest and gave him a hard shove. "Names mean a lot to me. I'm going to Escapade Island."

"You got the wrong, plane, lady."

Peering around Happy, Irene looked at Mr. Tanned-and-Buff in the aisle seat.

"You just landed on Eden Island," he continued. "Escapade Island is about twenty-five or thirty miles south. On a clear day, you can see it on the horizon."

"Shit," Irene muttered.

"It's fate, Irene. I was really worried about embarking on this new phase of my life on Friday the thirteenth, but when your son brought you on board and helped you into the seat next to mine, I was sure you were my destiny."

When he reached for her hands again, Irene slapped his away and curled her fingers into the front of his shirt. "Listen up, Happy. I want some answers. Exactly how did I get on this plane?"

"The flight attendant rolled you in a wheelchair. You were pretty out of it. She said your son had explained that you'd taken some meds because you were terrified of flying, and they were making you very drowsy."

"Drowsy." That would explain her fuzzy memories or lack of them. But she certainly hadn't taken any meds. "Which flight attendant?"

Happy pointed to a slender, pretty blonde who was beaming a smile at the departing passengers.

Irene had some questions for her, but her path was temporarily blocked. When Happy gripped her wrists, she swatted his hands away. "Hands off, or I'll hurt you."

His eyes gleamed into hers. "Oh, good. I've never experimented with the pain/pleasure thing before."

This time when he made a grab for her hand, Irene wrapped her fingers around one of his thumbs and bent it back. "Hands off, I said."

"Owww." Happy's breath hitched and then he closed his eyes and sighed. "Oooooh, that's good. That's very good. I knew I was right to book this trip."

As passengers in the rows around began to file more quickly off the plane, Irene's mind finally cleared. She'd been drugged and someone pretending to be her "son" had put her in a wheelchair and gotten her on this plane. Who? Could Butch have found out she was coming and decided to do this to her?

No. The final wisp of fog in her brain finally cleared and her stomach rolled. Whoever had done this to her was more likely after the Monet. Jumping up, she scrambled over Happy to get into the aisle. One glance into the empty overhead compartment pushed her panic button. "My suitcase." Leaning down, she grabbed Happy by the shirt again. "I had a carry-on. Where is it?"

For the first time since she'd seen him, Happy frowned. "You didn't have any suitcase."

Oh no, Irene thought.

Whirling, she ran up the now empty aisle to where the flight attendant still stood beaming her smile. "Your wheelchair is waiting."

"I won't be needing it," Irene said. "Describe my son for me."

The flight attendant's smile wavered a bit. Probably she thought she was dealing with a looney tune. Who else would ask for a description of her own son? But whatever thoughts were in her mind, she said, "He was a very nice man."

Irene managed not to scream. "What exactly did he look like?"

"He was tall and dark with a goatee and he was wearing one of those French-looking hats. What do they call them?"

"A beret?"

"Yes, that's it. And he spoke with a French accent. So intriguing."

"Yeah," Irene muttered. She was intrigued all right. And her mind was racing. The description the attendant had given her matched a man who'd sat one chair down from her in the airport bar. Had he been close enough to slip something into her beer? Short of being sold into white slavery—which she didn't think she was a candidate for—there was only one reason to drug her.

The Monet.

"He didn't happen to give you my suitcase, did he?"

"No."

Damn. Someone had drugged her, swiped the Monet, and put her on a plane to sex camp with a man who thought she was a dominatrix. Could things possibly get worse?

Happy tugged at her elbow. "If there's a problem, you can room with me, Irene."

Irene had a feeling things could get a lot worse.

3

"TWO ISLAND FLINGS," Cole said to the beaming Gari. Pepper smiled at the young man who'd greeted her so enthusiastically at the airport. He'd made a beeline for their table the moment that Cole had chosen it.

"Excellent choice." Gari said. "One drink and you will reveal all your secrets to each other."

Oh, good, Pepper thought. As if Cole's proximity weren't making it hard enough for her to concentrate, now she was going to drink a truth serum.

He'd stuck as close as a guardian angel since they'd arrived at the hotel, and right now he was in the chair next to hers, sitting so close that she was more aware of the heat of his body than she was of the sunlight pouring down on them. Why did he have to look so damn good? The khaki-colored T-shirt and shorts only emphasized the tanned skin and the subtly muscled body that until now had always been disguised by clothes. Just looking at him had her mouth going dry. Although he didn't look like a body builder, if this man blocked your path, you wouldn't get past him.

And her body didn't want to get past him. Her palms were literally itching to touch him. She fisted her hands in her lap, shocked at the sudden rush of greed streaming through her. The problem with that kiss in the penthouse suite was that she hadn't had time to really touch him. And she wanted to. All over.

"Pepper?"

"Hmm?" She shifted her gaze to his face and tried to gather her scattered thoughts.

"I asked if you were hungry."

Starved was the word that popped into her mind. But the craving inside of her wasn't for food. *Focus,* she told herself as she drew in a deep breath.

"Sure. Food would be good." She hadn't had anything to eat but airline snacks since she'd boarded the red-eye from San Francisco. Maybe eating something would help to keep her mind on…her aunt, the Monet. Touching Cole Buchanan was not on her current to-do list, she reminded herself.

Cole turned to Gari. "Pack us up a little picnic, including a Thermos with a refill of the Island Fling."

"Absolutely."

Food wasn't going to help a bit if she continued to sit there looking at Cole Buchanan. She put some effort into shifting her gaze away from him. She had two immediate problems: figuring out how to locate Irene and deciding how much she dared tell Cole. Time was definitely running out on the latter. Cole hadn't pressed her since they'd arrived at the resort. But the inquisition was coming. The setup was perfect. He'd chosen a table on the ocean side of the pool terrace where they were alone.

Most of the other customers of the poolside café had chosen tables on the resort side where palm trees and potted plants offered plenty of shade. As her gaze skimmed them, she recognized several people she'd flown in with, including the cowboy who'd nearly run her down at the airport. He'd evidently caught up with his "lady." The couple who'd stopped traffic by kissing were also there, and they were still wearing those long coats.

She shot a quick glance at Cole and found that he was looking at her in that quiet, patient way that he had. Anxiety tightened into a hard little knot in her stomach. How much could she afford to tell Cole Buchanan? She still hadn't decided. It would certainly help if she could find out how much he knew and what he was thinking. There'd been a lot of stuff in her PI class on "reading" other people. But this man was a pro. She wasn't going to "read" anything he didn't want her to.

"Confession is good for the soul," he murmured.

Her eyes immediately narrowed. "I don't have anything to confess." But now that she was looking at him again, she was tempted to just lay the whole problem in his lap. That would mean betraying Irene though—and she couldn't.

"Where's the Monet?" Cole asked.

"I have no idea."

The simple truth of that statement made her stomach clench, and a bubble of panic rose in her throat. She really didn't know where Irene and the painting were.

And she had no doubt that he was "reading" her with great success. Break time, she decided. Deliberately, she shifted her gaze inland to the poolside bar again. It was built on two levels so that it could service swimmers as well as guests who preferred dry land.

Gari was standing on the dry land side, and when he spotted her, he sent a two-fingered salute. He was wearing the same blue flowered shirt and white shorts that he'd worn at the airport and that the receptionist had worn when Pepper had registered in her aunt's bungalow. It seemed to be the resort staff's uniform.

She'd had to think quickly when Cole had escorted her to the registration line. She hadn't booked a room for herself since she'd intended to stick like fly paper to her aunt once they'd both arrived on the island.

The young woman behind the registration desk hadn't batted an eye when the name on the credit card had been Pepper Rossi instead of Irene. Thank heavens, Cole had slipped into the gift shop, and so he'd missed the whole transaction.

"Enjoy." Gari set down two scooped-out pineapples filled with pink liquid and topped with a straw and a colorful, little umbrella. Remembering what the young man had said, Pepper eyed the drink doubtfully.

"Try it. You'll like it," Cole said.

"That's what I'm afraid of," she replied.

"And take these." He pressed two pills into her hand.

When she met his eyes, he continued, "Aspirin. You rubbed your temples three times while you were standing in the registration line, so I got some from the gift shop."

Oh, good, Pepper thought. Not only did the man have eyes like a hawk and truth serum at the ready, but he was going to turn out to be a mind reader too. And she'd been so hoping her luck had changed. She popped the aspirin into her mouth and took the first taste of her Island Fling.

Smooth, sweet, and tangy, the liquid slid easily down her throat, and she was very tempted to take another swallow. Then another and another.

"Dangerous," she murmured. She'd had a similar

reaction the first time she'd had a chocolate milkshake. She'd given in to temptation and drained the glass then.

And she'd had the same reaction to Cole the first time she'd kissed him. Would she find it impossible to stop when she kissed him again?

She'd automatically thought *when*, not *if*, she mused staring down into the drink. Her mind seemed to be in tune with her body on that point. Very deliberately, she pushed the pineapple away.

"Why don't you tell me what's going on?" Cole asked.

She turned to look at him. It was a definite mistake, but she couldn't keep her eyes averted forever. His dark hair was still windblown from the ride, and his eyes were camouflaged by sunglasses. The now almost familiar itching sensation in her palms had her clenching her hands into fists again.

If there was ever a time to pretend to be someone else, this was it. But for the first time in her life, she didn't think it would help to try and be someone else. She didn't think there was any way to escape this overwhelming attraction.

He took a sip of his Island Fling, then set it back on the table. But he said nothing.

In one part of her mind, she knew exactly what he was doing. Lesson number five in PI school had been on interrogating witnesses. One of the suggested techniques was silence. If the interrogator said nothing, often the person being questioned would be tempted to fill up that silence.

Cole Buchanan looked so competent, and she'd gotten herself and her family into one huge mess. Each minute she sat in the sunshine, listening to the play of waves on the nearby sand, increased her desire to tell him everything.

But she couldn't tell him about Irene and her forty-year long-distance affair with Butch Castellano. Even if he could understand, she didn't want to betray her aunt. Irene had never told anyone—not even her brother and nephews—about her relationship with the former criminal. Only Pepper knew about the letters they'd exchanged over the years. Irene trusted her, and Pepper cherished that trust. No one had ever had faith in her the way Irene did. She'd never known her mother, but Pepper wanted to believe that her mom would have confided in her and trusted in her the way her aunt did.

Plus, if she told Cole everything and asked for his help, how would she ever prove to her family that she was good enough to work at Rossi Investigations? And what if he *didn't* understand why Aunt Irene had felt she had to steal the painting? No, she couldn't do it.

This time she let out a sigh as she took another sip of her Island Fling. Then she set it carefully back on the table. "Nothing's going on."

Cole leaned a bit closer. "Liar. Let's start with what I already know."

She was reaching for her pineapple, but he beat her to it and placed it out of her reach. "I wanted to loosen your tongue, but I don't want you incoherent."

She frowned at the pineapple. "That lethal, huh?"

"According to Butch Castellano, the owner, they don't call it the Island Fling for nothing."

"You've met Butch?" That couldn't be good, she thought. "How...how long have you been here?"

"I arrived yesterday evening."

She frowned at him. "Gari told me there's only one flight here a day and it gets in at noon."

"Yeah. This isn't the easiest place to get to. I arranged to charter a small plane right after you booked your ticket for today."

"Ah." Pepper's mind was racing. Perhaps that's what Irene had done. She glanced up at the sky. If she could just get away from Cole and make a few phone calls...

"I wanted to do a little investigating before you got here," Cole continued.

Her gaze flew back to his. What could he have found out? As far as she knew, Butch wasn't aware that Irene was bringing the painting. And Cole hadn't mentioned her aunt's name yet.

"I don't have all the pieces, but I have enough to tell you that you won't get away with it."

She lifted her chin. She wasn't sure what she would have said because the half-formed thought flew out of her mind the instant she looked beyond Cole's shoulder. Two men were climbing the steps to the poolside café, and she recognized one of them instantly as Evan Atwell.

There was no mistaking that almost white blond hair. It had always made her think a little of Spike on *Buffy the Vampire Slayer*. It took her a moment longer to place the tall man with the goatee and the beret as the man who'd taken the last seat on the plane.

As the two men stepped onto the terrace, she gripped Cole's arm and pitched her voice low. "Don't turn your head. Evan Atwell is coming up the steps from the beach. What on earth is *he* doing here?"

IT WAS COLE'S TURN TO frown as he studied her carefully. He could have sworn that it was bewilderment and concern he heard in her voice. With his free hand, he pulled the oversize sunglasses down her nose so that he could see her eyes. "You should know. You came here to meet him."

Her eyes widened in what he could have sworn was surprise. "No." Then lowering her voice, she continued, "Why would I do that?"

"Because he's your lover."

She frowned at him. "No, he's not. We were never lovers. And we broke up three months ago."

It was Cole's turn to frown. "You're still bringing him to your father's Sunday dinners."

Color rose in her cheeks. "Evan wanted to continue to see me as a friend. His mother liked me, and he's working up the courage to tell her we've broken up."

She'd broken up with Evan. And they'd never been lovers. A flood of feelings poured in, but Cole pushed them aside. There was no time to sort through them now. What in hell was wrong with Evan Atwell? he wondered. This man had dated the woman for three months without becoming her lover. He wouldn't have lasted through one night. Hell, he wouldn't have lasted through one kiss if the damn Monet hadn't disappeared.

Leaning back, he studied her for a moment. Gut instinct told him she was telling the truth. She was blushing as if he'd pulled something out of her that she didn't want to admit. His whole interpretation of the facts surrounding the disappearance of the Monet had centered on his belief that Pepper and Evan were lovers. And he'd been so sure. This threw a whole new light on the evidence.

Cole had never known his instinct to fail him. But Pepper Rossi had been clouding his senses from day one.

Pushing her glasses back up on her nose, she leaned in to him. "Let's get out of here. I don't want him to see me."

"Why not?"

She glanced at the two men who were making their way to the shade at the other side of the pool. "I'm not sure. It's just so odd that he's here. His mother's priceless Monet has been stolen. You'd think he'd be in San Francisco, holding her hand or at the very least pestering my brothers to find it."

"'Of all the gin joints in all the world'...?"

"Yeah." She grinned at him. "Exactly."

Cole simply stared at her. This time the flood of feelings wasn't so easily ignored. She'd never before looked at him in that easy intimate way. Come to think of it, she'd never smiled at him so openly and genuinely. He felt something inside of him opening.

"C'mon," she said, rising.

He took her hand as he drew her toward the bar. While he settled their bill and they waited for the picnic basket he'd ordered, she kept her back to Evan Atwell and peppered Cole with whispered questions.

"Did he sit down at a table?" she asked.

"Yes."

"What is he doing?"

"Just sitting with his companion."

"Very informative." Pepper risked a quick look, then turned back to him.

"Told you so," he said.

"It'll be just a few more minutes," said Gari. "We had to send someone up to the main kitchen for a Thermos."

Pepper pulled on Cole's arm. "We can skip the Island Fling. Let's get out of here before Evan recognizes us."

"Relax," he murmured. "I think your true identity is safe as long as you wear that wig."

"You're not wearing a wig," she hissed.

Before he could reply, a woman at a nearby table gasped. Someone else choked and started coughing. By the time Cole caught sight of the nude man and woman who were running around the far end of the pool, others had begun to applaud. One man cheered.

Pepper grabbed his T-shirt with two fists. "What?"

"A couple of streakers," Cole said.

She turned then. "The trench coat couple. I wondered why they wouldn't take them off."

"They have now." The coats were draped over the chairs they'd been sitting on. The elderly couple reached the beach and ran hand in hand across the sand. Some of the guests had risen from their chairs and the applause was blossoming into a standing ovation.

Pepper began to laugh uncontrollably. Her shoulders shook and she let out such a sweetly delighted sound, he had to smile.

"I'll be…all right," she gasped just before a fresh wave of giggles took over.

"Take your time," Cole murmured. He couldn't recall ever hearing her laugh before, and he found himself simply enjoying the bubbly sound of it. She was always so serious, so wound up and focused. Even in the picture that Luke had originally shown him, she'd had a serious expression. "If it helps any, they're out of sight."

"Good," she mumbled. Then another giggle erupted. "That's…good. I think I'm all right now. Did Evan see me?"

"We're both safe. Everyone was looking at the streakers. Now they're talking about them."

When Pepper finally looked up at him, there was a look

in her eyes that he'd never seen before. There was no trace of the wariness that he'd always detected, and for a moment he thought of nothing, of no one, but her. The realization streamed through him that he was in very deep trouble. Missing Monet or not, he was not going to be able to keep his hands off of her much longer.

He rubbed his thumb over the corner of her mouth. "Pepper, I—"

She took a step back from him, the wariness back in her eyes. "We should make our getaway. I personally don't need any more of that Island Fling concoction."

Cole might have been persuaded to abandon the picnic basket they were waiting for too if it hadn't been for the two men who were walking straight toward Evan's table. Instead, he drew Pepper with him behind a trio of potted palms that provided shade on the terrace. "Curiouser and curiouser."

"What?" Pepper hissed. "Is someone else taking off their clothes?" She pulled down a palm branch so she could peek over it.

Several beats went by before Cole spoke. He wanted to give her time to absorb the newcomers. The shorter man was Butch Castellano. As they watched, Butch sat down in one of the chairs at Evan's table and took out a cigar. The other, larger man moved behind him.

Once he'd figured out where Pepper was headed, Cole had researched the island and its owner. In his youth, Butch Castellano had acquired quite a rap sheet. Born into a prominent New Jersey crime family, he'd had a brief but successful career before his luck had run out. Either the young Butch hadn't been very smart or he'd taken the fall for someone higher up in the organization. Cole favored the latter explanation since, from what he could gather, the man had been smart enough to accumulate a fortune in prison while playing the stock market.

Butch Castellano reminded him of Al Pacino—one tough Italian. Now in his early sixties, he'd kept fit in prison, and whatever he lacked in stature was more than compensated for by the air of toughness that emanated from him. The fact that Butch was wearing shorts, flip flops and a shirt with tropical fish swimming across it did nothing to dampen that impression.

Butch's bodyguard wasn't any less formidable. Referred to as Mr. H by the staff, the man was well over six feet tall with the kind of body that Arnold Schwarzenegger used to have. He was wearing a variation of the Escapade resort uniform, white shorts and a blue tank, several gold chains and one diamond earring.

Pepper tugged his arm. "Very colorful. Who are they?"

Once again, he used one finger to pull her sunglasses down so that he could see her eyes. "You don't know?"

She shook her head. "No. You haven't given me a lot of time to socialize since I got here."

"That's your host, Butch Castellano, and his assistant slash bodyguard, Mr. H."

There was a quick flash of something in her eyes. It disappeared quickly, but if he had to guess, he would have said it was surprise. So she didn't know Butch Castellano? If that was true, then his theory about what was going on definitely needed revising.

After studying the two men for a moment, she said, "So that's Butch." Then she turned to him again. "Let's go to the beach. I need to think."

So do I, Cole thought as he gathered up the picnic basket from the bar. *So do I.*

At the foot of the short flight of steps that led to the beach, Pepper took her shoes off and tucked them into her duffel. Without the three-inch heels, the top of her head didn't come up to his shoulder, and Cole found himself remembering how small and fragile she'd felt in his arms two days ago. But the set of her chin and the way she faced problems head on testified to strength too.

And she was smart. She might act on impulse and get herself into scrapes, but she was definitely one smart cookie. If she wasn't involved in the theft, then what was she doing on the island? Had she helped Evan steal the painting because she was his friend?

Somehow he didn't think so. Even in his fairly short acquaintance with her, he knew she valued her family. Most of the scrapes she got herself into were an accidental consequence of her efforts to please them. He strongly doubted that she would place a friendship with Evan Atwell above that.

Another thought suddenly occurred to him. Was she here to somehow save Evan's sorry ass? No. He rejected that idea as quickly as it had formed in his mind. She'd seemed honestly surprised to see Evan when he'd appeared in the poolside café.

As they walked together in silence, Cole tried to clear his mind of the swirling thoughts. Long ago, he'd learned that if he just had enough patience, the answer would come to him. He glanced down at Pepper. Besides, he didn't want to think about the Monet right now. Instead, he wanted very much simply to enjoy the moment.

He hadn't released her hand, and she hadn't pulled away from him either. A gull swooped down toward the sea and then climbed swiftly back up to the azure-blue expanse of the sky. He watched it until the bird's wings were only a wispy pencil stroke of gray.

Had the slower pace of island life gotten to him? Or was it simply that it felt right somehow to be walking here in this place, with this woman? All Cole was sure of was that nothing, not even the theft of the Monet, seemed as urgent as it had back in San Francisco.

Though they'd been walking for some time, it wasn't until they reached a long outcrop of rocks that Cole realized they'd rounded a point of land that blocked off any view of the hotel. The beach here wasn't as pristine as the stretch in front of the resort. Shells of all sizes, broken palm leaves, and chunks of driftwood lay along the shoreline.

When they reached the far side of the cluster of rocks, Pepper withdrew her hand from his, waded into the water and sat down on a large flat rock. He watched her shrug off the duffel she'd slung over her shoulder, fold her hands together, and look out to sea.

She was withdrawing, and he wasn't about to let her do that. After slipping out of his shoes, he waded out and sat down on the rock next to her. "We have to talk."

Though she stiffened, she didn't move away, but merely turned to face him. "I wish you wouldn't sit next to me. I find it difficult to think when you're this close."

Her words sent a thrill shooting through him, and giving into impulse, he ran one finger down one hoop at her ear. "It's a mutual problem. But we're both going to have to adapt. Perhaps we'll even indulge some of the feelings we have for one another. I'm not going away."

The sudden heat of desire that he saw in her eyes nearly had him losing focus. But he managed not to touch her.

"I'm going to stick to you like glue until I have the Monet back in San Francisco."

She studied him for a minute. "What if I told you that I came here to take it back?"

"You stole it, and now you're going to take it back?"

She frowned. "I didn't steal it."

His brows shot up. "You may not have personally carried it out of Atwell's suite, but you kissed me to distract me long enough for your partner to steal it."

She lifted her chin. "And you know that because...?"

"You kept your distance from that day we met in your father's kitchen—despite the obvious attraction between us. I thought it was because of Evan. Then suddenly two nights ago, out of the blue, you ask me to kiss you."

The way her eyes had darkened and the frantic way her pulse had begun to beat at her throat distracted him. He could kiss her again right now. He could taste her again— have her. Need sharpened until it was an ache, and once more he had to clamp down hard on his control.

"I didn't have to be a rocket scientist to put it together. You kept me busy while someone else got out of the suite with the Monet."

She winced slightly, and then swallowed hard. "Yes. Okay. Maybe I did kiss you to distract you. But it's not what you think. At least, it's not exactly what you think. It's...it's complicated."

"Good," he said. "Because I was figuring it was pretty simple. That you'd helped your ex-lover Evan Atwell steal his own painting."

4

Friday, February 13—2:00 p.m.

PEPPER JUMPED UP from the rock. "You think that I helped Evan steal the painting? That's not true. Evan's not involved in this, and I've already told you he was never my lover."

"You dated him exclusively for three months. You're friends enough with him to continue seeing him even though you claim you've broken things off." Out of simple curiosity, he asked, "Why didn't you become lovers?"

A hint of color rose in her cheeks. "There was no chemistry. I liked him. He liked me. We had a lot in common. But that was it."

"You could have figured that out on the first date. Why did you go out again?"

"It seemed to please my father that I was dating Evan."

Of course, it would, Cole thought. Peter Rossi was planning a run for mayor in the next election, and the Atwells were a very well-connected family in San Francisco.

"Luke and Matt thought it was terrific. So did Evan's mother. We just sort of got carried along on the waves of approval."

"Ah." Cole thought he understood. If Pepper had married Evan, then that would have solved the "Pepper Problem" for Luke and Matt.

She met his eyes. "I know Evan. He would never steal the Monet."

Cole stared at her as feelings streamed through him: admiration for her loyalty and jealousy of the man who inspired it. She'd denied that Evan was her lover, but that didn't seem to matter. Her relationship with Evan still rankled him. Pepper Rossi had been able to push emotional buttons in him from the moment that Luke had shown him that photo six months ago. Luke had been so proud, bragging that his sister had agreed to move to San Francisco.

Oh, Cole had been attracted to women on first sight before. But never to a photo. One look at Pepper and he'd decided to take Luke and Matt up on the standing job offer that had been on the table since they'd thought of opening their office. The warning bells had jangled then, and they'd reached the pitch and volume of a five-alarm fire alert that first Sunday in Peter Rossi's kitchen.

With a sigh, Pepper sat back down on the rock beside him. "I have to admit it looks bad. But there has to be some explanation."

Right now, he wanted nothing more than to put his arm around her and tell her that everything was going to be all right. But he couldn't—not until he found out what connection she had to the disappearance of the Monet.

"Two heads are better than one." He opened the wicker basket he'd been carrying. "Why don't we have something to eat and pool our information?"

He tamped down his impatience while he spread a small cloth on a nearby flat rock and opened containers of cold chicken, fruit and buttered rolls. When he'd dished up two plates, he opened the Thermos and filled two plastic glasses. Handing her one, he said, "They do a nice job here."

She turned and looked out at the sea.

He took a sip of his drink and let her mull over her next move. Because that was what she was doing as she sipped her Island Fling. He could almost hear the wheels turning in her head.

He glanced at his watch and was surprised to see it was only a little after 2:00 p.m. Minutes seemed to slip by more slowly here on the island. Glancing back at Pepper, he studied her profile, taking in that lifted chin and the way she tightly clasped her drink. He'd interrogated reluctant people before. Instead of letting her push his buttons, he should be pushing hers.

With an inaudible sigh, he put down his cup and plucked hers out of her hand. Then he handed her one of the plates he'd filled. "You need to eat something before you have much more of that Island Fling. I don't want you fading on me."

When she'd taken a few bites of a chicken leg, he said, "Why did you decide to leave Philadelphia and move to San Francisco?"

She placed the chicken back down on the plate and turned to him. "You're trying to distract me."

He shrugged. "You don't want to talk about the Monet—so I thought I'd widen the scope of our conversation. Luke and Matt told me about how they'd been separated from you when your parents split up years ago. I don't have any family. If I suddenly learned that I did, and that they'd known where I was but hadn't contacted me for most of my life, I'm not sure I would have packed up and moved across the country to join them."

She broke off a piece of her roll. "I wasn't going to at first."

"What made you change your mind?"

She began to shred pieces of the roll. "I wasn't happy in Philadelphia. I never quite got the knack of being a Pendleton. Plus, the Rossis are persistent."

"Tell me about it," he said and had the pleasure of seeing her lips twitch.

"My father was the worst. He kept calling, and finally, Luke and Matt came to plead their case in person." Her mouth curved slightly as she met his eyes. "They can be persistent *and* persuasive."

Cole thought of Luke and Matt, who were as different as two brothers could be—a computer genius and an ex-cop, respectively. What they had in common was incredible charisma, no doubt inherited from their father, Peter. "I always thought they could sell the Brooklyn Bridge again if they put their minds to it."

She met his eyes then. "Why did *you* come here?"

It was the first personal question she'd asked him. A small sign of progress, he thought. What would she say if he told her the simple truth? A truth he still wasn't comfortable with. He'd moved to San Francisco because of a photo of a woman. Instead, he told her a truth he was more comfortable with. "I wanted a change from the kind of work I was doing. Your brothers had been after me for some time to join their firm."

She stiffened. "Yes, I suppose they were."

"But you still haven't answered my question. Why did you finally give in to them and leave the life you had in Philadelphia?"

"They convinced me that they wanted me."

The sudden trace of pain in her eyes had him frowning.

Did she still doubt that they wanted her? One thing he knew for certain was that her brothers loved her. Whatever mistakes their parents had made all those years ago, he was convinced that Peter and his sons wanted Pepper with them now. His first impulse was to try to set her mind at ease on that score. But then he remembered why he'd started this little interrogation. He needed information. There wasn't a doubt in his mind that Evan Atwell was involved somehow in the theft. And she was still protecting him. He needed to subtly work the conversation around to that.

"It must have been hard knowing that you had a family who didn't contact you all those years."

"They could have," she said flatly. "In fact, Irene did. Oh, I know that they thought they were keeping a promise they'd made to my mother on her deathbed. I've tried to understand that."

She set her plate on the rock. Then she pulled off her wig and ran fingers through her damp dark hair until it stood up in little spikes. "I still get angry if I let myself think too much about it. At first I blamed all of them. But I especially blame my grandmother."

"Why?" Cole asked.

She whirled to face him. "Because once my mother became ill, my grandmother was the one who orchestrated everything. She even admitted to it. More than that, she was proud of herself." She pushed up from the rock and began to pace back and forth in the ankle-deep water. A waiting seagull flew out of her way.

"What exactly did she do?" he asked.

"My parents' marriage was always volatile. Peter says that he and my mother had split before. He claims that they loved each other very much, but my mother could never quite get used to the life of a cop's wife. They'd have these arguments, then my mother would return to Philadelphia for a while and eventually they'd reconcile and she'd move back to San Francisco. The last time my mother left Luke and Matt with Peter because they were in school by then. She took me with her because I was a baby. Then she got ill. Cancer."

Cole watched her pace back and forth in the water. There were wounds there that hadn't completely healed.

"Peter says that they would have reconciled again. But when my mother learned that she was dying, my grandmother got involved. She got my mother to make my father promise that he would leave me with Grandmother and that he wouldn't try to contact me until my twenty-fifth birthday. In return, I would be raised as a Pendleton, sent to the best schools, and given everything that money could buy. I've thought about it a lot, and I can understand why my mother went along with the plan. She was dying and she wanted the best for me. Besides, my father had the two boys to worry about. She probably felt he had enough on his plate. Intellectually, I can understand it all, but emotionally…"

Cole watched her as she continued to pace. He could see temper and frustration building. The sun beat down on her from behind, waves lapped at her ankles. With her damp spiky hair and those huge almond-shaped eyes, she might have been some sea sprite, sprung from Neptune's court. She looked magnificent as she kicked water out of her way.

Then she whirled to face him, and Cole's mind went blank as he stared at her. Seconds, perhaps minutes ticked by before he realized that he'd totally lost the thread of what she was saying. Something about her grandmother.

She was looking at him as if she expected some kind of comment or reaction. He gave it his best shot and nodded.

"Exactly!" She threw up a hand. "I've tried to understand her. Really I have. But Grandmother could have released my father from that promise. The thing is she didn't want him to contact me. And she lied about my mother too. All my life, she held my mother up to me as a paragon that I could never measure up to. It wasn't until I talked to my father that I learned she wasn't a paragon at all. She failed at becoming a Pendloton just as much as I did."

"How so?" Cole asked.

"At seventeen, she ran away with my father. Both families were appalled, but Luke was already on the way. My grandmother has never forgiven my father. I think that's why she kept me with her all those years—as a kind of revenge. Tit for tat. You took my daughter and now I'll take yours."

Once again, Cole found himself clamping down on the urge to reach out and touch her. Not until he learned what he needed to know. "Revenge is a powerful motivator. What about your dad? Why do you think he never went back on his word and tried to get in touch with you earlier the way your aunt did?"

She met his eyes, and he saw a flash of hurt. "It's pretty obvious. He just didn't want me."

"So stealing a Monet and discrediting Rossi Investigations would be a way of getting revenge at last."

For a moment she simply stared at him. "You think that I—that I would do that to my family? How dare you?" She flew at him, grabbing fistfuls of his shirt. His plate of chicken went flying as he struggled for balance and lost. Wrapping his fingers around her wrists, he twisted his body so that he took the brunt of the impact when they tumbled into the shallow water. Then, anticipating her next move, he rolled with her until he could scissor his legs and trap her between them.

The struggle was brief. He was bigger and heavier, but she was stronger than he'd expected. When she finally stilled beneath him, they were lying in the shallows with the water lapping against them, staring at each other. Cole could feel that their bodies were already reacting: his own was hardening and hers was growing impossibly soft. She looked like some kind of pixie mermaid staring up at him defiantly.

He'd interrogated witnesses before, but never quite like this. If there'd only been murder he saw in her eyes, he might have had an easier time of it. But he saw the same hot lick of awareness that he was feeling. And he felt the heat, ricocheting from him to her and back again. How often had he fantasized about what it would feel like to have these soft curves, this strong, slender body beneath his? Already his mind was imagining once again what it would feel like to take that hot slippery slide into her.

He held himself perfectly still and tried to keep his brain on task.

"Since you won't tell me the truth about why you stole the Monet, I've had to come up with theories. If you don't like that one, try this. You resented me from the first day I joined Rossi investigations. For some reason you seem to think we're in competition."

"We are," she hissed through clenched teeth. "Now will you just get off?"

"Not yet. I haven't finished, and this is my favorite theory so far. You conned someone into helping you steal the painting so that you could recover it and kill two birds with one stone. In one fell swoop, you make me look bad, and you look good. Your brothers fire me and make you a partner."

She bucked under him, then bit out, "You're not even close."

He hadn't thought he was. "Then set me straight. What are you really doing on this island? Who stole that painting and where is it?"

"I don't know."

Anger and frustration rolled through him. They had no place in a good interrogation. But this one hadn't been going well from the get-go. And he was finding it harder and harder to concentrate. She'd set a fire in him from the moment he'd seen that photo, and what had happened in the Atwells' penthouse had fanned the flames almost beyond his ability to control them. "Okay. If you're not going to tell me what's going on, let's try this."

He brushed his mouth over hers. Her lips parted immediately, and without another thought he plunged in.

THE HEAT OF THE KISS exploded inside of her in one glorious wave. It was as if no time at all had elapsed since they'd kissed in the Atwells' suite. His mouth was hot and hungry, and every hard line, angle and plane of him was pressed tightly against her. All she knew was that she wanted to dive into that heat-filled wave—and to hell with the undertow.

When he cut off the contact and raised his head, she nearly cried out in protest.

"If you don't want to finish what we started the other night, you have to say so now."

Every single cell in her body wanted it, wanted him. Desperately, she tried to gather her thoughts. "I—"

He tightened his grip on her wrists. "The truth. I'll know if you're lying."

She tried to draw in a breath, but her lungs were still burning. And she could still taste him. "I want to, but we shouldn't. There are complications enough without—" She lost the thought and the rest of the sentence when she saw triumph flash into his eyes. And heat.

"This is simple enough," he said. "I want you and you want me. And I'm tired of waiting. Let's deal with this part first. Just ask me to kiss you."

His mouth was a breath from hers when he said the words. She simply couldn't resist. "Kiss me." Then she moved to close the small distance between them, and her mouth was as hungry, as desperate, as his. She felt that instantaneous explosion of greed that she'd experienced before. Here was the speed that she'd dreamed about, that she'd craved. Even as the thrill of it poured into her, she pulled her arms free and wrapped them around him.

The worries and fears that had haunted her for the past two days—ever since she'd come to grips with the fact that she'd actually helped her aunt steal that Monet—evaporated. There was no room for them in the floodtide of feelings that he was bringing her.

In between kisses, she said, "Don't stop. This time, don't stop." She'd wanted to shout the words, but they came out on a whispered moan.

"I won't." He traced a line of kisses along the line of her jaw.

She tried to arch against him, needed to melt into him.

Even as those wants and needs pounded at her, one thrill after another battered her senses.

She was so aware of everything. The sharp bite of the sea shells pressing into her back. The coolness of the water on her skin. And those hands. They were so strong, so demanding, so masterful. When one of them covered her breast, the arrow of pleasure was so intense that it bordered on pain.

Everything was happening so fast—and she wanted so desperately to hang on to each separate sensation. Sunlight filtered through the palms overhead, and she could feel it on her eyelids, see it form into a hazy red mist just before his head blocked it and his mouth covered hers again. She felt like a whirlwind of wants and needs had captured her, leaving her powerless to do anything but be swept away. And still she wanted more. More.

She was driving him crazy. And he wasn't about to do one thing to stop her. Because he had to have more. Since that first kiss, hadn't he dreamed day and night of her, of feeling this flash fire of desire again? Hadn't he known that if he followed her to the island, he would kiss her again? Only this time, he'd been certain that he'd be able to handle his reaction. Certain that lightning couldn't strike twice.

But it had. Now with her mouth on his, her body arching against him—demanding, searching, offering—he couldn't think, could barely breathe. The generosity of her response was more than he'd remembered, more than he'd fantasized: the scrape of her nails on his back, the lick of her tongue, the scrape of her teeth on his ear, the moans that vibrated against his lips at her throat. Each sensation battered at him until he wanted nothing more than to swallow her whole.

In the six months since he'd met her, he'd fantasized

scores of different scenarios. One of them had involved a beach. There'd been moonlight and champagne, and a long and sensuous seduction. He hadn't anticipated being jumped and rolling with her in seawater or being as rough and needy as a teenager high on hormones.

He hadn't anticipated *her.*

Gathering what will he had left, he lifted his head. Her lips were moist, parted, and swollen from their kisses. Her eyes were half-closed and clouded with at least some of what he was feeling. What was she—who was she—that she could do this to him?

"Cole..."

The desperation in that one whispered word triggered an explosion of feelings she'd stirred in him from the first. He crushed his mouth to hers and devoured her. With Pepper, everything was new. Hunger had never been unmanageable. Desire had never made him ache. Once again, control was slipping away as surely as the sand streamed from beneath them with each wave that pulled back from the shore. Fear shot through him, sharp and real, at the power that she had over him.

When he tried to draw back, she tightened her arms on him and said, "More."

Choice and will drained away in an instant. Levering himself off of her, he dragged at her clothes, ridding her of her T-shirt and pulling at the snap of her jeans. Her hands were as desperate as his, scraping his skin with her nails as she jerked his shirt loose and tugged at his belt.

When they were both naked, their clothes scattered on the beach, he pushed her back on the sand and took his mouth on a quick journey over her. He found her skin rainwater soft over her breast, smooth and taut down her torso.

The need to savor warred with the need to hurry until he reached her thighs. When they parted and she arched her hips in invitation, he had to linger, had to sample her hot, sweet center. One taste and he feasted.

He knew the moment the orgasm moved through her. She gasped his name, and he experienced the power of knowing that she thought only of him. When her body went limp, he ruthlessly used his mouth on her again. This time, he varied his timing, keeping her shimmering on the brink, spinning out the pleasure for her before he drove her to the next peak and beyond.

She was still trembling, still struggling for a breath when he finally drew back to take care of the condom. Blood pounding, heart hammering, he ranged himself above. "Look at me, Pepper."

When she did, when her eyes were open and on his, he thrust into her in one long, hard stroke. As he withdrew and pushed into her again, she moved with him, and his own climax began to build. Groaning, he picked up the pace, driving her and driving himself until pleasure exploded and shattered them both.

REALITY DRIBBLED BACK in bits and pieces. The first time Pepper opened her eyes, her vision was still blurred. As it gradually cleared, she saw the pile of rocks to her right and the ocean to her left. The sun beat down, and she smelled the ocean, and Cole. He still lay sprawled on top of her, and she wasn't sure if it was her heart or his that was still racing so furiously. Or both together.

Closing her eyes again, she tried to think. But pleasure and satisfaction were still streaming through her. Nothing had ever been like this. Like him. In a moment, she'd have to lecture herself for going with her impulses again…and worry about the consequences…and probably have a panic attack. But right now, she just wanted to stop time and savor the press of that hard, muscled body on hers.

He stirred then, lifting his head, and another bit of reality penetrated. He was still inside her. The realization shot a new rush of heat through her body. She quivered and felt herself tightening around him.

"Well, well," he said. "Are you all right?"

"I think so," she said. It was a lie. She felt a little like Humpty Dumpty after his fall. She drew in a deep breath. "We should go. Someone might come along."

He rubbed a thumb along her bottom lip. "From what I observed yesterday, this is siesta time on the island. People are either snoozing around the pool, or they're back in their rooms doing what we just did."

"We could go to my room," she said dryly.

"I'm not sure I can move yet," he said, bending down to lick one of her nipples.

Her breath caught in her throat as another wave of desire coursed through her.

"I want you again, Pepper."

"I don't think it's a…good…mmm." She lost the rest of her sentence when he moved his hips and she felt him harden inside her.

When he lifted his head, he was smiling. "Oh, it's going to be good. And it's going to take a lot longer this time. I promise."

5

"MARLENE, ARE YOU CERTAIN Ms. Rossi registered?" With the phone pressed to his ear, Butch Castellano paced back and forth in the office he kept off the hotel lobby.

"I'll double-check it, Mr. Castellano."

"And find out which room she's in. Call her and ask if there's anything she needs."

"Right away, Mr. Castellano."

Damn. Three hours had passed since the morning staff meeting when he'd seen the name *Irene Rossi* on the day's list of arriving guests. Renie was coming to the island. Three hours, and his nerves had yet to settle. Once he'd known that the one daily flight to the island had landed, he'd hung out in the office, watching the lobby, waiting for a glimpse of her at the registration desk. And when H had arrived to escort him to the poolside café for his meeting with Evan Atwell, he hadn't been able to think straight. That never happened to him. But he couldn't stop thinking about Renie. Why was she coming to the island? He'd told her not to. He'd explained to her that he'd considered it from all angles and decided it was best for them both if they just remained friends. Hadn't he made his feelings clear enough?

He strode over to the one-way glass window where H stood, watching the lobby. Good thing someone was keeping his mind on business.

Butch shot a look at his personal assistant. "I told her not to come."

H said nothing.

"She fell in love with a boy. She doesn't really know me. It just wouldn't work out. And her friendship is too important to me. Surely, she must have seen the logic of that. Why couldn't she just follow orders?"

"She's a woman," H said. "They don't think the same way we do. And they're hard to predict."

Butch grunted his frustration. H had been his cell mate for the last ten years he'd spent in one of upstate New York's finest penal facilities, and the single initial was the only name Butch knew him by. Standing six foot five in his stocking feet and built like a professional wrestler, H had a high intimidation quotient. That was no doubt why the staff and hotel guests called him *Mr.* H.

Over the years, Butch had come to value his friend for his qualities that were less immediately apparent. H had an excellent business sense, and best of all, he had a flair for interior design. It had been his idea to decorate and furnish the lobby like one of the old sugar plantations that had once flourished on the islands. Butch particularly favored the ceiling fans and the overstuffed cane furniture.

In his opinion, the décor made a perfect backdrop for his art collection. Butch shifted his gaze to the three French Impressionist paintings that now graced the walls of the lobby, and deliberately shifted his thoughts to the new Monet that he would soon acquire. That was what he should be thinking about.

"What do you think of Atwell?" he asked.

"Soft," H said.

This time Butch grunted a reluctant laugh. "And the Frenchy?"

H shrugged. "Slick. And *he's* not soft. I think the accent's a fake. I'm running a check on him."

Butch frowned and swore. "I shouldn't have missed that."

"The woman is distracting you."

No shit, Butch thought to himself. What else had he missed in that meeting? He frowned down at his cell phone. "What is keeping Marlene? All she has to do is pull up the registration record on the screen."

"The system is slow today."

Butch shifted his gaze to the spot on the lobby wall where he intended to hang the Monet. His fascination with the French Impressionists had begun thirty years ago when he'd taken a correspondence course in art history. His desire to begin a collection had been one of the reasons he'd decided to go straight. Renie had been the other reason.

In those early days behind bars, he'd had the foolish idea of trying to turn himself into someone who would be good enough for Renie. Her regular letters had not only inspired him but they'd kept him focused. And he'd dreamed of one day building a life with her. But it was a pipe dream. He couldn't change who he was or what he'd done with his life. And Renie had turned herself into such a success. She had her own TV show, for heaven's sake. And she had a family in San Francisco. She shouldn't give all that up for a man like him.

Butch took a cigar out of his pocket, stuffed it in his mouth, and tried to ignore the knot of nerves in his stomach. Now she was here on the island. He pulled out the cigar, then shoved it back in his mouth. Hell. He was a grown man of sixty-two. He couldn't recall the last time a woman had affected him this way. His palms were actually sweating.

"Tommy's busy," H said.

Grateful for anything that would distract him from his thoughts, Butch focused on the lobby. The registration desk was quiet but couples were lined up at Tommy's concierge desk. That was normal for this time of day.

"Should we hire him another assistant?" he asked. "That young Garibaldi is anxious to better himself."

"Gari wants to take over the flower shop. He works there every chance he gets, and Letitia says he has a real talent for floral design. Besides, Tommy can handle it," H said. "It takes him a little longer because he wants to match couples up with the perfect activity. In the long run, that will build repeat business."

"Right," Butch said. His cell phone rang and he snatched it up. "Yeah?"

"Mr. Castellano?"

"Yes, Marlene."

"I just pulled up the record. Ms. Rossi checked in at 1:00 p.m. Henry put her in Bungalow 3."

"Is she all right? Did you ask if there's anything she needs?"

"She's not picking up her phone. I checked with Henry and he thinks she and the man she was with headed for the pool."

"She was with a man?" Butch was appalled when the words nearly came out on a squeak.

"Yes, sir. Henry was clear about that. The man told the

bell captain that they could take care of the luggage themselves. All she had was a small duffel."

Butch glanced at H. "She checked in at 1:00 p.m. And
she was with a man."

H said nothing.

Butch pocketed the phone and then suddenly tossed
down his cigar. "Wait a minute. Wait just a damn minute.
I was standing right here at one o'clock. We didn't go to
our meeting with Atwell until one-thirty." He dredged the
details up in his mind. He'd been in the office for two
hours, pacing and chewing on his cigar much as he was
doing right now. Disgusted, he picked up his cigar and
shoved it back in his pocket. "How in hell did I miss her?"

"You haven't seen her in a while," H pointed out.
"People change in forty years."

Butch's stomach sank. Yes, they did. He shifted his
gaze from the lobby to his reflection in the glass. He certainly had. The last time he'd seen Renie face-to-face,
he'd been twenty-two. His hair had been black and wavy,
and his body had been rock solid. There wasn't a doubt in
his head that she still carried that image around with her
in her head. She'd always been such a sweet little romantic.

A sweet little romantic who'd brought a man to his
island to celebrate Valentine's Day!

Butch's eyes narrowed. "They're not at the bungalow,
not yet." Turning to H, he said, "Send two men, Angelo
and Armando, down to Bungalow 3. I want to know the
minute they show up."

"Yes, sir," H said and punched numbers into his cell.

"C'mon," Butch said. "We're going to the poolside café."

As FAR AS Friday the thirteenths went, Pepper was certain that this one was going to set a record. As she treaded water, she made a list of her current disasters. Not only had she lost her aunt and the Monet, but she'd just made love with the enemy. More than once.

How could she have done that? Was she really as disaster prone as her grandmother had always said she was? But as she watched Cole walk out of the water and pick his clothes up from where they'd been drying on the outcrop of rocks, she was reminded of exactly why she'd made love with him—and even worse, why she wanted to do it again.

It had been that way from the first. She couldn't look at the man without wanting him.

Pushing the thought aside, Pepper continued to tread water. She couldn't stay in the ocean for the rest of the day. And Cole would wait until she joined him. The man was relentlessly patient, and there wasn't a doubt in her mind that the minute she walked out of the water, he would start pressing her again about her involvement in the theft of the Monet.

Her options were limited. The island was small so even if she managed to shake Cole Buchanan she wouldn't be able to do it for long. Then there was the fact that her original plan to get the Monet back to San Francisco in time for the charity auction on Sunday night was clearly in jeopardy. With only one flight on and off the island each day, Irene wouldn't get here until Saturday and chances were good that Pepper wouldn't be able to leave the island until Sunday.

She needed to make a few phone calls to see if Irene had chartered a flight the way Cole had. Irene didn't have a cell so there was no way of contacting her directly.

Maybe if she told Cole everything and asked for his help…

But that would mean that he would once again be rescuing her from disaster, and she would be no closer to proving to her brothers that she could be an asset at Rossi Investigations.

Unless… As she began to swim towards shore, a plan took shape in her mind. When she stepped out of the water, she was careful not to look at Cole until she'd grabbed her jeans and T-shirt off the rock and hurriedly pulled them on. Only then did she meet his eyes. "I want to make a deal."

Cole was silent as he studied her. "What kind of a deal?"

She took a deep breath. "I'll tell you everything I know about the theft of the Monet, but in return, you have to back off and let me handle the case."

For a moment the only sound was the sweep of a wave as it hit the shore and the cry of a seagull. Cole's eyes were hidden once more by mirrored sunglasses, but Pepper was pretty sure she wouldn't have been able to read anything in them anyway.

"Why should I agree to that?"

"Because I'm asking you to. Look…" she raised her hands and dropped them, "it's not either of our faults that we're in competition for a partnership at Rossi Investigations. But you've got to admit that you have an advantage. Several, in fact. I'm perfectly aware that Matt and Luke gave me the job to make me feel at home and to humor me, and I know that my track record so far had been less than stellar. But I want them to take me seriously. Is that too much to ask?"

"No," Cole said, surprising her. "They *should* take you seriously."

His words brought a pleasure that warmed her. "Okay. Well, all I'm asking you to do is to give me a chance. How am I supposed to prove to my brothers that I'm an asset if you keep rushing in to rescue me all the time? I want you to back off and let me recover the Monet."

Another wave swept into shore, then he finally answered.

"I'll consider it. But I won't agree to anything until you tell me what's going on."

Pepper let out a breath she hadn't even known she was holding. At least, he hadn't said no. Yet. "This whole heist goes back to the Rossi curse."

Cole's brows shot up. "The Rossi curse?"

Pepper nodded. "The Rossis are doomed to be star-crossed when they fall in love. My dad and mom are one example, and Aunt Irene and Butch Castellano are another."

"Your aunt and Butch Castellano?"

Pepper nodded. "They fell in love when they were teen-agers, but my grandparents separated them by uprooting the family and moving to San Francisco. Then Butch made the separation long term by being sent to prison. The way Irene explains it, he took the blame for one of the higher-ups in the crime family. You have to swear not to tell any-one what I'm going to tell you next. Not even my father knows, and Irene swore me to secrecy. Do you promise?"

"Okay."

Pepper moved closer and lowered her voice. "For forty years, he and Irene corresponded, and the plan was that they would get together when he was finally released from prison. She claims that he's gone straight, and all the money he used to build this resort was earned legitimately."

"She's right," Cole said. "I checked Butch Castellano out as soon as I'd learned you booked a flight here. He's evidently a real whiz kid when it comes to playing the stock market."

Pepper stared at him. Why should it surprise her? After all, she was talking to the man who could give James Bond a run for his money.

"What does all this have to do with the theft of the Monet?"

"I'm getting there," Pepper promised. "When Butch was released from prison a year ago, he and Irene were supposed to get together and start the life they hadn't been able to build forty years ago. But then about a month before his release, Butch backed out of their deal. She's been after him for a year to change his mind, but he's stubborn. His excuse is that he still isn't good enough for her. Can you imagine that?"

But Cole didn't seem to be paying attention. Where had his mind wandered?

COLE WAS IMAGINING QUITE a few things—and not all of them had to do with the Monet. The most vivid image flickering at the edge of his mind was making love to Pepper again in a special place he'd discovered when he'd been exploring the island earlier. It would guarantee more privacy than this stretch of beach.

"Well?" Pepper asked.

Cole dragged his thoughts back to her original question. It was a loaded one. "I imagine he had his reasons."

"Hmph." She fisted her hands on her hips. "Well, they

didn't convince Irene. She thinks he's just trying to be all macho and protect her, so she decided to do something to prove that she's bad enough for him."

Cole's eyes narrowed as the light finally dawned. "Your aunt Irene stole the Monet?"

"She just borrowed it. She says he'll give it back once he knows it's stolen. Then I'll take it back to San Francisco."

Cole had a strong urge to shake his head to clear it. This was one scenario he hadn't foreseen. Oh, he'd met Irene at the Rossi Sunday dinners, and he'd been impressed with her. She'd created and sold a highly entertaining local TV show in which she demonstrated how vulnerable homeowners were to theft by demonstrating how easily their homes could be burglarized. Irene Rossi could easily have stolen the Monet. "Where is the painting?"

Pepper's brow wrinkled. "I'm not quite sure. I lost her in the Miami airport, and she missed the connecting flight here. Gari says there isn't another one until tomorrow. But perhaps she chartered a flight the way you did. What do you think?"

"You're sure she just didn't take off with it?"

"No. Of course she didn't. She plans on giving it back as soon as she makes her point to Butch. She's going to present it to him tomorrow on Valentine's Day."

Cole studied her for a moment. Up until this moment, he hadn't thought that Pepper Rossi was capable of lying. Was he wrong about that? "Let me get this straight. You helped your aunt steal the Monet so that she could prove to her old lover that she wasn't too good for him?"

Pepper considered his summary for a minute, then nodded. "In a nutshell, that's it. Except that I didn't know that I was helping her until she broke into the bedroom of the Atwells' suite. I knew that she was planning on doing something drastic, but not that she'd set her sights on the Monet. That thought only occurred to me when she showed up at the preview party. That's when I began to get this queasy feeling in my stomach that something bad was going to happen. When I went into the bedroom, she was there. I tried to talk her out of it."

"You could have given me a chance with her."

"I—" She raised her hands and dropped them. "I know, but Butch is being unreasonable. And Irene is going to give the painting back. Besides, I followed her just to make sure that Butch doesn't decide to return to his life of crime and keep it."

"And you kissed me in the Atwells' hotel room to distract me."

"Yes." She bit her lower lip, then added. "It was the only thing I could think of to do. I knew you'd stop her if I didn't do something. Plus…" she drew in a breath and let it out "…to be perfectly honest, I did want to kiss you. I know it doesn't make any sense, but I'd been thinking of kissing you for a while. Even though I knew it would be a mistake. Just like making love was a mistake."

For a moment Cole said nothing as a flood of feelings washed through him. They baffled him. Pepper Rossi baffled him. The only thing that he was pretty sure of was that she wasn't lying to him. There was a deep-down streak of honesty in her; it was one of the things that attracted him to her. And in spite of the fact that she was up to her neck in the theft of a priceless painting, he was determined to get her out of the mess. He'd never before had this urgent need to protect a woman. Even if her brothers hadn't asked him to help them out with the "Pepper Problem," he would have wanted to help her out of her scrapes.

But right now, the fact that she was in a jam and he had to figure out a way to fix it—all that had become secondary. He couldn't seem to stop thinking about making love to her again. Perhaps it was the island getting to him, but his gut instinct told him it was the woman.

"Well? Do we have a deal?" she asked.

"Why do you think that our making love was a mistake?"

Her brow furrowed. "For several reasons. First of all, we're just so different. Second, at work we're always in competition. And third, now that we've made love once, we'll probably want to do it again."

"And that would be a bad idea because…?"

"I can't afford the distraction." She began to tick items off on her fingers. "I have to find my aunt Irene, then I have to figure out a way to get the Monet back to San Francisco in time for the charity auction, and at the same time I have to keep my aunt from being arrested. Plus, I have to save the reputation of Rossi Investigations. All of which I had pretty much under control until Irene missed the plane from Miami. Now she won't be here until tomorrow. Plus, I need to figure out why Evan is here."

"So you agree that his presence on the island is suspicious?"

"Yes."

"Had you ever seen his companion before?"

"Just on the plane. He took the last seat on my flight, the one I was praying Irene would take."

"Do you have any idea why Evan would be meeting with Butch?"

"No. So I have a lot to figure out." She paused to meet

his eyes steadily. "I think we ought to treat the fact that we just made love as an isolated incident—something we did just to get it out of our systems." When he said nothing, she continued, "I have a lot on my plate right now."

Cole reached out to take the hand she'd been ticking items off on. "Yes, you do."

They both did. He wasn't quite sure when he'd made the decision—right then when she'd used the phrase *isolated incident* or back when he'd first laid eyes on her in Peter Rossi's kitchen—but he knew that making love to Pepper Rossi was not going to be a one-time deal. He'd known it when he'd been making his plans to come to the island. He'd bided his time for six long months, and he was through with waiting. "The thing is I don't think we've gotten it out of our systems." He sure as hell hadn't. "We're going to make love again. We'll be just as distracted thinking about it, so we might as well do it and enjoy ourselves."

Pepper sighed and sat down on the rock beside him. "I figured you'd say that."

He nearly smiled at her tone. "Maybe there's a way to work it into our deal."

Her eyes met his. "You'll go along with my deal? You'll let me handle the recovery of the Monet?"

Cole had already decided he could agree to that. After all, he'd be there if she got into too much trouble. "With one added stipulation. Since neither of us is in a position to do much about the Monet until Irene gets here, we'll have some time to enjoy each other. To explore this out-of-control attraction we have for each other. How does that sound?"

She didn't say anything for a moment, but Cole heard her breath catch. "You mean we'll…"

"We'll be lovers," he finished. He saw her eyes darken and the pulse at her throat begin to beat frantically. He pressed a finger to it. "Are you always this responsive?"

"I don't know, I—" She ran her tongue over her lips. "I've never felt this way with anyone else. I don't understand it."

Cole moved his finger to touch her lips. They were moist and soft. "Let's not worry about understanding it. There'll be time enough for that later. The only thing we have to do right now is enjoy it. Deal?"

When he took his finger away, she said, "With one more stipulation."

He hesitated for a moment, then said, "Fair enough."

"Whatever happens between us can only be temporary. When we get back to San Francisco, we go back to our previous relationship."

Cole studied her. If she really believed that they could do that, he wasn't going to try to convince her otherwise now. Not with words, and not when he could use much more persuasive means. He thought of the need she had to please her family and how she never felt like she quite measured up. The one thing he could do in the time they spent together was show her all the many ways she pleased him. "Our time on the island—no more, no less?"

"That's the deal."

"Accepted," he said.

In spite of his resolve to wait until they were in a more secluded area, he leaned toward her, unable to resist taking a taste of her lips. His mouth was just touching hers when they heard laughter from behind the rocks.

"We have to find some place more private," he murmured. "Any suggestions?"

"We could go to the bungalow."

"Good call." Keeping her hand in his, he scooped up the hamper and together they walked back toward the hotel.

6

Friday, February 13—3:30 p.m.

BUTCH GLANCED AT HIS watch for the fourth time in as many minutes. Then he let his gaze sweep the lobby again. The line at the concierge desk had been three to four couples deep all day. And Renie hadn't been among them. He'd checked with Tommy himself.

It had been over two hours since she'd checked in and so far she hadn't gone to her bungalow. Butch pulled out his cigar and stuck it between his teeth. When he and H had checked out the poolside café, they'd come up empty. The waiter, Gari, claimed that no one answering the description he gave had been there. But then maybe his description was wrong. H was right. He hadn't seen Renie for almost forty years. But her body size couldn't have changed. She'd been a slender little thing. And fragile. The fact that she was sixty now and not twenty wouldn't change that. And unless she dyed it, she'd have gray hair, he supposed. But it was hard to imagine her that way.

Butch pulled out a lighter, then shoved it back in his pocket. Where the hell was she? And what was she doing on his island with another man? Ever since he'd learned that she'd been with a man at the registration desk, his brain hadn't been working right. He thought after forty years that he knew her. She'd always been the sweetest thing. For years, he'd kept her image in his mind. She was so pretty with that short, brown hair and those huge eyes. The first time he'd met her, he'd drowned in those eyes. Picturing her in his mind, knowing that she was waiting for him, had gotten him through those first years in prison. That and her letters. If he hadn't already been in love with her, the letters she sent would have surely sunk him. He'd learned everything about her in those letters—her hopes, her dreams. In so many ways they'd never been apart.

And he wanted those letters to go on. But he had to admit that the sweet Renie that he'd pictured in his mind so many years ago was different than the woman who'd called him after he'd explained that they shouldn't be together on his island. She'd sounded royally pissed. But she'd come around. She always did.

When he'd told her forty years ago that she should take her parents' advice and build a life for herself out in San Francisco, she'd gone along with it. She hadn't been angry with him. And she certainly hadn't threatened him. But in the two hours since he'd learned she was on Escapade Island with a male companion, he'd had time to go over their last conversation in his mind. And what she'd said to him certainly constituted a threat. "Listen up, Butch. I'm going to prove you wrong. I let you push me away once. Not again. Just you wait!"

Just you wait. That wasn't like his Renie at all. He turned to H who was seated behind his desk going over work schedules. "You're sure she isn't in the bungalow?"

"Angelo checked the rooms, and there wasn't any sign that either she or her companion had been there."

Her companion. Jealousy sliced through him. Butch bit down hard on his cigar. "Angelo's still there?"

H nodded. "He's outside the bungalow, keeping it under surveillance. Should I call him?"

"No." Butch pulled the cigar out of his mouth. The end was chewed beyond repair. It was the third one he'd destroyed since he'd learned that Renie was on the island. Disgusted, he tossed it into a wastebasket. Then he ran his hands through his hair.

"Maybe we should send some men to comb the beaches. Maybe she went for a swim and ran into some trouble."

H glanced up from the schedule he was working on. "Maybe she's not as helpless as the woman you're remembering."

Butch whirled on him. "What are you saying?"

H shrugged. "I've watched her TV show."

"How? It's a local show."

"I asked a friend to tape a few and send them to me in the event that you might want to see one."

"Well, I don't."

H nodded and went back to work.

Butch reached for another cigar, then thought better of it. "You think I was wrong to break it off." It wasn't a question. Butch knew his old friend well enough to be pretty sure of what H's feelings on the subject were.

"*Wrong* is a strong word."

"What then?"

H glanced up. "I think you're still in love with her."

Butch threw up his hands. "Of course I am. That's why I broke it off. She could do better than me. She *should* do better than me."

"In the past forty years she's stuck by you. That says something."

"It says that she needs to be protected from her own stupidity. That's what I'm doing."

H's cell phone rang. He picked it up from the desk and flipped it open. "Yeah?"

A moment later, he said to Butch, "They've just arrived at the bungalow. What do you want Angelo to do?"

They. This time, it was more than a stab of jealousy that he felt. It was a punch of pure fury that hit him right in the solar plexus. He drew in a deep breath. "Tell Angelo to wait." Then he motioned to H to follow him.

On his way past his desk, Butch unlocked the top drawer, removed his gun, and tucked it into the waistband beneath his shirt. "I'll handle this myself."

COLE GLANCED AT THE bathroom door as he punched numbers into his cell phone. Pepper was still in the shower. He'd wanted very much to join her, but he'd talked himself into giving her time—into giving them both time.

He'd checked with the Miami airport, but Irene Rossi's name was not on the list of passengers scheduled for tomorrow's flight to Escapade Island. Not yet anyway. He'd also checked with the charter companies that flew out of the airport, but Irene hadn't chartered a flight either, at least not from Miami.

That was worrisome and increased his concerns about where Irene Rossi actually was. He wasn't going to share his concerns with Pepper yet. But missing a plane was one thing. Missing it while you were transporting a priceless painting was another.

Then there was the fact that ever since their arrival at

the bungalow, he'd had a very clear feeling that they were being watched. If they were, the guy was a pro because so far Cole hadn't been able to spot him. As a precaution, he'd locked the doors—not that they wouldn't give under the right pressure—and his gun was on the bedside table right next to the candles he'd lit.

To keep himself occupied while he was waiting for Pepper, he'd set the scene for a seduction. He was a man who'd always known how to get what he wanted. His days of trying to figure out what to do about Pepper Rossi were over. He was going to use every amenity that the island had to offer in his campaign to persuade her to give their relationship a chance beyond the time they were going to spend on the island.

Not that he'd had to do much. Escapade Resort was a natural setting for seduction. Impatient that his call hadn't connected yet, he disconnected and punched in the numbers again. As he waited, he glanced around the bedroom. The interior of the bungalow was a cool and dark escape from the sun beating down on the beach outside. Through the slatted shutters, he could hear the waves hitting the shore. There was a high surf on this side of the island. The bed was draped in mosquito netting that isolated whoever slept there from the outside world. No doubt about it, the people who ran the Escapade Resort knew romance. All he'd had to do was light the candles on the nightstand, pull a split of champagne out of the mini-bar, and pop the cork.

"Tell me you're on your way back with the Monet." Luke's voice on the other end of the call had Cole reining in his thoughts.

"Not yet," Cole said. "But I have a lead on it."

"All of our jobs could depend on getting that painting

back. If Althea Atwell sues us, we're going to take a hell of a PR blow."

"Yeah."

"Got any idea yet who took it?"

Cole sidestepped the question. He wasn't going to betray Pepper or her aunt, not even to his best friend and boss. "Evan Atwell is here on the island with a male companion."

"You're kidding."

The stretch of silence on the other end of the line told Cole his distraction had worked. He could picture Luke, his eyes closed, leaning back in his chair, mulling that one over.

Of the two Rossi brothers, Luke was the one who had a gift for figuring things out. He was a genius when it came to anything electronic. Matt was more of an action man. If you were holed up in an alley being shot at, Matt was the Rossi you wanted at your side. But if there was a puzzle to solve, Luke was your man. Together, the brothers made a good team.

It occurred to him then that what Pepper had to do was find and use her strengths if she wanted to make a place for herself. He glanced toward the bathroom door. Perhaps their deal—that he would back off and let her handle this case—could help her to do that.

"So, genius boy, what do you think?" Cole finally asked.

"I've got several ideas. You think Atwell set up the robbery?"

"I think it would be an amazing coincidence if he was just here to take in the island's amenities. Evan also had a meeting with Butch Castellano, the owner of the resort, and Mr. Castellano has a well-known reputation for collecting French Impressionists. Atwell's companion wears a goatee and a French beret. It would help if you could get a line on him."

"Will do. I don't like this turn of events one bit." Luke disconnected.

Ditto, Cole thought. There was nothing to like about Atwell's presence on the island. He couldn't get rid of the feeling that there was more going on here than Irene Rossi's scheme to lure back an old boyfriend.

He strode to the wide window that looked out on the beach. Then he moved back into the bedroom and peered through the slats in the window that looked out on a forest of palm trees. The hairs on the back of his neck rose to attention. Someone was out there all right. But who and why?

PEPPER USED THE SLEEVE of her Escapade Island robe to wipe off the steam that covered the bathroom mirror. She'd finished her shower fifteen minutes ago, and then she'd rubbed herself with lotion, brushed her teeth, and done what she could with her hair. Phone calls had been next. Irene wasn't booked to fly in on tomorrow's flight, and she hadn't chartered a flight from the Miami airport. That didn't mean that she hadn't been able to find another charter company, but Pepper was beginning to have the same bad feeling she'd had in the penthouse suite.

She glanced at the bathroom door. Cole might have some ideas. But she wanted to handle this herself. Besides, she was stalling. Nerves were dancing little jigs in her stomach. She looked down at the book she'd dug out of her duffel, the one that Gari had given her on the island's history. She'd leafed through it to postpone going back into the bedroom, but when she discovered herself caught up in the story of Adam, a plantation owner's son, who'd fallen in love with Elena, one of his slaves, she'd closed the book in disgust. She just couldn't seem to escape from tales of star-crossed lovers.

And what was she doing sitting here reading when she could be making love with Cole? When was she ever going to stop worrying that she would never measure up?

"Stupid," she whispered to the image she saw in the mirror. Still she hesitated. Glancing back down at the book, she couldn't help wonder if the island slave girl Elena had faced the same fears the first time she'd made love with her young master. Probably.

But this wasn't going to be the first time she made love with Cole. Strictly speaking, if she was keeping score, it would be the third time. Slowly, she ran her finger down the spine of the book. It was one thing to make love on impulse and quite another to know it was going to happen—to have to think and to plan.

Had Elena had some sort of plan the first day that Adam had summoned her? Probably.

But Pepper was lousy at plans whether it had to do with making love or anything else. Following her aunt to Escapade Island was a prime example. Her idea of how she was going to recover the Monet and return it to the Atwells without involving her aunt was vague at best. Her grandmother's main complaint about her echoed through her mind—that she always rushed headlong into things without thinking them through.

Come to think of it, that's what had gotten her into her current situation. If she hadn't gone with the impulse to kiss Cole to distract him, and if she hadn't gone with impulse again and made love with him on the beach, she wouldn't be here in the bathroom hiding.

Lifting her chin, Pepper fisted her hands on her hips.

Hiding in the bathroom was just ridiculous. She wanted to kiss Cole Buchanan again, and she wanted very much to make love to him. They only had the next twenty hours or so, and she was wasting precious minutes wallowing in self-doubt. Yet again.

She didn't doubt for a minute that Elena probably had her act together from the first moment she'd seen Adam. Meeting her own gaze in the mirror again, Pepper whispered, "Coward." Then another thought occurred to her. Hadn't she gotten the courage to ask Cole to kiss her that first time by pretending to be someone else?

Why couldn't she pretend to be Elena, the slave girl? Inspired, she rose, opened the door, and stepped through it.

The bedroom was so dim that it was the scent that hit her first. Vanilla and some other more exotic spice. Her eyes were drawn to the candles. Then she saw Cole standing at the foot of a huge bed that was draped in a sheer, gauzy fabric. He was wearing black briefs, and even in the candlelight she could make out his broad shoulders, the lean waist, and those strong, muscled legs.

Elena would have met her lover in much the same kind of room, and also during the day and in secret. And their time together would have been similarly limited—the curse of all lovers who came from different worlds.

A soft breeze made it through the slats of a shutter, stirring the gauze draping the bed and making the candlelight flicker. But she couldn't take her eyes off of Cole. Hunger for him built at a speed that she was still struggling to get used to. Hunger to touch him. All over.

"I was just about ready to come in and get you," Cole said. "Are you having second thoughts?"

"No." But she didn't move toward him yet. "Not about

making love to you again. I want to do that. It's just that…
my nerves are…"

He held out a hand. "What can I do to help?"

A warmth moved through her at the gesture and the
words. He was kind. Why did that surprise her—and why
hadn't she noticed that before? Without thinking she
blurted out, "Do you ever like to act out fantasies? I mean
when you're making love with a woman?"

"You want to pretend you're someone else?"

Even in the dim light, she could see his eyes narrow
slightly. He was going to think she was nuts.

"You already know that pretending helps me cope with
nerves. And you probably think that's crazy."

"No. I've used the same coping device myself on occasion. What do you have in mind?"

She moistened lips that had suddenly gone dry. "There
was this book I was reading in the bathroom. Gari gave it
to me, and it's filled with stories about the early settlers
of the island. One of them was a story of forbidden love
between the son of the plantation owner and one of his
slaves. Adam and Elena. For days and days, he watched
her in the fields, stole out to speak with her, left her secret
gifts, before he finally sent for her the first time."

"Once he laid eyes on her, he couldn't get her out of
his mind." With one finger, Cole traced the line of her
throat, and Pepper felt the touch right down to her toes.
"She filled his dreams at night and filled his thoughts all
day."

"Yes."

"His feelings for her grew so strong that he wasn't quite
sure how to handle them. But finally, he could no longer
resist the attraction. So he sent for her."

"Yes." Pepper moistened her lips again. "And she longed for him too because she'd learned what a sweet and gentle man he was. She wanted nothing more than to feel the warmth of his touch and to touch him in return."

"I think I can understand that," Cole said, his eyes never leaving hers.

She cleared her dry throat. "Well, I was just thinking that they must have met secretly in a place just like this, and I thought—I mean, if you wouldn't mind..."

"You're my mistress, Elena, and I've just sent for you."

Pepper let out the breath that she was holding. He didn't think she was nuts. "Yes. And I've made it clear that I desperately want this too. In fact, this isn't the first time we've met. Each day guards fetch me from the fields and bring me here to you."

He moved toward her then, slowly. "Each day when you get here, I take your clothes off and bathe you first. I like to touch you. I enjoy making you come just by touching you."

With the fantasy spinning in her head, Pepper struggled to find her voice. "Each time we meet the threat of discovery is heightened, and we know our time together is slipping away."

"I can have my pick of the slaves, but I'm not supposed to favor one. I can't help myself. Each time you leave, I know that I'll have to ask for you again because I have to touch you again." Cole reached out to her then, running one finger down the column of her neck to her collarbone. "I have to have you again. I've become addicted to you— to the pleasure we can give each other. I can't stop. I don't think I'll ever be able to stop."

Pepper was surprised that she could walk when he took

her hand and led her to the side of the bed. She'd never before been seduced by words alone.

Cole lifted a glass of champagne from the nightstand. When he touched it to her lips, she took a sip. Then he turned the glass and sipped from the same spot that she'd used. Her knees went weak.

"Have I told you how much I like your taste?" he asked.

"I like yours, too. I…want more." Pepper wasn't quite sure whether she was speaking as Elena or herself.

"Yes," Cole murmured as he set down the glass and reached for the sash of her robe.

She had one brief feeling of regret that she didn't have on something sexier underneath, and then she pushed it aside. Elena wouldn't have had anything fancy to wear. Like the slave, she was going to live in the moment.

The second her robe hit the floor, she took his hands and said, "I want to touch you the way you always touch me. All over. Will you let me do that?"

Even in the dim light, she caught the gleam in his eyes.

"Of course," he said. "Don't you remember the one rule we agreed to, Elena? Every request we make of each other must be granted. Without exception."

Pepper felt a dark, hot thrill move through her. Cole not only didn't think she was nuts, he was adding to the fantasy.

Her hand trembled as she pushed aside the gauzy fabric draping the bed. He climbed onto the mattress first and then pulled her up beside him. After she urged him back on the pillows, she straddled his waist. Just the feel of that smooth, hot skin beneath her began to cloud her mind. Inching herself forward a few inches, she placed her hand on either side of his face.

His low moan distracted her for a moment.

"What?" she asked.

"You feel so good on top of me, I'm not sure how much time I can give you to touch me."

As Pepper considered that, all the sensations moving through her intensified. She was aware of the sharp angle of his jaw and the roughness of stubble beneath her palms. She felt the hard heat of his stomach muscles pressed against her center. There was a growing feeling of emptiness right there, and she hungered for it to be filled. *In a moment,* she promised herself as she drew her palms down his neck and over his shoulders. Then she moved her hands slowly down the muscles of his chest absorbing the texture of the crisp dark curls that covered it until her fingers finally stopped at the apex of her thighs.

"Touch yourself now, Elena."

A tide of heat moved through her, so hot that she was afraid she was going to melt.

"Do it for me," he urged. "You promised to do anything I asked you to do."

It seemed such a wicked and wanton thing to do. And she was surprised at the strength of her desire to touch herself simply because Cole wanted her to. But the melting sensation inside of her was so intense now that she wasn't sure she had the strength to...

"Now."

It was the tight husky tone of his voice that had her rising just enough to insert her fingers into the soft heat at her center. Pleasure speared through her.

"Tell me what it feels like," he said.

Battling a fresh onslaught of sensations, she said, "Hot. My fingers are burning. And it's so wet."

"Go deeper," he urged.

Her hand seemed to be controlled by his commands because all of a sudden, her fingers slid in further. But... "Not deep enough. I want—"

"Soon. But first, pull them out and then push in again."

Once again her fingers moved at his command as if she were merely his puppet, and this time a fierce tightness began to build inside of her.

"Out and in," he murmured.

She could barely hear his words so focused was she on the sensations that were flooding through her. His skin was so hot, so hard against her thighs. And his hands were at her waist now, gripping her tightly as her fingers moved. Out and in. Out and in. Pressure built inside of her until that's all she knew, all she felt.

"Come for me, Elena. Come for me, now."

The whispered words, the urgency of them, moved through her, releasing the pressure in one colossal wave of pleasure that grew in strength as it moved through her.

When she could think again, she was lying on top of Cole, her face pressed into the curve of his shoulder, his arms holding her close. She wasn't sure that she could move, wasn't sure she wanted to.

"I didn't get very far with my plan to touch you," she murmured.

She heard the deep rumble of his chuckle beneath her ear. It was a nice sound, one she hadn't heard before.

"You can give it another try as soon as you feel up to it," he said.

"I think my arms are still about as operative as wet noodles," she said and had the pleasure of hearing his chuckle again.

There was a sudden explosion of sound from the other

room—the front door crashing open. In one smooth movement, Cole lifted her and pushed her aside.

"My gun," he whispered as he slid from the bed. "It's on the nightstand."

Footsteps pounded across floorboards as she slithered out of the bed, twisting herself in the sheet and nearly losing her balance. By the time she grabbed the gun, two men were in the doorway of the bedroom. She recognized them as Butch Castellano and the man Cole had identified as his bodyguard, Mr. H. Butch was reaching behind him for something. There was no time to hand the gun off to Cole. He was on the other side of the bed. So she raised it with both hands and pointed it at the two intruders.

"Put your hands in the air," she said.

But Butch had already drawn his gun and was pointing it at Cole.

The noise when she released the safety was loud and seemed to echo in the room.

Everyone froze and looked at her.

Despite that her hand was shaking, she kept the barrel pointed in Butch Castellano's direction and said, "Drop that gun and put your hands up."

"Renie—"

"If I were you, I'd put my hands in the air," Cole said.

For a moment no one spoke or moved. The only sound was the pound of waves on the shore.

"Renie, put that gun down," Butch said. "You know you won't shoot it."

"I wouldn't be so sure of that," Cole said. "And her name isn't Renie. It's Pepper."

"You keep out of this," Butch said, taking a step toward Cole.

Panic struck Pepper. Butch had a gun and he had it pointed at Cole. Her hand was shaking so hard that any minute she might drop the weapon she was holding. What was she going to do? She couldn't shoot Butch. She was pretty sure she couldn't shoot anyone. Before she was even aware that her brain had made a conscious decision, she aimed the gun at the ceiling and fired a shot through the thatched roof.

The sound was so loud that she thought she'd gone deaf. The others had frozen in place again.

Pepper registered the expressions on the two men's faces. Butch looked shocked, his companion thoughtful.

H turned his head and spoke to Cole. "I'll handle Mr. Castellano if you'll get the gun from her."

"No can do," Cole said. "Her hand might be shaking a bit, but she meant that last shot to go where it did. She's as good as I am at the practice range."

Pepper saw that her hand began to shake even more.

After three long beats, H said to Butch, "Lower your gun."

Butch did. Then he shot Cole one searing look. "You, I'll deal with later." He turned back to Pepper. "Renie, why are you—"

H put a hand on Butch's shoulder. "That isn't Renie."

Butch blinked and then put the gun back in the belt of his shorts. Pepper nearly dropped her own weapon in sheer relief, but she managed to get it onto the nightstand.

"You're not Renie?" Butch's eyes narrowed as he studied her. "You sure as hell look like her."

"She looks like Renie did forty years ago," Mr. H said.

"Perhaps it would help if I made some introductions," Cole said. "The woman who just shot a hole through the roof is Irene Rossi's niece, Pepper Rossi."

"Niece," Butch said. "You're Renie's niece?"

"Yes." She glanced up at the ceiling. "Sorry about that."

"I told you that you should watch one of her TV shows. People change in forty years," Mr. H commented.

Without replying, Butch turned to Cole. "And you are?"

"Cole Buchanan. I work for Irene's nephews at Rossi Investigations," Cole said.

Butch looked from one to the other of them, then said, "Where in the hell is Renie?"

7

"WE'RE GETTING OFF THIS island," Irene said, urging Happy along the shoreline.

"I don't see why you're so upset. You've got a room, and look at this place. It's paradise."

Irene glanced around. The sun sent sparks off the water that nearly blinded her to the shadow on the horizon that was Escapade Island. "This island is the wrong paradise." She pointed to across the water. "I have to get over there."

She just had to figure out a way to do it, and her first stop was going to be the marina she'd spotted from the room she and Happy had been assigned to in the hotel.

"You heard our commander-in-chief," Happy said.

Irene snorted. "That's a very apt description of her. She's running a regular sex boot camp here. Did you see those 'morning exercises' she's recommending?"

"Yeah." Happy's smile widened. "I thought they looked exciting."

"They looked anatomically impossible."

"We won't know until we try, will we? And besides, the morning exercises are only the first step in exploring your inner sex goddess."

Irene clenched her fingers into fists. She had never met a man in her life who exuded such positive energy. It made her want to slap him. But he might start moaning again.

"Look, Happy." She suppressed the urge to grab him by the shirt. "Let me make this clear. We're not trying out anything. The only person I'm interested in exploring my inner sex goddess with is on Escapade Island. My goal right now is to get there."

"But our commander-in-chief says that these little mix-ups occur all the time. People board the wrong plane in Miami once or twice a week. As she told us, there are a couple of guests stranded on Escapade Island who will be coming here tomorrow, and you can go back on the same boat."

"I can't wait until tomorrow." While the drill sergeant had been giving her opening spiel, Irene had had time to think about the Monet. She was willing to bet that whoever had drugged her and dumped her on the plane to Camp E.D.E.N. was now on Escapade Island. After all, a man who collected French Impressionists resided there. Butch had never kept that a secret. There'd even been mention made in the travel magazine that had written up his resort.

But she was putting the missing Monet out of her mind for the moment. First things first. She had to get to Escapade Island, and then she'd figure out what to do about the Monet. "There's got to be a boat that we can rent or borrow. Or steal."

"I don't know," Happy said. "She seemed pretty firm about it."

Irene shot him a withering glance. "That's because *firm* is her credo. If Hitler were ever reincarnated as a woman, she'd be him." *Just your type,* she thought. But she didn't say it. She didn't want to start him moaning again. As annoying as Happy Johansson was, it had occurred to her that he might have his uses. For one thing, she'd learned that he was a sailor, and she'd never operated a boat in her life.

When they rounded a curve of the shoreline and the marina came into view, she quickened her pace. "There's a boat—the one with the canopy."

Happy shook his head. "That's a paddle boat, and there's no way that you can paddle to Escapade Island. I wouldn't recommend it even along the shoreline."

Irene pointed to the canoes. "What about those?"

Happy shook his head again. "Not seaworthy enough. The commander-in-chief told you that the only boats available were for the lagoons."

"We're getting off this place somehow." The sun was still so hot that the horizon was hazy. But she could see the outline of Escapade Island in the distance, beckoning to her. It was so close. She had to get there. She couldn't and wouldn't let Butch buy a stolen painting. At the very least, she had to warn him. At best, she was going to steal it back. However that played out, she was not going to let anything stop her from having a little face-to-face chat with Butch Castellano.

When they reached the dock, a man stepped out of the small shack near the water. He was short, stocky and bald. He spit tobacco into a wave, then said, "Can I help you?"

"I need to rent a boat to get to Escapade Island," Irene said.

The man sent another spit of chew into an oncoming wave. "I've only got boats for the lagoons."

"Told you," Happy murmured.

Irene glared at Happy until he cleared his throat and

asked, "Surely you've got something—perhaps a small sail-boat?"

The man shook his head again. "Got no call for them. People who come to this island aren't much into boating. They have other interests."

Before he turned away, Irene grabbed his shirt and gave him a little shake. Behind her, she heard Happy moan.

"Isn't she something?" Happy asked.

Irene ignored him. "There's got to be someone on this island who has a seaworthy boat we could use."

The man, more alarmed than threatened, raised his arms in surrender. "There's a lady on the other side of the island who has a motorized raft. You might be able to get across on that."

"How do I get there?" Irene asked, releasing him.

He took a step back, smoothing his shirt. "There's no taxi service, so you'll have to walk along the shore. It's about seven or eight miles."

Turning, Irene gave Happy a shove. "Let's go."

"I love it when you shove me."

Irene swallowed a groan. He was a sailor, she reminded herself. And she needed to get to Escapade Island ASAP. Urging him along, she started walking along the white sand beach.

WHERE THE HELL WAS Renie? Butch's question echoed in Cole's mind as Pepper served drinks from the mini-bar to Butch Castellano and his bodyguard, H. The large man had requested them to drop the "Mister." Pepper was filling them in on the fact that she'd lost Irene in the Miami airport.

She'd pulled Cole aside in the bedroom while they were

dressing and asked him not to mention the Monet. Her plan was to enlist Butch's help to locate her aunt, but they wouldn't tell him about the painting. Not until her aunt was here on the island. He'd told her it was her call, her case.

Since Butch had asked his original question, they'd all moved from the bedroom into the living room. Butch was drinking beer, and H was sipping from a bottle of water.

When Pepper finished with her story, Butch said, "So let me get this straight. You followed your aunt here? Why?"

Pepper's cheeks colored. "She was coming to see you. And you'd told her not to come. I wanted to make sure she was all right."

After regarding her steadily for a moment, Butch nodded. "Fair enough. Then you lost her somewhere in the Miami airport and she didn't show up on the connecting flight. This guy with a French accent and a goatee was the last to board."

"And this French guy was the same man I saw here with Evan Atwell."

Butch's eyes narrowed. "You know Atwell?"

Pepper nodded again. "I used to date him."

Butch grunted and said, "Good thing you stopped. He's gay."

Pepper stared at him. "No, he's not."

"He and the Frenchman are a couple, right, H?" Butch asked.

"That would be my guess," H said.

"Evan and the man with the goatee?" Pepper asked.

"They're sharing the penthouse suite at the main hotel," H said with a small apologetic shrug. "That's not conclusive, but this is a couples resort."

Cole tucked the piece of information away. He'd had a

hunch that might be the case, but Butch's and H's near certainty convinced him. Both men seemed to be very astute.

"Well," Pepper said. Cole knew her well enough now that he could tell she was processing the information, using hindsight to put it together with what she already knew. But what he noticed most was that she didn't seem at all upset about the fact that Evan Atwell might be gay.

"I'm still worried about Aunt Irene," Pepper said. "She's not booked on tomorrow's flight, and she hasn't chartered a plane from the Miami airport. The more I think about it, the more I wonder if she really missed the plane. What if something else happened to her?"

"Foul play?" Butch frowned.

"I don't know. But I do know that she was dead set on getting to this island today. She wanted very much to see you, and she's a very focused woman."

Butch glanced at H. "Maybe she got on the plane to Eden Island by mistake. How many misplaced guests do we have right now?"

"Four. The cowboy and his lady friend and the two streakers."

Pepper's mouth turned up in a wry grin. "We had a glimpse of those streakers."

"They're running a very specialized resort over there on Eden," H explained. "They advertise it as a sex camp. It's very hedonistic, from what I gather. With the similarity in names, we often have mix-ups. Guests have a pina colada on their layover in Miami and get on the wrong plane. Every morning, one of our locals runs a boat between the two islands to relocate the misplaced guests."

Pepper turned to Butch. "Can you find out if that's what happened?"

"Yeah." As he spoke, Butch punched numbers into his cell phone. A minute ticked by and he finally repocketed the phone. "The boss lady who runs the place doesn't always pick up her phone." He raised his voice an octave. "She has better things to do like participating in an orgy." He spoke in a normal tone as he rose. "I'll send Angelo right over there. If Renie's on that island, he'll bring her back."

Cole gave H his cell phone number, and then Butch and his sidekick went out the door. Moving toward Pepper, Cole said, "I thought they'd never leave."

When he took her hand, she gripped his fingers tightly. "The more I think about it, the more worried I am about Irene."

"She might very well have just taken the wrong flight. Besides, from what I've observed, she's pretty capable of taking care of herself. And...." Cole lifted her hand and pressed a kiss to her palm. "Worrying never solved anything."

"What about Evan? Shouldn't we be trying to figure out why he's here and who this French guy is?"

"I have a confession to make. I called Luke while you were in the bathroom and he's trying to get a line on the Frenchman. I didn't mention either you or Irene. We have some time with regard to Evan and his friend, I think. After all, they aren't going anywhere. They'll still be here tomorrow, at least until noon." He pressed another kiss to her palm and gave himself the pleasure of hearing her breath escape on a sigh. "So there's really nothing either of us can do right now. If Irene's on that island, Butch will locate her. And I have a feeling that she'll be here on Escapade Island with the Monet a lot sooner than tomorrow at noon." Which meant that their time together might very well be less than twenty-four hours. He was stunned at how that thought pained him. He wanted every last minute he could have with Pepper almost as much as he wanted the Monet.

"In the meantime, I bet I can take your mind off of Irene and Evan," he said.

She smiled at him. "I'll just bet you can."

But when she turned toward the bedroom, he pulled her toward the outside door. "C'mon."

"But we didn't finish...the fantasy. You didn't finish..."

Cole turned and the concern he saw in her eyes melted something deep inside of him. "Don't worry." He leaned down to brush his lips over hers. "We will. I will."

"Where are we going?"

"To paradise," he promised.

SHE WAS DEFINITELY in paradise, Pepper thought as Cole sent the sailboat skimming across the cove. The boat itself was a rental and only built for two people, three at the most. The sun was a bright yellow ball in the sky, the sand on the shore was a nearly blinding shade of white, and the water beneath the boat was impossibly clear and blue. She could even see the ripples in the sand that the movement of the sea had made.

But it was the speed rather than the beauty that she found so exhilarating. So freeing. Worries, responsibilities, even her anxiety about Irene and the Monet—everything was whipped away by the wind. Cole was right. They couldn't have put a better man than Butch on the task of locating her. Then Irene could give the painting to Butch, and Butch could give it back. And if that little scenario didn't go as smoothly as Irene had predicted, Pepper would find a way to handle it.

Out here on the water, she somehow felt confident of that. And that was the only difference. Time, which had seemed to slow since she'd first set foot on the airport tarmac, had almost ceased to exist. She wondered if that was what it must have been like in the original paradise.

"Perfect," she murmured.

And so was the man who sat with his hand on the tiller. Through the amber-tinted sunglasses she wore, he looked like some kind of bronzed god. He was lean and hard, and dangerous. For some reason it was the dangerous quality that had appealed to her from the beginning. In a million years, she wouldn't have suspected that she'd be attracted to that type. Maybe she took after her Aunt Irene in that regard.

Droplets of spray glinted on Cole's skin, and she found herself wanting to taste them. She was almost getting used to the heat that grew within her whenever she looked at him. Almost.

He looked so natural sitting there guiding the boat across the water, as if he'd been born to do. But then he always looked so competent, so at ease. She envied that quality about him the most. And perhaps that was what drew her.

What else? She'd never before tried to analyze the attraction she felt for him. This was a man who'd desired her, pleasured her. She'd been held against that lean, hard body, pressed beneath it, and yet she knew very little about him.

She hadn't wanted to know about him. Once she'd read his résumé, she'd convinced herself that the less she knew the better. But now, she was curious. What had she learned since she'd come to the island?

"Penny for your thoughts," Cole said.

"I'm thinking that you're a surprising man."

"In what way?"

"For starters, you went along with my slave girl/plantation owner fantasy."

He smiled slowly. "That was my pleasure. I enjoyed meeting Elena."

Her eyes narrowed. "Really?"

He threw back his head and laughed. The bright sound was whipped away by the wind. "I believe I detect a note of jealousy in your voice."

She lifted her chin and lied. "Not at all. I'm just thinking of all the ways I'm going to enjoy Adam."

"Good. Adam is thinking about his next meeting with Elena right now. He's thinking of just how he's going to touch her."

Pepper felt her insides begin to melt.

"Would you like to know where I'm going to touch Elena?"

Throat dry, Pepper could only nod.

"I'm going to touch her throat where that pulse beats so fast. It beats that way whenever she's near me, and I want to feel it against my finger. I want to taste it."

Pepper felt her hands tighten on the edge of her seat. She was so hot, and the breeze was doing nothing to cool her.

"But what I really want to do, what I thought about doing all morning while I sat through a boring meeting in my father's office, is that I'm going to touch Elena just the way I asked her to touch herself the last time we were together."

The image that filled her mind was so vivid that Pepper had to grip the edge of her seat hard or she would have slid right to the floor of the boat. How could he affect her this way with words alone? And he knew exactly what he was doing to her. She could tell in the intent way he was looking at her.

"I wish we weren't on this boat," he murmured. "I wish I could make you come again right now."

If he kept talking, he might be able to do just that, Pepper thought.

"Duck your head," he said in a different tone. "I'm going to bring her around."

She did, and the boom just missed her head. The glance she got of the shore as the boat turned told her that they'd come very close to some rocks that were jutting out into the water at the edge of the cove. It gave her some satisfaction that he must have been as distracted by the fantasy as she'd been.

When she met his eyes, he was smiling at her. "We'd better keep Adam and Elena apart until we decide to beach this little boat." He tilted his head. "Why did it surprise you that I would go along with your fantasy?" he asked.

She thought for a moment, then said, "I didn't expect you to be…fun." Or perceptive or sensitive, she added silently.

"Why not?"

"You're always so quiet. At those Sunday gatherings, you're always on the sidelines, watching my father make pasta or Matt fire up the grill. And then there's your résumé. Ex-CIA? I've always thought that working for that outfit would be pretty grim. No offense."

"You're right. The CIA doesn't offer a lot of laughs. That's one of the reasons I took Luke up on his job offer."

"More laughs?"

"Less grimness."

"You must have gotten at least a few chuckles getting me out of scrapes."

His smile widened. "I did enjoy the Parakeet Caper."

The corners of Pepper's mouth twitched. He was referring to her attempt to lure a flyaway parakeet off of the roof of a house. She'd climbed a nearby tree to try to talk the bird down. And then she'd gotten the idea of climbing along one of the limbs and onto the roof. A half hour later, she'd finally gotten the bird to trust her, but then she'd discovered that there was no way she was getting off the roof unless she could fly.

The Allibrandi family had called Rossi Investigations and, of course, Cole had come to her rescue.

"It wasn't funny at the time," Pepper pointed out.

"Hey." Cole threw up a hand. "I didn't laugh, did I?"

No, he hadn't laughed at her—not ever. Not even when Luke and Matt had told that story and others at their Sunday gatherings. It occurred to her then that she owed Cole Buchanan for that and for other things.

"Thanks for letting me handle the situation with Butch this afternoon," she said. "With the gun, I mean."

"You did a good job. You had H scared."

His praise sent a thrill through her. "Really?"

"He couldn't predict what you would do, and that automatically gave you the upper hand."

"Maybe there is hope for me after all."

The smile faded from his face. "You have good instincts. You should trust them more and stop undervaluing yourself."

Before she could think of something to say, he told her to duck again and brought the boat around.

"Is sailing all you thought it would be?" Cole asked once they were speeding across the cove again.

"Better." She smiled at him. "Much better. I don't

want to go back to shore. I mean, the Elena in me does, but—"

"I know exactly what you mean." With a laugh, he patted the seat beside him. "Do you want to try sailing her?"

"Me?"

He nodded. "You."

"How badly do you want to capsize?"

Cole threw back his head and laughed. Then he extended a hand. "C'mon. I'll help you."

PARADISE WAS WEARING a bit thin, Irene thought as she looked at the stretch of white sand and turquoise-blue water ahead of her. As scenery, it rated full marks—ten out of ten. Still, after an hour of walking, it was beginning to annoy her.

She shot a look at the man walking beside her. "How much longer do you think we have?"

He smiled at her. "An hour or so. We're making good time so far."

Irene studied him for a minute. Did the man never lose that positive attitude? "You know you've been a good sport, coming along with me like this."

"No problem. I came here looking for a bit of adventure, and you're providing it in spades."

Irene stopped short. "If you're looking for a sexual adventure, you're not striking pay dirt here."

Happy's smile widened as he walked forward. "Yeah. I think I got that part. You've got a man on that other island. Why don't you tell me about him?"

Irene double-stepped to catch up with him. "Why would I do that?"

"To pass the time. As beautiful as it is, this scenery gets a bit boring after a while."

"Doesn't it though," Irene said. "The color of that water doesn't even look real to me. It's beginning to annoy me. Maybe I'm not cut out to live in paradise, you know?"

Happy chuckled. "Yeah. It's a nice place to visit, but I wouldn't want to live there?"

Irene frowned. "Yeah. I just thought about getting here. I haven't given much thought to what would happen next."

"So what's his name?" Happy asked.

She glanced at him, but he was looking straight ahead. She might as well tell him about Butch. What did she have to lose? And talking about it might help her to sort through all the thoughts that had been tumbling through her mind. "Butch Castellano. He owns the resort over there on Escapade Island."

"Ah," Happy said. "So he's committed to living here."

"Yeah. He decided to build his own retirement home and a business venture at the same time."

"Smart man," Happy commented.

Ahead of them, the beach curved sharply. As they rounded it, Irene saw another seemingly endless stretch of sand and water ahead.

"So how long have you known this guy?"

"Forty years," she said.

Happy missed a step. "I never thought to ask. Are you married?"

"No," Irene muttered. "I thought we were going to be. That was the plan, but a little while ago, he changed his mind, sort of. I came here to change it back."

Happy said nothing.

After a moment, she turned to him. "Have you ever fallen in love at first sight?"

Happy met her gaze, and for the first time, his expression was serious. "Maybe. Maybe I did on that plane."

She frowned at him and resisted the urge to give him a good hard shove. "Don't even start. You're too old to fall in love at first sight. You should know better. I was only eighteen when I first met Butch Castellano. So I have an excuse. I was just a kid and he was only a couple of years older, handsome as sin and just a bit wild. He rode a motorcycle."

"What happened?" Happy asked as they resumed walking.

"That was it for me. I fell in love with him, and I've never fallen out."

"Why didn't you get together and live happily ever after?"

"He had some family problems. He'd been born into a ____ dent of birth. My parents didn't approve ____ n't approve of me either, for that matter. ____ all ganged up on me. Even Butch. He ____ od enough for me and that he couldn't ____ rents packed up and moved from New ____ co. And I went along with it. I thought ____ when I was a bit older, everyone would see it differently. And then Butch went to jail."

"Bummer," Happy said. But he sounded pretty cheerful about it.

Irene frowned at him. "It wasn't his fault. He took the rap for someone, and while he was in jail, he went straight. Every single cent he's earned has been legit. And he's made a fortune."

"Okay, okay," Happy said. "I believe you. I take it you kept in touch with him all these years."

"Yeah. We were supposed to get together when he finally got out of jail. But he changed his mind. He drummed up some lame excuse about still not being good enough for me. He values our friendship and doesn't want to ruin it. It's bullshit. All of it."

"And you came here to set him straight?"

Irene fisted her hands on her hips. "Yeah. Not good enough for me. Ha! I showed him. I stole a Monet to prove to him that I'm bad enough for him."

Happy stopped short and stared at her. "You stole a Monet?"

She whirled to face him. "I did."

Happy's smile was the brightest she'd ever seen it. "You're a real pip of a woman, Irene. Your Butch is a stupid man if he doesn't see that."

"Yeah. But I had a better chance of proving it to him before that jackass Frenchman drugged painting. I'm betting he's on that island rig the damn thing to Butch. I can't let Butch b painting. That's why I have to get to the island."

"Right," Happy said moving forward. "Let's pick u pace, shall we?"

8

COLE KEPT HIS HAND over Pepper's on the tiller as the small sailboat raced across the cove. He was acutely aware that time was flying by just as fast.

Ever since Butch had come up with his theory that Irene might have taken the connecting flight to Eden Island by mistake, he'd known that his time alone on the island with Pepper was running out.

At any moment Butch might call. Cole was pretty sure that if Irene was on that island, Butch's man would find her and bring her back posthaste. And there was so much he wanted to show Pepper, to share with her. He wondered if Adam had felt this same kind of urgency with Elena.

"Think you've got the feel of it?" he asked.

"Maybe."

"I'm going to take my hand off. Ready?"

She nodded, and he lifted his hand.

"Now, push to the left a little."

She did, and suddenly they were cutting across the wind, picking up speed. When they were nearly to the other side of the cove, he told her exactly what to do to turn the boat in a half circle, warning her to duck when the boom came around. Seconds later, they were racing across the surface of the water once more, and she was laughing.

He knew that moment would remain with him for ever.

"What do you think?" he asked.

"It's amazing." She laughed again for the pure joy of it. "It's even more fun to be in control."

"Always. To the left now."

She did what he suggested, and he could see that she was beginning to get the feel of it. But he didn't move away. He didn't want to. He liked the feel of that small slender body resting against his side. He'd waited a long time to get this close.

"Where did you learn to sail?" she asked.

Without thinking, he said, "One of my foster parents was ex-navy. He kept a small boat, just a little bigger than this one, and the one summer I lived with him we'd sneak off for a sail whenever the weather was good enough." He hadn't allowed himself to think of that summer for years.

"What happened?" she asked.

"We had a great time. He talked about adopting me. A little to the left."

"Did he adopt you?"

"No. He died in a car accident over Labor Day weekend, and his wife didn't want the responsibility of a twelve-year-old. She preferred babies. You can't blame her." He hadn't thought of that rejection in years either.

She reached out and placed her free hand on top of his. "I'm sorry. You must think I'm very ungrateful the way I ranted on and on about how rejected I feel because Peter never contacted me until I was twenty-five. And my grandmother and I may have had our issues, but she didn't reject me either. She did her best to raise me the way she thought a Pendleton should be raised."

"It was a long time ago."

"You never got adopted?"

"No. I never expected to be after that. The longest I ever stayed anywhere was two years. By the time I met Luke in college, I was on my own. Your father and brothers have always made me feel a part of the Rossi family."

"Good." She tightened her grip on his hand.

He said nothing as a wave of feelings swept through him. Her concern had something inside of him softening again. He never spoke about his past. He seldom thought about it anymore. But she shouldn't be feeling sorry for him. "There's nothing about my past that I regret. For better or worse, it's made me the man I am today."

She studied him. "I've never thought about it much, but that's true about me too."

"Yes." He might have said something more, but just then the sail began to flap.

"A little to the left, now," he said.

The boat gathered speed again, and for a time, they concentrated on keeping it on course.

This time when they reached the other side of the cove, he let her bring the boat around by herself. Then as she was about to cut across the wind again, he stilled her hand on the tiller.

"What?" she asked.

He lifted his sunglasses and frowned as he ran a finger down her nose and along her collarbone. "You're turning pink. We'd better take a break and put some sunscreen on. The sun in the tropics can be dangerous."

But instead of heading toward shore, he helped her sail

the boat around the point at one end of the cove. The wind was brisker here, the waves a bit rougher. He took over the tiller and began to tack toward the land. Eventually, he turned the boat into a lagoon.

Water and wind stilled at nearly the same time. Cole let the boat drift a while before he lowered the sails, secured the boom, and dropped an anchor over the side. Here in the late afternoon, sun slanted through the palms, and the water was a deeper blue, but it was still crystal clear.

"This is lovely," Pepper said. "I think I saw this lagoon from the plane as we came in. How did you find it?"

"I did a little exploring after I arrived yesterday, and I thought of bringing you here."

She stared at him. "You did? I mean…that was before I told you about Aunt Irene and we made our deal. You still thought that I was a thief."

He unzipped her duffel and pulled out the sunscreen he'd bought at the hotel gift shop. "I thought you might enjoy it. Turn around. I'll do your back first."

But she didn't turn. Instead, she reached out to grab his wrist. Then she used her other hand to remove his sunglasses. "Why? Why would you have thought of bringing me here when you were certain that I took that Monet and when you suspected I might have done it to score some points off you?"

He regarded her for a moment. "Because I want you. I've wanted you from the first moment I saw you in your father's kitchen. Do you remember?"

She swallowed, then moistened her lips. "Yes."

"When you arrived, you were wearing a white linen dress, and there were pearls at your throat and in your ears." With one finger he traced a line around her throat where the pearls had lain.

An Important Message from the Editors

Dear Reader,

If you'd enjoy reading romance novels with larger print that's easier on your eyes, let us send you TWO FREE HARLEQUIN PRESENTS® NOVELS in our LARGER PRINT EDITION. These books are complete and unabridged, but the type is set about 20% bigger to make it easier to read. Look inside for an actual-size sample.

By the way, you'll also get a surprise gift with your two free books!

Pam Powers

Peel off Seal and Place Inside...

THE RIGHT WOMAN

she'd thought she was fine. It took Daniel's words and Brooke's question to make her realize she was far from a full recovery.

She'd made a start with her sister's help and she intended to go forward now. Sarah felt as if she'd been living in a darkened room and some-one had suddenly opened a door, letting in the fresh air and sunshine. She could feel its warmth slowly seeping into the coldest part of her. The feeling was liberating. She realized it was only a small step and she had a long way to go, but she was ready to face life again with Serena and her family behind her.

All too soon, they were saying goodbye and Sarah experienced a moment of sadness for all the years she and Serena had missed. But they had each other now, and that's what

She held

Printed in the U.S.A.
Publisher acknowledges the copyright holder of the excerpt from this individual work as follows:
THE RIGHT WOMAN Copyright © 2004 by Linda Warren. All rights reserved.
® and ™ are trademarks owned and used by the trademark owner and/or its licensee.

The Harlequin Reader Service™ — Here's How It Works:

Accepting your 2 free Harlequin Presents® larger print books and gift places you under no obligation to buy anything. You may keep the books and gift and return the shipping statement marked "cancel." If you do not cancel, about a month later we'll send you 6 additional Harlequin Presents larger print books and bill you just $4.05 each in the U.S., or $4.72 each in Canada, plus 25¢ shipping & handling per book and applicable taxes if any.* That's the complete price and — compared to cover prices of $4.75 each in the U.S. and $5.50 each in Canada — it's quite a bargain! You may cancel at any time, but if you choose to continue, every month we'll send you 6 more books, which you may either purchase at the discount price or return to us and cancel your subscription.

*Terms and prices subject to change without notice. Sales tax applicable in N.Y. Canadian residents will be charged applicable provincial taxes and GST.

"I remember," she said. "The Friday before, Matt and Luke had told me that they'd hired you. They were so full of praise, so happy that you'd finally agreed to accept a job. I was so annoyed at you and so jealous, and when I saw you with them at the party, I was more jealous than ever."

His brows drew together. "Why?"

"You seemed to fit in so well with them. You were standing with Luke and Matt and you were so relaxed and at home."

He smiled. "I wasn't relaxed. I was thinking of how quickly I could get you out of that dress and wondering if I'd ever have the chance to do it."

"I was thinking that I would never be able to compete with you, either at work or with my family. I wanted to hate you. But I wanted you too."

"Pepper—"

"That's why I left Evan and went into the kitchen. I needed a moment to gather my thoughts and compose myself."

"I followed you into the kitchen because I couldn't help myself, and the moment that I looked into your eyes, I couldn't think at all."

"Me, too. I couldn't understand how I could feel the things I was feeling about you. When you took the sliver of glass out of my hand, I nearly kissed you. I was feeling the same way when I kissed you in the Atwells' suite. I could have stalled and kept you outside long enough for my aunt to get away with the painting. But I'd been wanting to kiss you for so long. I don't understand it."

Her words had him feeling an ache deep down that stunned him. Her eyes were huge, and he was close enough to see the brown flecks in that deep golden color.

Her hair stood up in spikes from the spray and the wind. Once again, he thought she looked like some kind of sprite that would exist only in an enchanted place.

No woman had ever made him think in such a fanciful way. No woman had ever made him ache like this. He didn't understand it either, and he wanted her so much that he didn't dare to touch her. If he did, he would take her quickly—and he wanted to do more for her, for them both. Setting the sunscreen down, he pulled a towel out of the duffel and spread it on the bow of the boat.

"Do you suppose that Adam and Elena ever met in a place like this?"

He turned back to her. She was asking if he wanted to slip into the fantasy again. Maybe if he did, he'd be able to keep a better hold on his control. Taking her hand, he raised it to his lips. "I think they came here every chance they got. It was far too dangerous to keep meeting in his rooms. The word might spread to his parents that he was favoring one slave over another."

"Even when they met here, they wouldn't have long," Pepper said. "She would be missed in the fields."

"He'd have to get back to the plantation. So they'd meet on the beach or here where they couldn't be interrupted." He took her hand and drew her toward him. "Turn around and stretch out on the bow of the boat."

PEPPER MANAGED TO do what he asked though she wasn't sure how. She felt so weak and the feeling in her body only grew as he began to rub the sunscreen into her shoulders and the back of her neck. At first the shade provided by the overhead palms had provided relief from the sun, but here in the lagoon there was no breeze.

The cream felt cool, but his hands were warm as he began to rub them over her. Sensations streamed through her. The bow of the boat was hot from the sun, but it was nothing compared to the heat that was beginning to build inside her.

"I've been thinking about touching you like this," Cole said as he moved his hands in long, gentle strokes down her back.

He wasn't giving her a massage exactly. He wasn't concerned with her muscles—only the skin, and he wasn't missing an inch of it. His hands were so light, moving down her arms to her fingers and back up again. Far away, she caught the faint sound of the sea pushing into the shore. Overhead, a seagull called, and palm leaves whispered in the wind.

Had Adam been this gentle with Elena? Could she have lain here just like this, floating on a cloud of pleasure?

The slow, patient brush of his hands, the steady repetition of the pattern mesmerized her, sensitized her. Then he pressed only his fingers down the length of her spine, and the arrow of heat that shot through her made her gasp.

"You're so sensitive," he murmured. "It's addictive."

"Don't stop." Her voice was shaky.

He drew his hands down one of her arms and began to slowly spread the sunscreen between her fingers. "I'm not going to stop until I've touched every single inch of you. Do you understand?"

"Mmm," she murmured. Was he thinking of Elena now or of her?

He began to stroke the backs of her thighs, her calves, her ankles, and the heat grew more intense. When he began to rub sunscreen over the soles of her feet and between her toes, she didn't think she could stand it any more. "Please," she murmured. And she wasn't sure whether she wanted him to stop or go on. "Please."

"Soon," he promised.

Trapped between pleasure and torture, her eyes drifted shut and her world narrowed to this one man and his touch.

WHEN HE COULD NO longer resist, Cole turned her over and began to rub sunscreen on her shoulders and chest. She wore a simple one-piece tank suit of some thin, stretchy material that he could see her nipples through. They were already erect and hard. It took all of his control not to touch them. Instead, he tortured them both by merely using his fingers to spread the cream down her throat and along the material that rode low across her breasts and high on her thighs. By the time he got to her inner thighs, his intention to go slowly was fading and his control was beginning to slip. Her body was already arching toward him. At some point, he'd lost the thread of the fantasy he'd been weaving, and he wanted her out of it too. Setting aside the sunscreen, he wiped his hands on the edge of the towel she was lying on and then stretched out beside her.

"Pepper?" he murmured. "Open your eyes."

When she did, he saw that they were wide and misted with desire. "Say my name."

"Cole."

He had to strap down on his control. Then he said, "I'm going to touch you inside now." He slipped a finger beneath the edge of her suit and into her. When the soft wet heat tightened around his finger, he nearly lost it. "I'm touching you just the way you touched yourself in the bedroom. Do you have any idea how much I wanted to do this?"

She arched high against his hand and he held her as the orgasm moved through her.

Afterward, he wasn't sure how he managed to rid them both of their suits. All that he could think of was being inside of her. Being a part of her. When he'd settled himself over her, he framed her face with his hands. "Open your eyes."

When she did, he said, "Say my name. Tell me you want me."

"Cole, I want you."

9

"DAMMIT!" Butch slammed down his phone and tossed the cigar he'd just ruined across the room.

H ducked, then gathered up the shreds of the mutilated cigar and disposed of them. "Problem?"

Butch rose from his desk and began to pace. "The problem is that woman. Damn her."

"I take it that Irene Rossi caught the connecting flight to Eden Island by mistake?" H asked.

"Yeah." Butch reached in his pocket for a cigar, then recalled that he'd already destroyed it. "But Angelo says the camp boss lady lost her. She claims Renie checked into the hotel with a Mr. Johansson, and then the two of them disappeared. They don't know where she is. What kind of a place are they running? She claims that couples disappear all the time, that they're encouraged to do that." His voice turned falsetto again. "What better way to seek out all the sensual delights that Eden has to offer."

Butch whirled and pointed a finger at H. "And she's with a man. I'm going to go over there myself."

"You've forgotten your meeting with Evan Atwell."

Butch stopped short at the door to his office. "What do I care about that? I want Renie."

H said nothing, and for a moment Butch concentrated on what he'd just blurted out. He wanted Renie. Could that be true?

"Don't say a word," he said to H. And the man wouldn't. That was why Butch liked him, why they made such good partners in business. H never interrupted when Butch was thinking something through. "I just want to make sure she's safe," Butch said.

"Of course. But Angelo's very competent. And Mr. Vanetti will be at our meeting in Atwell's suite to verify the authenticity of the painting. If that goes well, as I assume it will, we're joining Atwell at nine-thirty to discuss a price."

"All right. I'll stay here and take the meetings."

"Shall I inform Pepper Rossi that her aunt is on Eden Island and that we're going to bring her here just as soon as possible?"

"Yes." Then Butch added, "Dammit! What's Renie up to?"

H said nothing.

Butch began pacing again. "Why couldn't she just have understood that we should continue to go on as we were? She has her life—a good one—and I have mine here. It's worked for forty years. And getting together might ruin all that. We're too different. If we get together, it could turn out to be a disaster, and I don't want to lose her. She can't know what her friendship has meant to me. Why can't she understand that?"

This time H spoke. "She's a woman. They're different than we are. And not just biologically. They think differently, too."

"Tell me about it." Butch opened the drawer of his desk

and took out a new cigar. "And isn't it the French who say, 'Vive la différence'?"

"That they do."

"Well, they're stupid. And speaking of the French, have you gotten anything back yet on the Frenchman with Evan Atwell?"

"I'm still working on it," H said.

PEPPER SWEPT HER HANDS back and forth in the water with just enough force to keep herself afloat. Cole was treading water only a few feet away.

"You told me that you were taking me to paradise, but I thought were talking about the sailing," she said.

"You didn't think I was talking about my masterful techniques as a lover?"

The feigned look of insult on his face had her laughing, and if his hands hadn't gripped her waist just then, she would have slipped beneath the surface of the lagoon.

"Well, that too," she said. "But I've never been any-where quite this beautiful." They'd rowed the sailboat to a spot where the lagoon had widened into a pool of sorts. Water poured from an outcrop of rocks above in a sheer curtain that fell a few feet from them. There was a small cave behind the waterfall that they had yet to explore. And flowers she'd never seen before bloomed everywhere. She cupped water in her hand, lifted it, and then let it fall back into the lagoon. "This color—it can't be real."

"It's as real as the place," he said.

Treading water again, she glanced around. She was aware of the stillness, of the dappled sunlight that managed to make its way through the canopy of palms overhead, of the soft splash of the waterfall. But most of all, she was aware of the fact that her legs were almost brushing Cole's beneath the water. She might not be sure of the reality of her surroundings, but she was sure that Cole was real.

And both the man and the place would be gone at the end of twenty-four hours. Something twisted around her heart.

"Adam and Elena must have come here often."

"You're fascinated by their story, aren't you?" Cole asked. "Do you know how it ended?"

She shook her head. "I didn't read that far. But what chance did they have of a happy ending? They reminded me of my parents. It must be hard to find love and then lose it."

"Yes, I suppose it is."

A cell phone rang. But before Cole moved away to the shore, she had seen the shutters come down over his eyes. She wondered how often he'd found the love of a family and then lost it. Turning in the water, she watched him pull himself out of the lagoon. He was so different than what she'd expected him to be.

"Yeah?" He spoke the one word into his cell and then listened.

It had to be Butch or H, Pepper thought. Had they located Irene? It shocked her to realize that she hadn't thought much about either her aunt or the Monet since they'd begun sailing. She'd better remember that she'd come to this island on a mission. After swimming to the side of the lagoon, she climbed out and sat beside him.

"Okay, I'll let her know," Cole said. "Thanks."

Pepper let her gaze sweep the lagoon. Lovely as it was, this was just an interlude. The reality was a missing Monet.

Cole closed the phone and was about to set it down when it rang again. "Yeah?"

There was a brief silence. Then Cole said, "Interesting. I can't talk right now."

This time when he disconnected, he turned to her and said, "Your aunt is somewhere on Eden Island. According to the woman who runs the place, she's gone off with a man to find a way off the island. Castellano's man is looking for them and he'll bring your aunt back here."

Pepper frowned. "Irene has gone off with a man? I don't think so. She's crazy about Butch. What if someone's kidnapped her? I'm getting that feeling again that something's wrong. Maybe we should—"

Cole touched her arm when she started to stand up. "I think Castellano has it covered. And I don't think she's been kidnapped. According to Butch, your aunt has been highly visible and made quite a stir about getting back here ASAP. A kidnapper would hardly allow that."

She searched his face. "You're sure?"

"Since Butch isn't going over there himself, I'm betting that Angelo is highly capable. Butch is clearly besotted with your aunt."

"You think?"

"He had blood in his eyes when he came crashing into our bedroom. If you hadn't grabbed that gun, he might have shot me first and asked questions later."

"Suppose you're right and Butch really is head over heels. I know for a fact that she's over the top when it comes to him. So why don't they just get together? Instead, she's stolen a priceless painting. And a man who's gone straight for forty years is thinking of shooting people. What's wrong with them?"

"People do stupid things when they're in love. Shakespeare used to call it madness—and he got a lot of mileage out of that theme in his comedies and tragedies, not to mention the sonnets."

Pepper stared at him again. "I would never have pegged you for a Shakespeare scholar."

"I'm not. I've just worked a lot of jobs where I've had time to read."

"Stakeouts?"

"Yeah. You could call them that." He plucked a flower from one of the plants that grew along the edge of the lagoon and tucked it behind her ear.

When she realized that he wasn't going to elaborate, she asked, "Why did you come to work at Rossi Investigations?"

He studied her for a moment, then nodded. "Okay, I guess you deserve to know that. I came because your brother offered me the job, and I wanted to get out of government work."

It wasn't the whole answer. She was certain of it. And she suddenly realized how little she knew about him. "What kind of work did you do for the CIA?"

Once again he hesitated. Then he said, "I killed people for them."

Her eyes widened. "You worked black ops?"

His mouth twisted wryly. "Nothing that adventurous. Mostly, I worked on a hostage rescue team as a sniper. I was often called in for situations where I had to wait hours on end to get the right shot. I never missed."

Something cold and hard in his voice had her taking his hand and linking her fingers with his. "That had to be a lonely life. No wonder you wanted to get away from it."

She thought of the family gatherings Peter insisted on having every Sunday at his house, and for the first time, she tried to see them the way Cole would see them. Matt was in charge of the grill, Luke mixed the drinks, and her father made an audience out of everyone as he prepared fresh pasta. Italian music blared out of a speaker system, and neighbors were invited so that they wouldn't complain.

Compared to the sedate gatherings at her grandmother's, the dinner was loud and confusing and somehow welcoming at the same time. It had held an almost overwhelming attraction for her. She'd wanted so much to belong, to fit in. But now she realized that considering his background, those Sunday get-togethers must have been equally appealing to Cole.

Thinking about it, she slipped her arm around his waist and leaned her head against his shoulder.

COLE FOUND THE GESTURE almost unbearably sweet. Understanding. He'd never asked it of anyone. Never expected it. He put his arm around Pepper's shoulder and simply held her. How could she do this to him—push buttons that had feelings he couldn't even identify moving through him? Perhaps, he'd never understand why or how she affected him this way. Maybe it wasn't important to understand. Maybe he only had to accept.

For a while they sat in silence except for the fall of the water and the whisper of the palm leaves above them. Cole could feel precious minutes slipping away. He wished that they had nothing more to do than sit here and make love again. But there was the Monet. It would ease his mind a great deal if they knew for sure that Irene had it. And he wanted to know more about the Frenchman with Evan Atwell.

"I've been thinking about Evan Atwell and his friend," Pepper said.

Meeting her eyes, he smiled. "Me, too. Great minds evidently think alike."

"If they're a couple coming here to celebrate Valentine's Day, why didn't they come on the same plane?"

"Good point."

"And I've thought about something else. I don't know why I didn't remember sooner—I've been so focused on Irene and you."

"What is it?"

"Irene said that there was someone else on the hotel roof when she got there that night."

"Another thief?"

"Looked that way to her. She shot him with a tranquilizer."

Cole stared at her for a minute. Finally he shook his head. "I don't imagine that made her very popular with the other thief. But it does throw a slightly different light on the situation."

"That's what I was thinking. There were two thieves after the Monet that night. What if there still are? What if the other thief stole the painting from Irene and then sent her off to that island?"

"We won't know that for sure until Irene arrives. Unless you want to tell Butch the whole story and ask him point blank if he's been contacted about a Monet."

She shook her head. "No. Not until Irene gets here. If she still has the painting, I want her to be able to give it to him. So I guess we just have to wait."

He handed her his cell, and she shot him a curious look.

"There's something that you can do. Right after Butch called, I got a report from Luke."

"He found out who this Frenchman is?" Pepper asked.

Cole shook his head. "So far, he's learned that Evan hasn't been seen around town with anyone who fits this man's description."

"Could H and Butch be wrong about them being a couple?"

Cole shook his head. "I wouldn't bet on it. It's more likely that Evan and his friend have been very discreet. How would Mrs. Atwell feel if her son were to come out of the closet?"

She paused to consider his questions. "Not good, I suspect. Maybe that's why he wanted to continue to date as friends after I broke up with him. If Evan and the Frenchman wanted to keep their relationship a secret, this island is secluded and far away from Mommy." She glanced around. "It's the perfect place for a clandestine tryst." She turned to Cole. "And that could be the only reason they're here."

"Could be," Cole agreed. "But…"

"The timing's very suspicious. Why this island at this particular time, right after Evan's painting is stolen? It all keeps coming back to that."

"Bingo." He nodded at the cell phone. "Luke could use a name."

She stared at him. "You're letting me get the name?"

"It's your case."

She hesitated for a moment, deciding who to call. There was Butch or H. But both might have questions about why she wanted to know the name of Evan Atwell's companion. In the end she dialed the resort number and asked for the reception desk. Luck was with her and she got the same young woman who'd registered her.

"Escapade Resort. Marlene speaking."

"Marlene, this is Pepper Rossi. I'm not sure you remember me."

"Of course I do, Ms. Rossi. What can I do for you? Mr. Castellano says that you're to have anything you want during your stay on the island."

All the better, she thought. "I have a request that you might find a bit unusual. Can you give me the name of the man who's staying with Evan Atwell? Evan and I are old friends, and I want to arrange to have a gift basket made up. But I need the name of his friend so that I can put both names on the card."

"No problem. It'll take me just a minute to look it up."

Pepper kept her fingers crossed and counted to ten.

"Here it is. Jean Claude Rambeau. Would you like me to take care of the basket for you?"

"No. I want to make some of the selections in the gift shop myself. But thank you, Marlene. Oh, one more thing. Can you find out what Evan's plans are for the evening? I'd like to have the basket delivered shortly before midnight."

"I'll check with Tommy."

Placing her hand over the phone, she said to Cole, "I have an idea."

"Tommy says they have reservations at the poolside café at nine-thirty," Marlene said. "Then at midnight, they're having a late supper in the main dining room."

"Thanks, Marlene." She handed the cell phone back to Cole. "Evan's friend is Jean Claude Rambeau."

Cole punched in numbers and relayed the name to Luke. Then he turned to her. "Good job."

"Thanks."

"What's the idea you had when you were talking to Marlene?"

"I'm thinking of accidentally running into Evan this evening. Maybe that would stir things up."

He smiled at her. "Not a bad idea."

"How would you have gotten Jean Claude's name?" she asked.

"I would have probably called Butch."

"I thought he might have questions."

"Good point. And he could have offered a name but chose not to."

"Do you think Butch is hiding something?" she asked.

"I think he's an astute businessman who plays his cards very close to his chest. Calling the receptionist was a nice move, by the way."

"How long will it take Luke to check out Jean Claude?"

"Hard to say, but your brother is the best. You're a lot like him, you know."

"Me?"

The shock on her face had a little flare of anger shooting through him. "Didn't your family in Philadelphia ever tell you when you'd done something right?"

"No. But I didn't give them much cause. I really wasn't cut out to be a debutante. I had to keep pretending to be one. I kept imagining myself as tall, blond and beautiful— like Britney Spears or Paris Hilton or Jessica Simpson. The game got old."

He took her chin in his hand and turned it so that she had to meet his eyes. "Why are you still playing the same game with your brothers and your father?"

"What do you mean?"

"You're still wearing masks with them."

Color rose in her cheeks, but she didn't look away. "You see everything, don't you?"

"I see what you're doing because I've worn a lot of masks myself. If you stop wearing them, you might discover qualities in yourself that you like."

She said nothing, and after a moment he continued. "I had to play the fitting in game a lot, and I learned that I had a better chance if I played to my strengths. At Rossi Investigations, you should do the same thing. You have good instincts. And you have Luke's brain. Matt's the one with the street smarts and the brawn. They make a good team, because they don't try to be what they're not. And they could use you because you're something that they're not. You're a woman. And even if you didn't turn yourself into a perfect Pendleton, you have class. Plus, you have the same kind of determination that your aunt does. Think about it."

She would, Pepper decided. But right now, she was thinking about the boy who'd had to fit in with more families than she could imagine.

Cole took her hand and drew her to her feet. "While we're waiting for your whiz-kid brother to work his magic, I have an idea about what we can do to pass the time."

"So do I," she said. "I'll race you to the cave." Then she dove into the lagoon.

10

PEPPER GLANCED AT herself in the mirror that filled one wall of the small room. She was dressing for a date with Cole Buchanan, and for some reason the idea had nerves tangling in her stomach.

Cole had proposed the idea when they'd been sailing back from the lagoon. After all, he'd argued, they really hadn't gone out on an official first date yet, and since they were going to "accidentally" bump into Evan and Jean Claude at the poolside café, why not combine their sleuthing activities with a date?

Cole had overcome her one objection that she didn't have anything to wear by escorting her to one of the shops that opened off the main lobby of the hotel and placing her in the capable hands of Gari's friend Reynaldo.

The small trim man who'd given her a quick tour of his shop was the polar opposite of Gari. While Gari radiated charm and enthusiasm, Reynaldo was soft-spoken, astute, and totally focused on business. His shop offered an array of exclusive designer merchandise, from dresses and shoes to cosmetics. There was even a glass display case totally devoted to jewelry from Cartier. Sometime during her tour, Cole had disappeared.

A knock at the dressing room door had her turning as Reynaldo stepped into the room.

"Why don't we start with these sarong dresses? They're all made by craftsmen here on the island." Reynaldo wore his long, dark hair pulled back in a sleek ponytail, and in place of the island uniform of white shorts and blue flowered shirt, he wore impeccably pressed white trousers and a short-sleeved navy silk shirt. In spite of his small stature, the man managed to radiate the authority of a five-star general.

Pepper glanced at the selection of sarongs he was holding. "They're all so beautiful. But…this is not what I usually wear."

The look he gave her held understanding. "I hear you. I worked in New York for several years, and I'm still getting used to the more informal attire of the island. But you have an advantage. You're only going to be here for a short while. You don't have to make a permanent change. A visit to Escapade Island is the perfect opportunity to try something different and—shall we say a bit wild?"

Try something different and a bit wild? Pepper swallowed a nervous laugh. That's exactly what she was doing, wasn't it? Only it wasn't just a sarong she was trying on—it was Cole Buchanan. And it was only temporary.

Instead of relaxing her, the thought had a band of pain tightening around her heart. Her time with Cole Buchanan was running out. Tonight might not only be their first date. It might very well be their last.

Turning her so that she faced the mirror, Reynaldo held two sarong dresses in front of her. One was splashed with the red flowers she'd seen blooming everywhere on the island. She could imagine the slave girl Elena wearing it. The other sarong was plain white.

And Cole had remembered the white linen dress she'd worn the first time they'd met.

"White is definitely your color," Reynaldo said.

"Yes." It was her color, and if it was going to be her first and last date with Cole she wanted to be herself tonight.

"Try it on," Reynaldo commanded. Then, as quickly as he'd entered the room, he left.

After discarding her jeans and T-shirt, she slipped into the sarong. Then she stared at herself in the mirror. The woman staring back at her was not the Pepper Rossi she knew.

"If you're decent, I'd like to take a peek," Reynaldo said from outside the slatted door.

"Come in." *Decent* wasn't exactly the word she would have chosen to describe what she looked like. Pepper wasn't even sure she was going for decent. The dress certainly wasn't. She would have called the look provocative. She'd never worn anything like it.

"Turn," Reynaldo commanded.

Pepper did what he asked. The thin material of the sarong hugged her breasts and waist before it draped over her thighs to just above her knees. On the side where it tied, a good half of her thigh was revealed.

No, this wasn't something that Pepper Rossi would have worn. But then she'd never before dressed with the sole purpose of pleasing a man.

Reynaldo clasped his hands together and for the first time the serious expression faded from his face, and he smiled. "Exquisite. Simply exquisite. Your man is going to be smitten. You look like a goddess."

Pepper frowned. "I'm not going for goddess. I'm going for me."

Reynaldo's eyes widened and gestured toward her image in the mirror. "But that *is* you. Look."

Pepper did what he asked. She looked sophisticated and together, with a hint of the unexpected. Straightening her shoulders, she drew in a deep breath and studied her image more closely. Cole had said that if she quit hiding behind masks, she might discover qualities in herself that she would like. Could this be what she looked like when those masks were peeled away?

"You need shoes." Reynaldo's tone had turned brisk and businesslike again. "Contessas might be able to go barefoot, but never goddesses. What size?"

"Six," Pepper said.

"I have just the thing." Whirling, he sped out of the room.

Pepper studied her image in the mirror. Goddesses were always confident, she supposed. And it would be an interesting break from the slave girl fantasy. What would it be like to make love with Cole if she pretended to be a goddess?

No. Pepper slammed the brakes on her wandering thoughts. She wasn't going there. The whole idea of this "first date" was that they were going to be themselves and get to know each other. Besides, if this was to be her last night with Cole, she wanted him to remember *her.*

Last night. She pressed her hand against her chest to ease the ache around her heart as she thought of that. But they'd made a deal that they'd enjoy this time together on the island. And then it was over.

A chime sounded, indicating that someone was coming into the shop. It was probably Cole, she thought. And she wasn't ready. Through the slats in the door, she heard Reynaldo welcoming customers. "Mr. Atwell, Mr. Rambeau, so nice to see you again. How can I be of help?"

Evan and Jean Claude. Whirling, she peered through the slats.

"The diamond-and-gold cuff links," Jean Claude said.

Reynaldo used his key on the display case, and handed them to Jean Claude. "They're lovely, aren't they?"

"Exquisite," Jean Claude murmured, holding them up to the light. "Don't you agree, Evan?"

"They're too expensive," Evan said.

She couldn't see the expression on Evan's face, but his tone was less enthusiastic than Jean Claude's.

"How much are they?" Evan asked Reynaldo.

"Ten thousand," Reynaldo said. "The diamonds are a carat each and they're flawless. They're by a young Italian designer."

"Do you like them?" Jean Claude asked Evan.

"Yes, but I think we should wait. We don't know yet—"

Jean Claude put a hand on Evan's arm. "You bought the ring for me yesterday, and I saw you looking at these. Indulge me and let me buy these for you as a Valentine's Day gift."

"Yes. Okay," Evan agreed.

Jean Claude turned to Reynaldo. "Wrap them. And put them on the room tab."

"But of course," Reynaldo murmured as he hurried to another counter.

Pepper's nerves knotted when Jean Claude drew Evan closer to the dressing room door.

"You worry too much," Jean Claude said in a soft voice.

"We haven't closed the deal yet," Evan said.

"We will. Relax."

"Here you are, Mr. Rambeau."

Pepper watched the two men turn in unison and walk back to the counter. After taking the package, they left the shop. Her mind raced. What was the deal that they hadn't yet closed? Was it with Butch?

The sinking feeling in her stomach had her thinking that her suspicion was dead on. Did they have the Monet and were they in the process of selling it to Butch? But they hadn't mentioned the painting. And she still didn't want to think that Evan was involved in stealing his own painting.

The knock on her door had her jumping. Then Reynaldo stepped into the dressing room, a box in his hands. "Wait till you see. In these, you can dance until dawn. Sit."

She did what he asked and then watched as he pulled a red velvet bag out of the box and extracted a pair of white sandals. Then he dropped to one knee and extended his hand. "Your foot."

She gave it to him. The heels on the sandal were impossibly high, the straps thin, and when she spotted the designer name on the bottom of one shoe, she had to swallow hard. The price tag was going to be four figures. Not even when she was a Pendleton had she bought that particular brand. "You must have some very rich guests staying here."

"Oh, yes. Celebrities have taken a fancy to this place because it's so out of the way. And Mr. Castellano wants us to encourage repeat business, so every other month I fly to New York and do some buying." He leaned closer and spoke in a low voice. "I could name one movie star who's staying here right now, but we promise complete confidentiality."

"I understand." While he buckled the ankle straps, she asked, "Was that Evan Atwell I just heard in the shop?"

"Yes, do you know him?"

"I used to date him in San Francisco. Does he come here often?"

"I believe this is his first trip."

"And his friend? I've never run into him before."

"Mr. Rambeau is turning out to be one of my best customers. Yesterday he bought a two carat diamond pinkie ring and today a pair of cuff links. He has a good eye. They were the most valuable pieces of men's jewelry in the shop. There." He stood and stepped to the side of the small room. "Rise and walk."

She did, and the sandals couldn't have fit better if they'd been made especially for her.

She sighed. "They're lovely, but—" But she was going to buy them anyway. Why did she have to have such a weakness for shoes? It was the only authentically debutante gene she possessed.

"Don't worry about the price. Your gentleman is putting them on his tab."

Pepper's eyes narrowed. "My gentleman?"

Reynaldo's eyes twinkled. "Tall, dark hair, looks a little like James Bond on vacation."

It was such an apt description of Cole that Pepper nearly smiled. But she couldn't let him buy her such expensive shoes. She pushed through the door of the dressing room and stepped into the shop. Cole turned from where he stood at the counter.

"I'm not going to let you buy these shoes," she said as she walked toward him. But she nearly stumbled when she drew close enough to see the look in his eyes. He was surprised. In fact he was staring at her as if he'd never seen her before.

Well…good. Maybe she'd chosen the right dress after all. The goddess look and the shoes might just be worth it.

"You like the dress?" she asked.

"What?"

She bit back a satisfied smile. She hadn't just surprised him. She'd stunned him. But despite the thrill that moved through her, she said, "I can't let you buy clothes for me."

"Okay."

"Good." She turned to take the jeans that Reynaldo had carried out of the dressing room and handed her credit card to Reynaldo. While he hurried away to get the authorization, she drew Cole aside. "While I was in the dressing room, Evan and Jean Claude came in and bought a ten thousand dollar pair of cuff links." Then she filled him in what else she'd overheard.

"Interesting," Cole murmured.

"I know nothing that they said constitutes proof, but I'm beginning to think they might have the Monet. Jean Claude could have stolen it from Aunt Irene in the airport and then somehow put her on the plane to Eden. I hate to think that Evan could be involved, but this isn't looking good."

"No."

"Tell me that they could be working on a different kind of deal."

"They could be working on a different kind of deal. We won't know until your aunt can tell us just how she got on the wrong plane."

"No word yet?"

Cole shook his head.

"I hate this waiting."

He smiled at her. "Welcome to the world of investigative work."

Reynaldo returned to the counter, and when she'd signed the bill, Cole put a hand on her wrist. "If I can't buy the dress and shoes, then you have to accept the other presents I've bought for you. Think of them as early Valentine's Day gifts. Deal?"

She met his eyes, but she couldn't read anything there. "Gifts in the plural?"

"Yeah. I like to make a good impression on a first date."

A smile tugged at the corner of her mouth. For the first time she noticed the bag he was holding. "How many presents exactly?"

"Uh-uh. First, do we have a deal?"

She glanced at the bag again and saw that it carried the logo of the flower shop. So that's where he must have disappeared to while she and Reynaldo were busy in the dressing room. Flowers were safe enough. "Deal. Now tell me how many presents?"

Instead of answering, he pulled out a small box and took out one of the island flowers. She caught the delicate exotic fragrance. "The florist attached it to a comb so it would stay in your hair."

"Let me." Reynaldo plucked the flower from Cole and fastened it near her ear. Then he turned her so that she could see herself in the mirror behind the counter. But it wasn't her own image that she looked at. It was Cole's. She wanted always to remember the way he was looking at her right now. It had something moving through her in a steady warm stream.

"Do you like it?" he asked.

"Yes." She very much liked what she was looking at. He was wearing a khaki shirt and khaki slacks which were a perfect complement to his bronze-colored skin.

Then she saw that he was removing another box from the bag. "I was going to give you this at midnight, but since you wouldn't let me buy you the dress and the shoes…"

This box was not from the florist shop. It was small and the name of the jewelry designer was still visible beneath the blue bow. Cartier. Her eyes flew to his.

"We have a deal," he said. "I'm going to hold you to it."

Yes, they did have a deal. But she wasn't thinking about her agreement to accept the presents. She wasn't thinking much at all, not with the flood of emotions pouring through her. Her fingers shook as she pulled away the ribbon and opened the box. Then she had to blink at the brightness of the stones shining up at her. The spray of diamonds in each earring reminded her of fireworks, hot and bright on the Fourth of July. Tears pricked behind her eyes. Hesitantly, she touched one of the diamonds with her finger to test if the heat were real. But the stones were cool. She knew she had to say something, but she wasn't sure she could speak past the tightness in her throat.

With one finger, he lifted her chin so that she had to meet his eyes. Then he used the same finger to trace the path of a tear as it ran down her cheek. "You don't like them?"

"I love them." She set the box on the counter, then took them out and fastened them in her ears with shaking hands. She turned to look at him. The only other thing she could think of to say to him was "You shouldn't have," and it sounded so trite.

"Beautiful," he said.

"Jewelry fit for a goddess," Reynaldo said as he gathered up the empty boxes.

"I was talking about the woman," Cole said as he lifted her hand and kissed her fingers.

"That too," Reynaldo agreed.

Taking a deep breath, Pepper managed a smile. If she had just one more night with this man, she was going to make the most of it. "This is turning out to be a very expensive first date for you."

He smiled as he tapped the shoe box on the counter. "You're not getting off cheaply yourself."

She linked her fingers with his. "What do you say we make sure we get our money's worth?"

THE MOMENT HIS CELL phone rang, Butch lurched across his desk to get it. When he heard Angelo's voice on the other end of the line, he said, "Tell me you've got good news."

"Good news and bad news."

Butch frowned. "Explain."

"I tracked her to a fishing cabin on the far side of the island. She rented a boat there and she's gone."

Butch felt his heart sink. "What do you mean she's gone?"

"The woman who owns the cabin says she was hell bent on getting to Escapade Island tonight. They left about an hour before I got here."

Frowning, Butch glanced at his watch. It was 9:30. The sky was darkening now, so that would give her another half hour of daylight. The trip between the islands usually didn't take longer than that. "Hold on, Angelo." Butch turned to H who was watching the lobby through the one-way glass. "They borrowed a boat and they're on their way here." Then he frowned and spoke one word into his cell phone. "They?"

Angelo cleared his throat. "That's part of the good news. The man she was with is ex-navy and he sailed once in the America's Cup. She should be in good hands."

It didn't sound like good news to Butch. He was almost afraid to ask what the bad news was. "And?" he prompted Angelo.

"The boat they borrowed started out on the far side of the island, and it's nothing more than a motorized raft."

"Shit," Butch said

"You want I should try and find them?" Angelo asked.

"Hell, yes, I want you to find them. I want you to search every inch of the water between that damn island and this one." By the time Butch flipped his phone shut, H had turned from the window.

"Trouble?"

"Hell, yes." Butch began to pace. "She's out there on a raft floating around with some ex-navy man who's competed in the America's Cup."

"Sounds like she's in good hands," H said.

Butch whirled on him. "I don't want her in someone else's hands. What the hell has gotten into her?" He pounded a fist into his palm. "I want her right here in my hands."

H said nothing. Butch badly wanted to throw something at him because he knew just what his friend and partner was thinking. "When she gets here, I'm going to tell her that." He jabbed a finger at H. "And you're going to handle the sailor."

H said nothing for a moment, then reminded Butch, "Right now, we've got a meeting to go to."

11

Friday, February 13—9:30 p.m.

IRENE LOOKED OUT OVER the water. It was dark, black in fact, and the moon was playing hide-and-seek behind an increasingly thick layer of clouds. But what worried her the most was that they were moving much more slowly than they had been an hour ago. No, that was an outright lie. What had her stomach tied in knots had nothing to do with the fact that they were presently stalled halfway to Escapade Island.

"I thought you were supposed to be some kind of super sailor," Irene said, darting a glance at Happy.

"Even the best sailor needs a little help from the wind."

Irene glanced up at the sails. They'd been filled before. Now they were flat. She'd already asked him if the motor could go any faster.

"Not to worry. Those clouds are a good sign. I expect the wind to pick up any moment."

She decided to believe him. What choice did she have? He was the sailor.

"You got a plan for getting the Monet back?" Happy asked.

He was trying to distract her. All in all, he was a very nice man. How different her life might have been if at eighteen, she'd fallen in love with him. Instead, she'd fallen for Butch. "I figure I'll locate the Frenchman, and then something will come to me."

"If you need some help, you've got a volunteer."

"Thanks. I suspect that my niece is on that island too, and she'll help us out."

"You think she's on the island?"

"She was following me, and I'm assuming she made the right connection. Pepper's a PI, a good one, and she wants to make sure the painting gets back to the owner."

"She doesn't trust you to take care of that?" Happy asked.

"She probably doesn't trust Butch. And she'll be concerned about me."

For a few moments, the silence stretched between them. "I'm not worried about getting the Monet back. I'm a little worried about seeing Butch again." In fact, her stomach felt like a troupe of circus acrobats was practicing in it.

Happy said nothing.

Irene let the silence stretch as she considered. The man was a good listener. She'd learned that much about him on the eight-mile hike along the beach. He rarely interrupted and he never judged or criticized. Maybe it would help to talk to him about what was bothering her.

"I've changed," she said.

"So has he," Happy said.

Irene gave a snort. "Not as much as I have. Men don't as a rule. He's probably still handsome. You don't lose that as you age. I was never beautiful. But at least when I was younger, he thought I was pretty."

"You're a fine-looking woman, Irene. Besides, it sounds to me like he fell for more than your looks."

"You think?"

"He sided with your parents and sent you away, didn't he? That sounds like love to me."

"Yeah it does, doesn't it? I mean people make stupid decisions when they're in love, don't they?" Suddenly, she felt better.

"And they tend to see the people they fall in love with through rose-colored glasses."

"Well, that should help some." The wind suddenly picked up as if it was in tune with her spirits.

"Hang on," Happy said as the sails filled.

Please, God, Irene prayed as the boat shot forward, *Don't let Butch be quite as stupid this time around.*

As GARI TOOK AWAY Pepper's empty plate, she said, "That was marvelous."

"Can I get you anything else?"

"Another bottle of champagne," Cole said.

"Right away, sir."

The moment that the waiter hurried away, Pepper leaned toward Cole. "If I drink any more champagne, I'm going to need a nap. And Evan and Jean Claude haven't even arrived yet."

"Don't worry. I'm not going to uncork the bottle until midnight. I have some special plans for it."

She smiled at him. "I can deal with that."

She looked relaxed. That had been his plan. He had a pretty good idea that once her aunt arrived, the proverbial shit would hit the fan. His gut instinct told him that Irene would not have the Monet with her. This might be the last time they could spend like this while they were on the island.

Pepper rested her head against the back of the chair and pointed at the sky. "Look at the stars. There must be thousands up there. I never knew there were that many."

Cole didn't even bother to glance up. Ever since Gari had seated them at a table—the same one they'd been at earlier in the day—he hadn't been able to look at much besides the woman who sat across from him. Lanterns were strung on the other side of the pool and around the bar, but here the illumination came from nature. And she was stunning in moonlight.

"Why can't I see this many stars in San Francisco or in Philadelphia? I mean they have to be there, right? The galaxies just didn't multiply overnight."

"Light pollution. In a big city, you can't see many stars because the intensity of the city lights blocks them."

She rested her chin on her hands and studied him. "You're a regular encyclopedia. Where did you learn that?"

He shrugged. "I took a wide variety of courses in college, and I already told you, I read a lot." A glance at his watch told him that Evan and Jean Claude would arrive at any minute—if they kept their reservation.

"Why don't we dance?" Without waiting for an answer, he took her hand and led her to the terrace above the pool bar where they'd cleared a space for dancing. The music was being provided by a local group, and the songs had catchy rhythmic beats.

As he drew her into his arms, she said, "You're really into this date thing."

"I've waited a long time."

In a move that had her eyes widening, he swung her out and pulled her back into his arms. Then in a series of steps, he led her between other couples until they were at a railing that offered a view of the sea. She hadn't missed a beat, and she was laughing and a little breathless as he swung her out again and pulled her back into his arms.

"You're a good dancer," she said.

"Good?" He made it sound like an insult. Then he twirled her out and this time he turned her in two fast circles before he drew her back.

"Where did you learn to do that? You must have taken lessons."

"I did. When I was eighteen, I dated a dancer—Mary Jane Simonelli. She was older and she was eager to teach me everything she knew."

Pepper met his eyes and her laugh came quick and easy. "I'll just bet she did."

"Of course, I've practiced quite a bit since then."

He ran his hand down her back and spread his fingers over her bottom to draw her closer.

"I can see." Her eyes had darkened, and her breath had hitched.

"I also asked you to dance because I wanted to hold you like this." For a few minutes, he indulged himself, keeping her pressed to him and letting her swamp his senses. This was what he'd wanted to do since she'd walked out of that dressing room. In the high heels, her hair just brushed his chin. The exotic scent of the flower she wore over her ear blended with a scent that was uniquely hers—something that promised spice and heat.

He ran one hand up her back and down again and felt a tremor move through her. All during dinner he'd been imagining how the silk of the sarong would compare to her skin. The material was smooth and cool. Her skin was even smoother and hot.

The bow at her shoulder taunted him as it had all evening. An instant—that's all would it take for him to have her out of the whisper of silk she was wearing. Minutes—that was all he needed to lead her to a secluded place on the beach. She would go with him, and he could quench the fire that had begun to build in him again. Even as the images flooded his mind, he pressed her closer, moved his hips against her.

"Cole—"

"Mmm?" He leaned down and tasted the skin at her shoulder. It was sweet, hot. And another tremor moved through her.

"This isn't dancing."

He drew in a breath and tried to gather his thoughts. He'd promised her a date. And hadn't he promised himself that he would take the time to seduce her? Still, it took all his resolve to create a little distance between them. "You mean Mary Jane Simonelli steered me wrong?"

"No. I THINK SHE WAS probably a very skilled teacher." Too skilled. Being a little jealous of an imaginary slave girl was one thing, but every time she imagined Mary Jane dancing with Cole, or even worse, making love with him, something inside of her twisted.

"If you tell me she taught you how to kiss, I might have to trace her and do something really nasty to her."

With a laugh, he lifted her so that she was seated on the railing. "I'd rather you did something nasty to me. Shall I tell you what I have in mind?"

She narrowed her eyes. "Don't tell me you're into dominatrix stuff."

He laughed. "I've never been tempted to try it. You know, you're a pretty good dancer yourself."

"My grandmother arranged for me to have private lessons with a young man who came to the house. I'd like to tell you that he looked like Patrick Swayze in *Dirty Dancing,* but he didn't. And his behavior was depressingly proper."

"I'm glad." He snagged her fingers and raised them to his lips.

She shot him an amused look. "It was okay with me, too. He was at least thirty-five—ancient-looking to a sixteen-year-old. And he was a task master too. I had to do hours of ballet exercises at the bar to develop poise before we got to the ballroom stuff. But enough about me. I want to know something else that you're good at." She held up a hand when he opened his mouth. "Something that will surprise me."

She'd been peppering him with questions all evening, claiming it was what people did on a first date. She'd pried out of him that he'd had a double major in college—literature and anthropology—and that he was widely read. They'd even discussed some of the books they'd both enjoyed.

So far he'd told her only what he wanted her to know. But he was surprised at how much he wanted to confide in her. He wondered why. Because she'd understand?

"I'm a pretty decent cook."

Real surprise registered in her eyes. "No kidding. Where did you learn? No, wait—let me guess. You read cookbooks too."

He smiled. "Some. But your brother Luke got me interested in cooking in college. We moved out of a dorm and into an apartment as soon as it was allowed, and he was always in the kitchen whipping up something. The rest I've picked up from watching cooking shows on TV. Where did you learn to cook?"

She wrinkled her nose. "I didn't. My grandmother had a temperamental chef who never allowed anyone in the kitchen. But show me a place setting of silver, and I'm a real whiz kid. You *cannot* trip me up."

"Time out," Cole said. "Back up. You don't cook, but you always bring something to the Sunday family gatherings at your dad's."

She leaned closer. "I just pretend I'm Julia Child when I'm in the kitchen and I whip something up."

He studied her. "Liar."

She laughed then and the sound carried, bright and carefree, on the breeze that was coming in from the sea. "You're right. Although I did my best to pretend to be her. I even bought her original cookbook on French cooking. It was a disaster. I ended up dirtying every single pan in my kitchen and the result was still totally inedible. I would have signed up for a cooking class, but I was already taking the PI class. So I went to Plan B. My Pendleton background is good for something. I found a really good caterer, and I have this cordon bleu chef make something for me. Then I put it in one of my own bowls and take it to my father's. I figured that was what you were doing, too."

I could teach you to cook. Cole barely stopped himself from giving voice to the thought. If he offered now, it would bring up the topic of what their relationship might be when their time on the island was up. And he didn't want to bring that into the discussion. Not yet. Not on a night when she was more relaxed than he'd ever seen her.

He could also point out to her that her brothers and her father wouldn't care if she didn't know how to cook. They loved her for who and what she was. But she wasn't quite ready to accept that. She was still too afraid of not measuring up to their expectations.

No, he'd tell her neither of those things tonight.

"What *are* you an expert at?" he asked instead.

"Well…" She thought for a minute. "A lot of stuff, actually. A Pendleton had to know how to play the piano and tennis, how to dance and how to ride. Sometimes my grandmother would hire tutors to come to the house. Other times— like for the riding lessons—the chauffeur would drive me."

In his mind, Cole pictured the young girl being driven to one lesson after another so that she would measure up to being a Pendleton. He was beginning to see why she was so determined to learn what she needed to know to fit in at Rossi Investigations. "It sounds like you had a busy life."

"Actually, some of it was fun. I found that I liked learning new things. And I managed to add some lessons that were more interesting. I once snuck away to Atlantic City and took courses on how to play Black Jack and poker."

His brows rose. "Those don't sound like they're on the Pendleton required list of skills."

She grinned. "I told you I didn't really fit in there."

He thought of his own efforts and failures to fit in.

"You know, this first date thing is turning out well, I think. All told, we have more things in common than I would have thought." She began to tick them off on her fingers. "Curiosity and a love of learning new things, though you're self-taught and I'm a lesson freak, so we have different styles. And then there's the fact that we both want very much to be a part of a family."

His eyes narrowed. "You're going to have to elaborate on that."

She leaned toward him a little. "As a lit major, you must have read the Brontës. Remember Jane Eyre and Heathcliff?"

He nodded, wondering where she was going.

"Well, we're like them—I'm Jane and you're Heathcliff. We're both on the outside looking in and wanting to fit in to a family. In this case, it's the Rossis."

"I'm not sure I like the analogy. Your ending is happy. Mine isn't."

"Don't worry about it. You're much more inventive and competent than Heathcliff ever was."

He threw his head back and laughed. "Thanks for the compliment."

She reached over to pat his hand on the railing. "That's how it was meant. Heathcliff was pretty clueless as far as Catherine was concerned."

He kept her hand when she would have withdrawn it and linked his fingers with hers. "You're a surprising woman, Pepper Rossi." Even in the moonlight, he could see the blush that rushed to her cheeks.

Suddenly Pepper's eyes widened and she leaned closer. "Don't turn around."

"What?"

"Evan is finally here. He and Jean Claude are sitting down at a table on the other side of the pool." She slid down from the railing and turned her back on the pool.

"Why don't you want him to know you're here? I thought your plan was to go over and surprise him."

"I've revised it since I overheard them talking in the gift shop. I mean I can't very well walk up and ask Evan if he's selling the stolen Monet to Butch, can I? Well, I suppose I could, but I'm not sure his answer would be truthful. And besides, once I go up and let him know I'm here, my cards are all on the table, and he's still holding all of his."

"Right. What's Plan B?"

She glanced up and met his eyes. "I'm going to do a little eavesdropping."

"You've got good instincts." He reversed their positions so that her back was to the railing and his back was to the pool. "Jean Claude is looking this way."

Then his own gaze became riveted on the path that led down from the main hotel. "To borrow a phrase from Yogi Berra, it may be 'déjà vu all over again.' Butch and H are on their way down." He watched where the two men headed. "They're sitting down with Evan and Jean Claude."

The look she shot him was filled with mischief. "C'mon. Let's eavesdrop."

"Your call," he said as she took his hand and drew him along the edge of the dance floor.

IT TOOK LONGER THAN she would have liked to reach the potted palm trees that were clumped near Evan's table. They'd made it there without attracting any notice from the men at the table, but that was when her luck had run out. The band was playing close by, making it difficult to hear anything.

Evan was the only one she had a full view of through the palm leaves. He looked nervous. She could see Jean Claude and H in profile, and Butch's back was to her.

She breathed a sigh of relief as the band ended a piece. But Gari showed up just then to serve champagne. He uncorked the bottle, offered it to Jean Claude to taste and then filled four glasses. No one spoke during the ritual, and

Jean Claude was the only one who drank champagne. By that time, the band had begun the next song, and the woman drummer took a solo.

As the sound built in speed and volume, it stirred something primitive in her—probably due to the fact that Cole had crouched right behind her. His body was pressed so tightly against hers that she could feel each breath he took in and let out. They hadn't been this close on the dance floor, and she was powerless to block out the sensations. His chest felt hard against her bare back, and his arms were around her. The sarong wasn't helping a bit. When she'd dropped to her knees, the slit on the one side had widened, and Cole's hand was resting on her exposed thigh. She could feel the imprint of each one of his fingers. To say that he was interfering with her concentration was putting it mildly.

The one thing she'd decided was that the four men were not enjoying each other's company. The Frenchman pushed a folded piece of paper across the table toward Butch.

Just then the drum solo ended, and there was a moment of silence before the crowd broke into applause. None of the men at the table clapped. By the time the clapping died down, Butch and H had risen, turned and walked away.

Evan frowned at Jean Claude. "You're making a mistake."

Jean Claude placed his hand over Evan's. "You'll see. I'm more experienced at this than you are. He'll come around when we meet in the morning at nine."

"How can you know that?"

"I've done my homework. Castellano's an astute businessman. He's not going to give an inch this early in the game. But in the morning, he'll make a counteroffer."

"But we're running out of time."

"No, we're not. Drink your champagne. We've come too far not to get the best possible price, and Castellano's pockets are deep." He patted Evan's hand. "In the meantime, we may as well enjoy the amenities of the island. They're serving a late supper in the dining room in honor of Valentine's Day. I heard that the menu is exquisite, so I made us a reservation."

Pepper could see some of the anxiety fade from Evan's face. "Yes. All right." It occurred to her that Evan was bowing to his friend's advice and wishes the same way he'd always bowed to his mother's.

Cole hunkered even closer, pushing her down as the two men rose and walked away. A few moments ticked by before he rose and helped her up. Then he began to draw her in the opposite direction.

Pepper dug in her heels. "Wait." She circled around the palms and using only two fingers on the very lip of the champagne glass, she plucked it from the table.

Cole didn't comment. He merely took her free hand, and drew her with him around the far end of the pool until they reached their table.

"We didn't learn much, did we?" Pepper asked as she placed the glass on the table and sat back down in her chair.

"Tell me what you noticed," Cole said.

"Evan is nervous. And the Frenchman is older-looking without the beret. Plus, he seems to be in charge."

"What else?"

"There's clearly some kind of negotiation going on between Evan and Jean Claude and Butch. The folded paper might have been a price or a bid on something, and Butch didn't accept it. But Jean Claude is convinced that Butch will change his mind by morning." Warming to her theme, she leaned toward him. "Evan is just going along with everything."

"You think Jean Claude is calling the shots?"

Pepper nodded. "Definitely. And he's giving off very bad vibes. And…I'm becoming more and more convinced that he has the Monet. Go ahead. Tell me that we don't have positive proof of that and that Irene could still have it."

"I could tell you all that, but I think your first scenario is more likely."

"Yeah. I wish I knew what to do about it."

"You want to go to Butch and tell him everything?"

She studied him for a moment. "That's what you'd do. Right?"

He nodded.

She thought for a minute. "No. We have until 9:00 a.m. to warn Butch that he might be purchasing a stolen Monet. I want to give my aunt at least that long to get here."

"Okay. In the meantime, we have a nice set of Jean Claude's fingerprints." He pointed at the glass. "What do you want to bet that Luke will have some luck with them?"

She lifted her hands and displayed her crossed fingers.

"Nice move taking that glass, by the way. And your idea of eavesdropping was productive too."

She felt a ribbon of warmth move through her, sweet and steady. And she knew that she was blushing again. "Thanks. I can lift the prints if we can get some scotch tape. Lesson number sixteen in PI class. And we can fax them to Luke, right?"

"You're amazing," Cole said. "Let's get right on it because I have other plans for the rest of the evening."

12

"ANGELO HASN'T CHECKED in for over an hour," Butch said as he joined H at the one-way glass that looked out on the lobby.

"There's a lot of water between here and Eden Island. You told him not to call until he'd searched every inch of it again," H said in a mild tone. "Plus, it's been dark for over an hour. I don't imagine he's having an easy time locating that raft."

Butch ran a hand through his hair. There was nothing to worry about. Angelo had spotted the raft about halfway between the two islands shortly before it had become dark. But before he could get within shouting distance, darkness had fallen. Even with a full moon, Angelo's job was a tough one. Butch glanced at his watch. "She should be here by now."

"Relax. The weather is good. And remember, she's with someone who raced in the America's Cup."

Butch grunted. "Yeah. That has me wanting to dance a little jig."

"Do you want me to tell Ms. Rossi that her aunt has rented a boat and is on her way?"

Butch shook his head. "Yeah. But don't tell her it's a

raft and we've lost track of it. There's no need to worry her. I'm worrying enough for the whole damn Rossi family."

As H dialed Cole's number and delivered the message, Butch pulled out a cigar, but just as he was about to stick it between his teeth, he extended his hand and stared at it. "Dammit. I haven't been able to enjoy one of these since I learned Renie had booked a room here. And now she's off in a boat with some sailor she picked up on an island that runs a damn sex camp."

He waved a hand at the lobby. "This should be a night for celebrating. The main restaurant has been booked for two seatings. The lobby bar is packed. Couples are dancing on the veranda, and the dance floor at the poolside café is full. The weekend is going even better than we'd expected. Finalizing that deal with Evan Atwell will be the icing on the cake. And I'm not enjoying any of it."

H said nothing.

"Don't you dare say it." Butch pointed a finger at him. "I'm not."

For a moment the silence stretched.

Finally Butch said, "Okay, I'll say it. Maybe I was wrong about Renie and me."

H said nothing.

He shoved his hands in his pockets. "When she gets here I'll tell her, and we'll settle this thing once and for all."

H glanced at Butch. "Remember, I have those videotapes of her TV show in San Francisco—if you're interested."

Butch's eyes narrowed thoughtfully.

"In any negotiation, it's a good idea to know everything you can about the other party," H commented.

Butch thought for another minute, then nodded. "Maybe you're right. Speaking of knowing the other party, have you been able to dig up something on Jean Claude Rambeau?"

H shook his head. "There is no such animal. At least not someone who meets Frenchy's description."

"He's using an alias?"

"That would be my guess," H said.

"Why?"

"Precisely."

"Shit. If that's the case, you might have more luck tracing fingerprints. I should have thought about that sooner. We could have had Gari bring us the glass he used at the pool."

"I requested Gari to do just that, but Mr. Rambeau was a step ahead of us. The glass wasn't there when Gari went back to the table. Fortunately, I have the slip of paper he gave you."

Butch took his cigar out and then shoved it back in his pocket. "Dammit. I haven't been thinking straight all day. That woman has my brain going into a complete meltdown."

Just then Butch squinted and moved closer to the glass. Cole Buchanan and Pepper Rossi had just stepped up to the main registration desk.

"They make a nice couple," H said.

Butch grunted. "Did you run a background check on Buchanan?"

H nodded. "I couldn't find anything disturbing. He's ex-CIA. That was pretty easy to access. But there were some files I couldn't get into."

Butch turned then to stare at his friend. "Files exist that *you* couldn't get into?"

H shrugged. "With some time, I'll get in, but this is a busy weekend. Classified government files are always a challenge. And I didn't think it was urgent."

"She's Renie's niece. I wouldn't want her hurt."

"Henry is escorting Buchanan and Ms. Rossi into the business office," H said.

Butch glanced at his watch. "At 11:15 on the eve of Valentine's Day. What kind of business could be that pressing?"

H punched a number into his cell phone.

While Butch waited for the information, he tried to gather his thoughts and plan his next move. That had been his problem all day. Ever since he'd learned that Renie was coming to his island, he'd been on the defensive. And that had never been his best game. It was high time that he took control.

H repocketed his cell. "They sent a fax. Henry got the number, but he didn't see the message."

"No matter," Butch said as he watched the two young people walk out of the lobby. "It can't be that important." Turning to H, he said, "I've decided I want to see those tapes."

H pushed a button on the remote, and on the wall to his left, a curtain pulled back from a large plasma screen. He pressed another button and the screen came to life.

Butch stared at the TV as the credits flashed onto the screen, then the title *Are You Safe?* But he was only vaguely aware of the words. His attention was completely riveted to the tiny figure, dressed in some kind of black ninja outfit as it rappelled down the side of a hotel. Seconds later, the figure landed on the balcony of one of the rooms and pulled off his mask. Her mask.

Renie. He would have known those eyes anywhere. His Renie was a cat burglar?

COLE LEANED HIS ELBOW on a rock ledge and watched Pepper in the moonlight. Irene was fine and on her way. They'd know soon whether she had the Monet, or whether Evan and his friend had indeed stolen it. And then there'd be the task of recovering it. Somehow, he suspected that part was not going to go smoothly. And he wasn't sure if he could keep his word to Pepper.

One way or the other, he meant to get the Monet back to Althea Atwell, and Pepper might not like him butting in on her territory.

Always a planner, he'd surprised himself by acting on impulse and bringing her here to the same spot on the beach where they'd made love earlier.

He'd intended to take her back to the cove. He'd even had a basket packed to provide ambience—champagne, a tablecloth, a half-dozen candles, chocolate-covered strawberries, grapes, cheese and some caviar.

But as they'd walked out of the hotel, the lagoon had seemed too far, and their time together was running out. Meanwhile, the beach was deserted.

Glancing around, Cole didn't regret his impulse. He'd spread a cloth and lit candles in a place where the fall of rocks blocked the wind. The surf was up, the waves tumbling into a lacy white froth as they pushed onto the shore. Other than that, the night was quiet.

Watching Pepper sip champagne in the moonlight, he felt something that he'd felt only twice before in his life. The first time was when he'd settled into the home of the man who'd taught him to sail. Then he'd felt the same thing when

Luke had invited him to San Francisco for the summer. He'd been eighteen, a college freshman, and walking into Peter Rossi's house, he'd felt as if he'd come home.

That he was experiencing a similar emotion on a deserted and moonlit beach had little to do with the setting or even the ambience he'd created and everything to do with the woman who was holding her glass out for more champagne.

He topped off her glass. He'd wanted her from the moment he'd first seen her picture. Since that first kiss in the Atwells' suite, the desire had only escalated. He was coming to realize that he would always want her like this, Always need her.

The thought, the word, stunned him. He hadn't allowed himself to need anything or anyone for a very long time. But she'd snuck up on him. Oh, he'd known that he wanted more from her than an island fling and he'd set out to sway her feelings in that direction.

Just what had been his agenda? To extend their affair once they got back to San Francisco. But now he realized that he wanted much more than an affair with Pepper Rossi.

Just what was he going to do about it? A decision would have to be made, but not tonight. Right now, he simply decided to give voice to the thought that had filled his mind all evening. "You're beautiful."

Her gaze flew to Cole's. Her hand trembled, spilling a little champagne, and he saw surprise in her eyes.

He suppressed the little flare of anger. "Hasn't anyone ever told you that before?"

She shook her head. "Why should they? I'm not beautiful. My mother was. Luke looks like her, tall and blond, like the Pendletons. Matt's inherited the best of both worlds—he's tall like a Pendleton and dark like the Rossis. And as handsome as sin."

Cole's lips curved. "He considers it a curse."

"Right. Unless he's dealing with a woman and it gets him what he wants." She tilted her head to one side. "I envy you."

"Why?"

"You knew them all those years that I didn't."

"I envy you too. They're your brothers. They're just my friends."

"They don't think of me that way. They think of me as the Pepper Problem."

He set his glass aside. Why was he surprised that she'd heard the phrase? She was a smart woman. "You're wrong about the fact that they don't think about you as their sister. That's the whole problem. They love you and they want to protect you. That's what brothers do with sisters. If I had one, that's exactly what I'd do."

"They want to put me on a shelf and drag me out for family gatherings. That's what my grandmother wanted. And she wanted me to marry 'well' because my mother hadn't. She wanted a marriage for me that she could put on display for others to admire. I'm not going to allow my father and my brothers to do what *they* think is good for me. That's what Irene did forty years ago. She tried to please her parents, and look where it's gotten her. She's stolen a Monet, probably lost it, and she's on a boat somewhere trying to get to a man who thinks it would be best for her if they never got together."

"You're not going to end up like your aunt."

"No." She met his eyes directly. "I'm not."

"And you're wrong about your brothers. I'm not saying that they don't want to put you on a shelf. They're proud of you and they want to show you off. They feel guilt for the years you've lost. But it's not all they want. More than anything, they want you to be happy. And you've got persistence. It won't be long before they see that you're turning into a damn good PI."

Her eyes widened. "You think so?"

"I do." He set his glass aside. Then he took her glass and set it next to his. "You never give yourself enough credit. I told you I was impressed by what you did tonight when you grabbed that glass. I was a step behind you there."

Her lips curved in a smile. "The way I recall it, you weren't anywhere near a step behind me. You were practically glued to my backside. And your hands were just inches from where I wanted them to be. It's a wonder I could think at all."

He leaned close and brushed his mouth over hers. "The point is you thought of getting Jean Claude's fingerprints, and I didn't. I think you have the makings of that super sleuth you want so much to be."

She drew back. "I'm never going to be able to handle the gun part."

"You did an effective job with Castellano and H earlier today. Ideally, a gun should act as a deterrent. You don't always have to shoot people with it. Besides, no one is perfect at everything."

"You are."

He shot her a quick grin. "My curse." Then his grin faded. "You have other strengths—not the least of which is the lightning-fast way your mind works. Like it did tonight when you decided to grab that glass. You should capitalize on those strengths and forget worrying about what you can't do. And now…" He drew her hand to his mouth and kissed her fingers. "Why don't we concentrate on what we both can do well?"

NERVES. Pepper could feel them knotting in her stomach as Cole leaned down to brush his mouth over hers. She tried to will them away. This was what she wanted, what she'd been looking forward to all evening. The dinner, the dancing—that was all a prelude.

Any second now he would deepen the kiss and her fears would be swept away. But he surprised her by withdrawing and then just touching his mouth to hers again. It wasn't like any other kiss he'd given her. His lips were feather-light on hers, pressing lightly and then withdrawing as if he were tasting her for the first time.

It was only then that she realized she might have been tasting him for the first time too. His flavor was different. Without the explosion of heat she'd always experienced before, he tasted more complex, more intense. She wanted more.

It was only as she tried to lift her hand and pull him closer that she realized how weak she had become.

He drew back then and said, "There's no plantation owner tonight, Pepper, and no slave girl. There's just you and me, and we're on equal footing."

It was what she wanted, what she'd planned. And it was just ridiculous that she was trembling. A little ribbon of fear moved through her—fear that she might come up short when he compared her to Elena. But she shoved it aside. Strengths—she had them, and this was Cole, a man who'd fascinated her much more than a plantation owner who had nothing better to do than to fool around with a slave girl.

The one thing she could give him was the truth. She managed to raise her hands and frame his face with them. "I want you, Cole, more than I've ever wanted any man." She saw the dark flash of pleasure in his eyes, and her courage increased. "I've been thinking of making love with you ever since we left the lagoon."

He took her wrist and drawing her hand to his mouth, he pressed a kiss to her palm. Once again the warmth and the weakness moved through her.

"All through dinner and dancing, even when we were hiding in that forest of palm trees, I was wondering how fast I could get you out of this dress." When he began to undo the knot at her shoulder, his fingers fumbled.

Another small thrill moved through her. This was Cole and she was unnerving him. Once the knot was freed, the silk parted and pooled around her. She wore nothing beneath.

"And I was wondering if you were naked under that dress."

The rough edge to his voice dried her throat, and she had to moisten her lips. "Perhaps I should have told you."

"We'd never have made it through dinner." Cole's gaze locked on hers. *"You're beautiful,"* he repeated.

A fresh thrill moved through her as she let herself believe him.

Cole began to taste her again, slowly. One moment his lips were pressed firmly against hers and the next he was tracing her lips with his tongue as if she were some delicacy he couldn't get enough of. He was only touching her with his lips and his tongue and yet she felt as if he were touching her everywhere.

She was floating, and the pleasure was so sweet she began to ache. There was a part of her that wanted him to hurry. She wanted his hands on her. But there was another part of her that wanted this moment to go on and on.

When he finally drew back, she felt her heart flutter.

He framed her face with his hands and regarded her in that intent way he had. "I want you to know that it's me touching you. And it's going to be me inside you."

When he brushed his mouth softly over hers again, she felt her heart take a slow tumble.

She was in love with Cole Buchanan. Before she could think about that, Cole increased the pressure of the kiss and began to feast—tasting, nipping, sucking—until the weakness in her body became an ache.

She murmured his name and he heard it above the surf. It was what he'd been waiting to hear. His name. As he felt the softening of her muscles that signaled surrender, ripples of delight moved through him. But he wanted more. He'd have more. Drawing away, he urged her back so that she was lying on the blanket. Then he simply looked at her, naked in the moonlight.

"Cole?"

"I want to look at you." Reynaldo had been right. In the moonlight, she did look like a goddess. He wanted to store away the memory, he realized. He needed it.

Pepper's lips curved slightly. "What if I tell you that every time you looked at me that way in the office, I wanted you to touch me?"

"What if I told you that I knew it?" He brushed one finger over the pulse that even now was beating rapidly at her throat. "This was a dead giveaway. You nearly drove me crazy." Bending lower, he replaced his finger with his mouth and once more sampled the sweetness of that telltale pulse.

Then as his own desire quickened, he began to use his hands on her, tracing curves and angles, skimming over strong arms, firm thighs, and exploring the impossibly soft skin over each breast.

Time spun away. He knew that he couldn't stop it, but he was determined not to hurry. Not this time. When they were away from the island, she would remember this and so would he. Leaning over her, he kissed her again and again. He wasn't even aware when his hands stopped moving. He only knew that he could have gone on kissing her forever

Finally, he drew back, and shifting his body downward, he took his mouth on the same journey his hands had taken earlier. He wanted to absorb her—her scent, the texture of her skin, the small sounds she made. He wanted her to absorb him. And he was learning about her too. Scraping his teeth along her collarbone made her sigh. Using his tongue on her nipple made her breath hitch. When he caught the peak of one breast between his teeth, she moaned his name and his blood began to pound in a primitive rhythm.

Pepper hadn't known it was possible to float on a sea of such intense pleasure. Anticipation and arousal swirled inside her and tangled with the promise of satisfaction. She thought he'd already shown her all the ways that her body could experience pleasure, but there were more doors that he opened up for her as he nibbled long the bone at her hip and his fingers traced patterns on the back of her knee and her inner thigh.

Then his mouth moved lower still until he found her center. There, his tongue lingered—tracing, teasing and trapping her in a world where pleasure became almost too much to bear. Even then he showed her more. When the first orgasm shot through her, she could only call his name. But he didn't stop, and he built her second climax more slowly. It was torture. It was paradise. She wasn't sure there was a difference as she felt her whole body strain upward until the release erupted and shot through her, catapulting her to a new peak.

She was still falling when she heard her name.

"Pepper, open your eyes. I want you to let me see where I'm taking you."

She did, and once Cole looked into her eyes, he knew nothing but Pepper. He'd made love before. He'd made love with this woman before, but this was new. This was different. At some point when he'd been so focused on giving her pleasure, he'd lost a part of himself. Now she was all he was aware of. There was nothing else. The sound of the sea had faded along with the candlelight and the moonlight.

He was only aware of her eyes, hot and dark and fastened on him. There was only Pepper, small and strong, soft and seductive. Passion and desire tangled with emotions he couldn't understand as he slipped into her and gave himself to her.

13

COLE WASN'T SURE how much time had gone by—seconds, moments, an hour? They were still tangled together on the blanket. But he'd pulled her on top of him and her head was resting on his shoulder. The candles were still flickering nearby, and the sound of the surf had picked up. He was aware that his heart was no longer racing, but he was still holding on to her as if his life depended on it. When a wave dampened one of his feet, he said, "I think we're going to have to move."

"Mmm." She made a negative motion with her head. "Don't want to."

"I think the tide's coming in."

"That old spoilsport."

Cole couldn't have agreed more. It suddenly occurred to him that he could have gone on holding her just like this for a very long time. And he might have risked it if there hadn't been a sudden shout.

"Ahoy, there!"

Pepper shifted off him and they sat up together. In the shaft of moonlight that cut a clear wide path across the water, Cole made out the shape of a boat and watched as a wave shoved it closer to the outcrop of rocks that extended into sea.

"Anybody there?" The shout was a little louder this time.

Grabbing his trousers and slipping into them, Cole called, "Are you in trouble?"

"He is if this isn't Escapade Island," a female voice shouted. "Is it?"

Cole felt Pepper stiffen beside him.

"It's Escapade Island." She grabbed her sarong, tying it around her as she scrambled to her feet. "Aunt Irene, is that you?"

"Pepper?"

"Are you all right?" Pepper raced knee deep into the water as the boat surged toward her.

Cole reached her side just as a second wave brought the boat within ten yards. A small figure slipped over the side and Pepper and her aunt waded toward each other. Cole turned his attention to the man at the tiller.

"Need some help?" he asked.

"Appreciate it," the man said.

Cole grabbed the side of the boat and began to urge it toward the sandy beach. This close, Cole saw that the vessel was nothing more than an inflatable raft equipped with a small sail and a motor.

He let out a low whistle as the short, portly man slipped over the side and joined them in the water. "My hat's off to you if you sailed this all the way from Eden Island."

"Irene wanted to get here tonight, and this was the only thing on that island that was seaworthy enough to make the trip. I'm Happy Johansson, by the way."

"Cole Buchanan." He hitched a thumb toward Pepper's aunt. "So how do you know Irene?"

"Met her on the plane to Eden." He lowered his voice. "And if I can be frank, it's the most exciting thing that's happened to me in years. God, I love a take-charge woman."

"I hate to be the bearer of bad news, but you've got some pretty stiff competition."

Happy sighed. "Yeah, I got that. She couldn't stop talking about him on the way over. But I think I'll hang around, in case things don't work out the way Irene's planned."

"She told you about her plan?"

Happy grinned. "About stealing the Monet to prove a point to her boyfriend?"

"That would be it," Cole said.

"She's a pip, isn't she?"

Cole couldn't have agreed more. "She's got the Monet then?"

"No. I expect the young man who drugged her and put her on the plane to Eden Island nipped it. But she's confident it's here on the island somewhere."

Cole glanced over at the two women now deep in conversation. No doubt Irene was filling Pepper in on her adventure. For a few minutes Happy and he worked in silence, steering the boat away from the rocks and helping the sea guide it onto the beach. It took only a matter of seconds to drag it away from the reach of the tide. Once the raft was secured, Happy glanced over to where the two women were standing by the rocks in the moonlight, locked in a tight embrace. "Is that her daughter?"

"Pepper is Irene's niece," Cole said, turning to him. "They'll need a moment to catch up and you look like a man who could use a drink. I hope you like champagne."

Happy's smile grew even brighter. "You just became my new best friend."

Cole poured him a glass. "Can Irene describe the man who drugged her?"

For the first time, Cole saw the laughter completely drain from Happy's eyes.

"I can," he said. "He spoke with a French accent and he was sporting a goatee and a beret. If he's here on the island, I'd like to have a few moments with him."

"He's here," Cole assured him. "And you'll have to wait in line."

FOR A LONG MOMENT, Pepper held on hard to her aunt as feelings swamped her. Delight and relief that her aunt was finally safely on the island, regret because she knew that her time with Cole was almost over. "Don't worry about the Monet. I was so worried about you—ever since you missed the plane. And I know you're wondering why I'm here."

Stepping back, Irene glanced at the remains of the beach picnic. "Not really. It looks like you were having a little tryst with Cole Buchanan." She shot a glance toward Cole who was pouring champagne into a glass for Happy. "I approve. He's a definite step up from Evan Atwell. Suits you, too."

"No, I mean you've got to be wondering why I'm here on the island."

"You followed me," Irene said.

Pepper stared at her. "My disguise didn't fool you?"

"It was damn good, but I figured you'd follow me, and the shoes were a big clue."

Pepper drew in a deep breath. "It's not that I don't trust

what you said you were going to do. I know that you intended to return the painting. But I didn't know that much about Butch. And I figured since you're in love with him, you might not be seeing him in an objective light."

Irene waved a hand. "I would have done the same. But Butch will not accept a stolen painting. He's legit."

"I think you're right. The people who work here like him, and he seems to be a very nice man."

Irene grabbed her hands. "You've met him? How is he? What did he say? You didn't tell him I was coming to the island?"

Pepper shook her head. "He already knew. You were on the guest list. When I checked into your cabin, he thought that I was you. And when he came barging through the door, he seemed upset that Cole and I were…well, sharing the cabin."

Irene's eyes widened. "He barged through the door?"

"I had the distinct impression that Butch Castellano was jealous of me," Cole said as he and Happy joined them.

Irene shot Cole a narrow-eyed glance. "Jealous?"

"He thought you had come to the island with another man," Pepper said. "Cole nearly had to dodge a bullet."

"Really," Irene said and she looked pleased.

"The important thing is that you're here now," Pepper said.

"But I don't have the Monet," Irene pointed out.

"Cole says the Frenchman who drugged you and nipped the Monet is here on the island," Happy said.

"His name is Jean Claude Rambeau," Pepper added.

"You know him?" Irene asked.

Pepper shrugged "We have some information about

him. He's here with Evan Atwell. They're a couple, and they're sharing the penthouse suite. So far Butch has had two meetings with them. I'll bet my PI license that they're negotiating the price of that Monet."

"Time out," Irene said. "This Rambeau stole the painting from me and Butch is having meetings with him?"

"In a nutshell," Pepper said.

"Shit," Irene muttered.

Cole pulled out his cell phone. "I'll get in touch with Butch, and we'll straighten this whole thing out."

"No!" Irene shouted.

"Wait," Pepper said in an only slightly calmer voice.

Cole closed his cell. "You don't think he'll cooperate?"

"Of course, he will," Irene said. "He`ll be only to happy to save my ass. That's why he made the big sacrifice and swore to stay out of my life forty years ago. If you tell him about this, Butch Castellano will ride to the rescue again and he'll continue to think of me as poor little Renie who needs to be protected and saved from ruining her life. I stole the Monet to erase that image forever from his mind. Unless I get it back, how can I convince him that I'm bad enough for him?"

Cole stared at her. "You want to steal it again?"

"Of course she does," Pepper said. "If she doesn't steal back the Monet, she hasn't made her point."

Cole glanced at Happy. "Are you following this?'

Happy laughed. "Nope." He patted Cole's arm. "But I wouldn't argue. It's female logic. I've raised three daughters, and I've never gotten the hang of it, but I've learned not to argue."

"After all," Pepper continued, "if you steal something back, it isn't really stealing, is it?"

"See?" Happy said. "There's really no rebuttal for an argument like that."

Cole couldn't have agreed more.

As the two women began to talk to each other again, Happy pitched his voice low so that only Cole could hear. "The other thing you ought to watch out for is that the older one is very forceful—though I would say it's her most endearing quality."

"Yeah, well when the younger one gets an idea in her head, she's no slouch either." Then he raised his voice. "Ladies, I think we should continue this discussion in more comfortable surroundings."

THE MORE COMFORTABLE surroundings turned out to be the two-bedroom suite that Cole had booked when he'd arrived on the island on Thursday. They'd decided against using Irene's bungalow because Butch would probably be keeping his eye on it, not to mention the hole in the ceiling that needed repairing.

Pepper glanced up from the diagram that Irene was drawing and took the room in for the first time. It boasted a spacious living room and even a small kitchen where she was surprised to see Cole and Happy cooking something.

"I'll come down to their balcony from the roof, jimmy the lock on the door and go into the suite," Irene said. "When I'm finished, I'll simply walk out the front door of the suite and take the elevator down three floors."

"Something tells me it's not going to be that easy," Pepper said.

Irene met her eyes. "Don't tell me you've got one of your feelings again."

Pepper nodded, and Irene patted her hand. "Relax. I've

got a real natural feel for locks. One of our Rossi ancestors was not as sweet and pure as my parents would have had me believe. I'm not going to have any problem getting into the suite."

"I'm not worried about your getting in," Pepper said. "It's getting out that has me worried."

Irene shrugged. "Frenchy and Evan will be busy negotiating with Butch.

"What if the meeting ends early? What if the Monet isn't just hanging on the wall waiting for you? What if they've put it in a safe?"

Irene rubbed her hands together. "I'm pretty good at opening safes too, especially the cheap kind that hotels provide."

Pepper studied the diagram again. Nothing her aunt said eased the knot of apprehension in her stomach. But she couldn't see anything specific to fault in the plan. If everything went well, she would be in and out of Evan's suite in ten, maybe fifteen, minutes. Still…

Pepper drew in a deep breath. "I'm going with you as backup."

Irene stared at her. "You sure you want to do that? You don't like heights."

Pepper nodded. "It's only one floor down. I can't let you go in there alone."

Irene glanced over at the kitchen. "He's a good influence on you."

"Yeah," Pepper said letting her gaze follow her aunt's. She thought of the fact that since they'd come up to the suite, Cole had kept out of her way. He hadn't hovered over her as she'd half expected him to. Instead, he'd taken Happy off to the kitchen and busied himself inspecting the contents of the refrigerator. He'd kept to that part of the deal. And he'd keep the rest of it too. An island fling. But once they got back to San Francisco…

No, she wasn't going to think about that now. She pressed her hand against the tightening sensation in her chest. "He believes in me more than I believe in myself."

Irene nodded ruefully. "That's a nice quality in a man. Happy over there thinks I can walk on water. Now, if I can just bring Butch around to think that way…"

As if he was aware that the women's eyes were on him, Cole turned. "Breakfast is nearly ready. Have the two of you—"

Whatever else he would have said was interrupted when there was a knock at the suite's door.

For a moment everyone froze in place. Then Irene bolted up from the couch. "It that's Butch…"

Cole waved her back down. "I'll handle it."

But before he could even reach the door, Pepper saw an envelope slide beneath it. Cole looked through the peephole, then picked up the envelope, opened it and scanned the information on the single sheet of paper.

"What?" Pepper asked.

His expression was unreadable when he looked up and met her eyes. "A fax from Luke. I told them to deliver it here. Frenchy's real name is not Jean Claude Rambeau. It's Maurice LeBlanc. Interpol has a nice thick file on him, and he's a nasty character. Luke's worried."

"This Frenchy's a thief?" Irene asked.

"A skilled one," Cole said as he pocketed the fax and returned to the kitchen.

"He must have been the guy I shot with the tranq gun

on the roof at Evan Atwell's hotel," Irene said thoughtfully. "I've been wondering who that was."

"You shot him with a tranq gun?" Happy asked.

"I didn't want to hurt him," Irene explained.

"Well, Le Blanc doesn't have your scruples," Cole said. He looked from one to the other of the two women. "Let's eat while you tell me your plan."

"So HOW ARE YOU going to steal the painting back?" Happy asked after everyone had dug into the meal.

Irene sprinkled salt onto her eggs and passed the shaker to Pepper. "We're going to rappel down from the roof to the balcony outside of the penthouse suite. That should take about fifteen seconds tops. It's on the top floor."

Cole already didn't like the plan. Two words stuck in his mind. *Rappel* and *we*. He put down his fork and repeated the first one. "Rappel down from the roof? Why not just go in the front door?"

Irene shook her head. "That would involve bribing one of the maids or distracting her while someone else swiped her master key card. It would take too much time, and too many things could go wrong."

"I can follow that," Happy said around a mouthful of scrambled eggs.

Despite that he didn't like it, Cole could see the logic in it too. "You said *we.*"

Irene nodded as she tore off a piece of toast. "Pepper wants to come with me. She has a feeling I'll need some backup."

"I have the same feeling," Cole said. "I'll go in with you."

"No." Irene and Pepper spoke the word in unison.

Cole knew he'd made a mistake. But he wasn't sure he

cared. Not with his mind filled with the image of Pepper rappelling down from the roof. And not with the information that Luke had dug up on LeBlanc. "It's too dangerous." The look on Pepper's face told him that he was just getting himself in deeper, but he went ahead anyway. "Here's what I didn't tell you about LeBlanc. He's not just one of these legendary second-story men who cut a romantic figure. He's killed to get what he wants. In fact, according to the information that Luke got from Interpol, LeBlanc likes to kill. I wouldn't give Evan Atwell much of a chance once LeBlanc gets his hands on the money."

Both women paled a little and Pepper put down her fork. *Good,* he thought and pushed ahead. "Here's the way it's going to go. I'll take care of getting Irene in the suite. Pepper, you and Happy will stand guard—one at the stairwell and one at the elevator so that we're not interrupted. Then we'll bring the painting down here."

"No." Pepper's voice was quiet, but it made Cole feel as if he'd just dug his own grave, laid down in it and pushed the dirt back on top of himself.

Irene was staring at him as if she'd just seen him for the first time. "You're just like Butch."

Cole almost winced. "I'm just being practical." When he heard what he'd just said, he did wince.

Pepper rose. "Could I please see you in the other room?"

He followed her, desperately trying to think of a way to dig himself back out. As soon as they were in the bedroom, he closed the door and turned to face her. A new strategy just didn't seem to be within his reach. "I can't let either of you do it."

She folded her arms across the chest. "Yes, you can. We

have a deal. For twenty-four hours I'm in charge. That's what we agreed to."

He said nothing, knowing that he'd backed himself into a corner. He reached for her but she stepped back. "Pepper—"

"You can't back out," she said. "I've kept my part of the bargain, haven't I?"

Cole felt the words slice him to the bone. She called what they'd shared a bargain. He'd let the romance of the evening they'd spent dancing and making love on the beach together cloud his mind. Pain twisted hard in his belly, but he ignored it. He'd survived rejection before. And she was right. They had a bargain.

"Yes," he said. "You've held up your end of the deal very well." He wasn't going to think about her feelings, or lack of feelings, about their time together on the island. Right now, he had to focus totally on the job at hand. Letting the two women steal the Monet and at the same time keeping them safe.

He stepped back and turned to open the door to the living room. "Let's go over the details."

14

BUTCH GLANCED UP FROM the papers he'd been shoving around on his desk. H was in his usual spot at the one-way window. The lobby was quiet, but the resort hadn't quite gone to sleep yet. The last time he'd checked, the hot tubs and the pools were still in use.

"Why don't you go to bed?" he asked H.

"Why don't you? Angelo found the raft on the beach. And it had been secured. There's every reason to believe she's here on the island somewhere safe and sound."

"Yeah." Butch longed for a cigar. He glanced at the last one he'd mangled, which he'd left on his desk as a reminder. "She's on the island. So is the super sailor. But she isn't in her bungalow, and she hasn't tried to contact me."

H turned to him then. "I've got more bad news."

Butch's eyes immediately narrowed. "Something's happened to her?"

H shook his head. "This isn't about Irene. It's about the Frenchman. I got a match on the fingerprints I lifted off that paper."

Now Butch did take a fresh cigar out of his drawer and began to roll it between his fingers. At least the cigar was something he could control. "Tell me."

By the time H had filled him in on Maurice LeBlanc's background, Butch had his cigar lit and was leaning back in his chair. "Sooo, we've got a professional thief on our hands. And he thinks he's clever too. He seduces Atwell, convinces him to approach me with an offer to sell the Monet. Once LeBlanc gets the money—" Butch paused to snap his fingers "—poof! He disappears with the money and I'll lay odds he's planning on taking the Monet too."

"That would be my guess," H said. "And Evan Atwell will get stuck with the tab that LeBlanc has been running up on the room. Close to twenty-five thousand dollars. The scheme might have worked, too. Atwell provided the perfect cover. Should I call the police?"

Butch shook his head. "I don't even want to think how quickly a man like LeBlanc could break out of our little island jail." He took another puff on his cigar, enjoying himself for the first time all day. "Besides, I want to handle this myself."

"He has to figure that we'll want delivery of the painting before you part with the money."

Butch nodded. "So he won't make his move until after that." He clamped his teeth down hard on the cigar as the plan began to take shape in his mind. A few moments later, he pulled the cigar out and smiled. "So we'll give the mighty LeBlanc a taste of his own medicine. We'll steal the painting out of the suite while he's meeting with us tomorrow morning."

PEPPER STIRRED IN Cole's arms for the third time since they'd gotten into bed. She wasn't going to be able to sleep. And it wasn't the upcoming heist that was bothering her. It was the expression that she'd seen in Cole's eyes when she'd said, "I've kept my part of the bargain, haven't I?"

For a moment, she'd seen the flash of pain. Then he'd masked it. If she could have snatched back the words, she would have. But they'd been said. And she couldn't, she wouldn't, back down from the plan to help her aunt.

Since then, Cole had been polite. He'd even made helpful suggestions. She'd discovered during their strategy session that he was a whiz at organization. In the morning, Happy was going to locate some good sailing rope so that she and Irene could climb down easily from the roof. Cole had even thought of coding numbers into their cell phones so that they could keep in communication during the heist.

He was still going to keep guard, but not outside the door of the penthouse. She and Irene would handle the heist completely on their own. Cole was going to be watching from a spot outside the hotel. As he'd pointed out, someone needed to keep watch over the comings and goings of LeBlanc and Evan—not to mention Butch and H.

Not once had Cole threatened to interfere again. So why—when she was getting exactly what she wanted—did it feel like a heavy weight was pressing on her chest?

The answer to that was pretty simple. She'd hurt him, and she wasn't sure what to do about it. But there was no sense in discussing it. He, more than anyone she'd ever met, understood her reasons for what she was doing. In the time they'd spent together, he'd come to know her so well. She was beginning to think that he understood her better than she understood herself.

Shifting again, she studied his profile in the waning moonlight. He was such a strong, competent man. And she was in love with him. Even as panic and joy and a mix of other feelings flooded through her, she wondered what she was going to do about that.

A problem for another day, she decided. Tonight she knew what she wanted and who she wanted.

"Cole?"

"Hmm?" When he turned to face her, his eyes were open. He hadn't been sleeping either.

"I—" She paused and drew in a deep breath. "I know you're angry with me."

"I'm not angry with you," he said.

"I want to make love with you."

His smile was slow. Seeing it and feeling the rush of warmth it always brought her only tightened the nerves twisting inside of her.

"I thought you'd never ask."

When he reached for her, she placed a hand against his chest. "Not as part of our deal. I want it to be like it was on the beach—just you and me."

He didn't say a thing. But the hands that gripped her and lifted her on top of him were hard. And she could taste desperation when he took her mouth with his.

IN THE OTHER BEDROOM of the suite, Irene moved out onto the small balcony to review her battle plan. In her mind, she looked at it the way she would if she were plotting out one of her TV shows. There wasn't a doubt in her mind that it would work. Any small detail she'd overlooked, Cole had managed to eliminate with his suggestions. The man had a good mind. He and Pepper were well suited, she thought.

Dammit. She badly wanted a beer. But to get one she'd

have to go back into the kitchen and that might wake Happy. Despite his rather odd preference for a dominatrix type of woman, she liked him. He'd helped her out in a pinch, and she'd known and worked with enough men to know that was something to value highly. He'd be a good catch for some woman.

But it wasn't her.

Irene gazed out at paradise. The moon had dropped in the sky to the point where it was nearly touching the sea, and a few of the stars had begun to fade. The resort lights were still on, illuminating paths, landscaped terraces, and the pool. But there were only a very few guests or staff members wandering about.

Paradise at night could be a very lonely place. Irene leaned against the balcony railing and thought about that. She thought about what life might be like here if she could convince Butch that they hadn't lost their chance.

So far she hadn't let herself think about what she would do if she failed with Butch. And dammit, she wasn't going to think about it now.

She was a one-man woman, and by damn, she was going to get him whether he liked it or not.

15

COLE'S POSITION IN a cluster of palm trees about twenty yards from the front of the hotel gave him the best view he was going to get of the penthouse balcony. He would have preferred to be in the hall or at the very least on a neighboring balcony, but he'd made a promise to Pepper, and he would do his best to keep it.

He still didn't like the plan—especially the part where Pepper and Irene would be inside that suite looking for the Monet. Irene wasn't dealing with one of the clueless homeowners who agreed to let her break through their security systems for her reality TV show. LeBlanc was a pro, and Cole doubted that they'd be able to merely pluck the painting off the wall. There was no way of telling how long it would take them to locate the painting. And there was no way of knowing just how long Atwell and LeBlanc would be meeting with Butch. It was the part of the plan that he had the least control over. He was going to have to depend on Butch and H. Unknown to them, they had a part in the plan, and Cole couldn't be certain of how they would act once things got rolling. The one thing he'd insisted on was that the two women wait for his signal before they started their descent from the roof.

The thing about plans was that at any point something could and probably would go wrong. And he was a good three or four minutes away from that suite.

Cole made himself take a deep breath. One of Pepper's many strengths was that she was able to think on her feet. And her instincts were good, he reminded himself.

He glanced at his watch, 8:55, then at the front of the hotel. Happy was posted in the lobby, and the moment that Atwell and LeBlanc were ushered into Butch's office, Happy would let him know. That would be his signal to call Pepper on her cell and let her know the coast was clear.

His cell phone rang. He flipped it open and Happy said, "They just went in."

"You've got the message with you?"

"Affirmative."

"Wait two minutes and then deliver it to Butch."

"Aye, aye, sir."

Cole shook his head and nearly smiled as he repocketed his cell. He liked Happy. Beneath that jovial exterior, there was an intelligence and a resourcefulness that Cole couldn't help but admire. There wasn't a doubt in his mind that the man would get the message to Butch.

The problem would be Butch's reaction. Cole had made the note both brief and explicit.

If you want to see Irene, make some excuse to leave your meeting and follow the man who delivered this note. The Monet will wait. Irene won't.
Cole

The key was not to alarm Atwell and LeBlanc. There

wasn't a doubt in his mind that Butch Castellano could keep his cool. The question was—would Cole, knowing the danger Pepper was in?

IRENE WATCHED AS Pepper glanced at her watch—again. She and Pepper had been squatting near the small abutment that ran around the roof for a quarter of an hour—plenty of time for anxiety to tie her own stomach in knots, so she could imagine what her niece must be going through.

"It's nine-oh-five," Pepper said. "Why hasn't Cole called?"

"Relax," Irene said. "You know the plan. He wants to make sure that Atwell and LeBlanc are in Butch's office."

"They should be in there by now. Their meeting was at nine."

Irene was thinking the same thing, and the thought had her own nerves twisting. They both needed a distraction. She put a hand on Pepper's arm. "You don't have to go with me."

Pepper met her eyes. "Yes, I do."

Irene shook her head. "You don't have to prove anything to that young man, you know. He's crazy about you."

Pepper blinked. "It's just…chemistry."

Irene laughed. "Sure, that's part of it. Butch and I started out that way at first. Lord, we couldn't keep our hands off of each other. But that initial explosive attraction grew into something else. That's why when my parents approached him, he agreed to the separation."

"He'd fallen in love with you," Pepper said.

"Yeah. Of course, I didn't understand that at first. It's only hindsight that's twenty-twenty. What I'm a little worried about is whether Butch still loves me. During the boat ride over here, Happy said something that makes sense. People who are in love do stupid things. And maybe that's why he's acting like such an idiot now. He still loves me, and love sometime interferes with brain functions."

"Tell me about it," Pepper said.

Irene tightened her grip on Pepper's hand. "What I'll tell you is don't let Cole talk himself into thinking that it's best for you if he backs out of your life."

Pepper stared at her. "You think he would?"

Irene tapped a finger on the side of her head. "Love and logic don't mix. But don't make the same mistake I did. My advice is to take action before you have to steal a damn Monet twice to convince a stupid, stubborn man he's wrong."

Pepper threw her arms around her aunt and gave her a hard hug. Irene felt the prick of tears behind her eyes and was about to blink them away when her cell phone vibrated in her pocket. Drawing back, she flipped it open.

"You're good to go," Cole said.

Irene shot her a wink. "Here comes the easy part."

COLE POCKETED HIS cell phone just as Happy and Butch joined him in the cluster of trees.

"Where's Irene?" Butch asked.

"You'll see in a minute," Cole said, meeting Butch's cold, hard eyes. "Where are Atwell and the Frenchman?"

Cole wouldn't have thought it possible, but Butch's eyes grew harder and colder. "They're in my office. Where's Irene? Is she all right? And what in the hell are we doing hiding in these palm trees?"

"First I need your word that you won't interfere with what Irene's trying to do. You could put her in danger."

Butch grabbed the front of Cole's T-shirt. "I'm tired of

this game. I'm going to ask you one more time. Where is she?"

Cole stood his ground. "Your word. Irene's and Pepper's lives may depend on it."

Five seconds ticked by. Neither man blinked. Then Butch said, "I won't interfere."

"There she is." Happy spoke for the first time. Butch and Cole shifted their gaze to where Happy was pointing and watched Irene swing her leg over the edge of the roof.

"What the hell...?" Butch said.

Cole put a hand on his arm when he would have moved.

"You gave your word. I'm going to hold you to it." It was all he could do to get out the words as he watched Pepper drop her legs over the edge of the roof. She could do this, he told himself.

"What the hell is going on?" Butch asked.

Happy patted his shoulder. "Irene's stealing a Monet to prove she's bad enough for you. Isn't she something?"

"Yeah," Cole said, never taking his eyes off Pepper.

"Shit," Butch said.

WITH HER ARMS braced firmly on the narrow ledge of the abutment, Pepper peered over her shoulder. She purposely didn't let herself look at the ground. She just wanted to judge the distance to the floor of the penthouse balcony. It wasn't close. And it was much narrower than the one outside Cole's suite had appeared. Her stomach pitched.

"Big mistake," Irene said as she tested the rope she'd tied to one of the steel ventilation pipes that dotted the rooftop. "Never look down—rule number one for any good cat burglar."

Pepper wrenched her gaze away from the balcony and looked at her aunt. "How can you do this?"

"I love Butch. Always have, always will."

"I didn't mean that. How can you rappel down from roofs?" She was thinking of the time that she'd gotten stuck on that roof and Cole had come to rescue her.

Irene shrugged and shot her a grin. "I took up rock climbing shortly after my parents made me break up with Butch. It was my feeble shot at being a rebellious teen."

Pepper smiled at her. "Been there, done that. But I never did anything more dangerous than cut off my hair or learn to play poker. I wish I'd had the nerve to think of rock climbing. It would have come in handy."

Irene reached over and tested Pepper's rope. "It'll be over before you know it."

In Pepper's mind, the possible implications were not quite as comforting as she was sure Irene intended them to be.

"Okay. Now, remember that the end of the rope is knotted around your waist. If you make a mistake, you'll only fall to the end of the rope."

"Kind of like a bungee cord, only there's no bounce at the end."

"Exactly," Irene said. "You can watch me go first and then I'll talk you down. Or we can do it together."

Though she was tempted by the first choice, Pepper knew that they'd save time with the second. "Together."

Turning her head, she watched her aunt clasp the rope between her two hands and slowly lower herself off the ledge they were both balanced on. Then holding her breath, she did the same. The resulting surge of adrenaline nearly made her dizzy.

"Now, keeping the rope between your legs, you're going to make sure your toes are touching the wall."

"Got it," Pepper said.

"This is the toughest part. You're going to do three things at once. Let the rope slide a bit between your hands at the same time that you lean back and plant your feet flat on the wall."

Drawing in a deep breath, Pepper gave it a whirl. But just as she leaned back, her foot slipped, and the next second, she was dangling from the wall and the rope began to slip between her hands. Out of the corner of her eye, she caught Irene's movement as she walked backward down the wall, but her heart was pounding so hard that she couldn't hear what Irene was saying. All that she knew was the rope was slipping through her hands. Just as her palms began to sting in earnest, her feet landed hard on something and her knees nearly buckled. Glancing down, she saw that she was on the railing of the balcony.

Fear swamped her, and for one long moment she teetered. Then she tightened her grip on the rope and one hard pull had her tumbling forward onto the balcony floor.

A second later, Irene landed beside her and pushed her down until they were out of sight below the railing.

"Excellent," her aunt said.

Pepper dragged in a much needed breath, and pressed a hand to her chest because she was afraid that her heart was going to pound right out. "Right. My foot slipped."

"Who cares?" Irene said. "It's not like we got a bunch of Olympic judges out there deep-sixing us with low technical scores. In second-story work, form always takes a back seat to efficiency, and you beat me down." Irene patted her on the shoulder. "You did good."

"Thanks." It was over, Pepper told herself as she pried her fingers loose from the rope. Rappelling down from a roof was going on her list of never-to-be-repeated experiences.

"Now for the fun part." Irene rubbed her hands together and turned her attention to the balcony doors.

Pepper was beginning to think that her aunt had a strange idea of fun. But she had to admire Irene's skill. In less than three minutes, they were inside, and for a moment neither of them moved. The windows were all shuttered to keep out a direct hit from the morning sun, so the interior of the suite was filled with shadows.

Pepper listened hard. The only sound was the steady tick of a clock. As her eyes adjusted to the dimmer light, she made out the tall grandfather clock in the corner.

Letting her gaze sweep the rest of the living room, she saw that it was twice the size of the one in Cole's suite. If she hadn't known better, she would have believed that she had been transported back in time to the mansion of a rich plantation owner.

The bungalow had been lovely, and Cole's suite had been luxurious, but neither could compare to this one. The floors were a honey-colored wood dotted with oriental rugs. And in spite of its size, the room seemed filled with overstuffed furniture, painted screens and huge potted plants. There was even a grand piano in the far corner.

"The damn place is huge," Irene whispered. "And I don't see the Monet."

Pepper scanned the walls. She counted six paintings, but none of them was the one they were looking for. Now that she was getting her bearings, she could see that even though it was larger, the suite had the same two levels and general layout as Cole's. The main entrance was down a short hallway to their left. She pointed to the two doors on the upper level to their right. "Let's try the bedrooms."

"C'mon." Irene led the way. "You take the one on the left."

Pepper crossed her fingers as she entered the bedroom, but a quick glance around told her that the stolen painting wasn't hanging on the wall. The bed was neatly made and the closet empty. Clearly, Evan and LeBlanc were using the other bedroom.

Turning away from the closet, she scanned the room again, then turned her attention to the bed. They weren't sleeping in this room, so perhaps...

She looked beneath the bed, then circled it, lifting the mattress until she was sure the painting wasn't there either. Fisting her hands on her hips, she looked around the room again. Time was slipping past, and the fact that Irene hadn't appeared in the doorway told her that her aunt's search was similarly unsuccessful. She felt a knot of anxiety tighten in her stomach and forced herself to ignore it.

What she needed to use were her instincts. Hadn't Cole told her they were one of her strengths? Moving back to the door of the bedroom, she looked into the main room. Another thing she was good at was imagining herself as someone else.

If she were a master thief and had a priceless painting, where would she hide it?

In her mind, Pepper pictured LeBlanc walking through the front door of the suite with the painting in his suitcase. What would he be feeling? Excitement and perhaps the remnants of an adrenaline rush because he'd just successfully stolen the painting from Irene. But apprehension, too, and caution—because he'd let the Monet slip through his fingers once.

He couldn't afford to make that mistake again.

Then too, there was the fact that he was about to strike a deal with a man who was an ex-mobster. Would someone like LeBlanc believe that Butch Castellano had reformed? Could he afford to believe that?

No, Pepper thought as she stepped out into the main room of the suite. LeBlanc wouldn't hang that painting on the wall or hide it under a mattress. There had to be a safe somewhere in the suite.

"Irene?" she called softly. "I have an idea."

Without waiting for her aunt to join her, Pepper started down the stairs to the living room proper. It was then that she heard the sound.

She stopped short. It hadn't come from the other bedroom. While she was still trying to identify it, she heard another sound—the door to the suite opening. Her heart leapt into her throat and she dropped to her knees behind the nearest sofa.

Less than a second later, Irene joined her. Not daring to speak, not needing to, they each crawled toward their respective ends of the sofa and peered out. The darkly clad figure at the door wasn't moving. He was listening, just as she and Irene had when they'd come in through the balcony doors. Even as that thought entered her mind, Pepper registered something else. The figure was too tall for Evan and too broad-shouldered for LeBlanc.

Besides, Cole would surely have called her if their meeting with Butch had broken up.

As if satisfied that the suite was empty, the figure moved purposefully forward, descending the steps into the living room proper and striding toward the fireplace. A moment later, he had removed a painting and was working on opening a wall safe.

Another thief, she thought as anger and fear tangled inside of her. No way! She'd just rappelled down from the roof of a building, and no one was going to get that painting but Irene. A glance over her shoulder told her that her aunt was on the same wavelength. Irene had disappeared.

As Pepper crawled out from behind the sofa, she spotted her aunt moving on her hands and knees from one piece of furniture to the next in a zigzag pattern toward the fireplace. The woman moved like a cat. Pepper prayed that she could do the same.

On instinct she moved toward the door, her only thought being to block the thief's exit. *How* was the problem. When she reached one of the potted palms that flanked the three-step flight of stairs, she paused. If she moved up them, she would be in plain sight.

When she glanced toward the fireplace, she saw the thief removing the rolled-up painting from the safe. Things were happening way too fast. In another minute he'd be on his way toward the door. She glanced around for a weapon, something. Anything.

"Put your hands in the air."

The low deep voice had Pepper jumping. She didn't recognize that it belonged to Irene until she turned back and saw that her aunt had a bamboo cane poked into the thief's back.

"Now, just put the painting back in the safe and walk very slowly toward the door."

For a moment, no one moved. It reminded Pepper of a scene in a movie that was freeze-framed. Then everything happened in a blur as the same scene went into fast-forward.

In one graceful movement, the thief whirled, shoved Irene to the floor and bolted toward the stairs. With adrenaline streaming through her, Pepper rose and pushed with all her might on the large palm tree. For an instant it didn't move, and then it pitched forward, catching the thief at the knee.

The Monet went flying high into the air. The thief went flying, too, pitching forward over the tree and then skidding across the tiles of the entranceway until his head thwacked hard into a heavy and ornately carved credenza. He uttered one moan, then didn't move.

Pepper turned back in time to see Irene run forward to catch the Monet as it arced through the air. The scene reminded her of one of those miraculous Hail Mary passes during a tightly contested football game.

"Got it," Irene said.

16

"WE HAVE TO DO something," Butch said, taking a step forward.

Cole grabbed one of his arms and Happy grabbed the other. "You gave your word not to interfere."

"That was before...you don't understand. One of my men should be in that suite right now taking the Monet out of the safe."

Cole stared at him. "You're stealing the Monet? I thought you'd gone straight."

To Cole's amazement, Butch flushed. "I have. But... hell, this whole thing with Irene has me...unnerved."

"She's really something, isn't she?" Happy said.

Butch shot him one look and then turned back to Cole. "When I got the information on LeBlanc, I decided that stealing it was my best move until I know more about just how he got his hands on the painting."

Cole's eyes narrowed. "You know about LeBlanc?"

"Yeah. H finally traced him a few hours ago. It wasn't easy. The guy's one slick operator. How'd you get onto him?"

"A colleague of mine—one of Irene's nephews—traced him through some fingerprints I faxed him."

Butch studied him with some interest. "You swiped the glass at the poolside café?"

Cole shook his head. "Pepper did. She has good instincts."

"She's a lot like her aunt," Happy said.

Butch pinned him with a look. "You are beginning to annoy me. The only reason that I haven't punched you before this is because you got Irene here safely. But you'd be well advised to button it."

For the first time, Cole saw Happy's ever-present smile waver a bit. "Sure thing. Not a problem."

"So?" Butch shifted his gaze back to Cole. "We're just supposed to wait here and let the best thief win?"

Cole's lips twitched. "Something like that."

"My money's on Irene and Pepper," Happy said.

Butch sent him a glare.

Happy murmured, "Sorry."

Butch glanced up at the now empty balcony. "I don't like it."

"You're in good company," Cole said. "And you're going to like it even less if the ladies don't come out on top."

Butch met his eyes. "Why won't I? We'll have the painting. They'll be safe."

"If Irene isn't successful, my guess is that she'll want to steal it again. She has this idea that she needs to prove she's bad enough for you."

"Yeah." Happy's smile was at full wattage again. "She's a real pip."

A cell phone rang and both Butch and Cole reached into their pockets. Butch flipped his open. "Yeah."

A second later he swore under his breath. Then he

turned to Cole. "Time for Plan B. Atwell and LeBlanc just walked out of the meeting."

"NICE WORK," Irene said, gazing down at the prone body of the thief.

Pepper's heart clutched. "You think I killed him?"

As if on cue, the man moaned again. Pressing a hand to her chest, Pepper felt her heart begin to beat again. "Thank heavens."

"I wonder who sent him," Irene said.

"Could we wonder about that later?" Pepper asked. "I have a feeling that we ought to get out of here." Now that they had the painting, she was getting that same queasy feeling she always got when something was about to go wrong.

Irene, still clutching the rolled-up Monet under one arm, was frowning now and she'd begun to tap one foot. "This guy had a key that got him in, he knew where the painting was, and he did not crack that safe. He had the combination."

"Yeah," Pepper said, taking her aunt's arm and pulling her toward the door. "But we have the painting, and he doesn't."

Irene dug in her heels. "What if Butch sent him here to steal it?"

"Butch?" Turning, Pepper stared at her. Even as she opened her mouth to object, she could see the logic of Irene's suspicion. But there was also another explanation. "It could have been Evan or LeBlanc who sent him."

"But why would they want to steal it?" Irene asked.

"I don't know, but we have to get out of here, Irene. This painting seems very popular. As far as I'm concerned this guy on the floor is the last Monet thief I want to run into today."

"Good point," Irene said.

This time when Pepper took her arm, she didn't resist. Pepper opened the door and checked the hallway. Clear. Still keeping her hand firmly on Irene's arm, she moved quickly toward the elevators.

"If Butch did try to steal this painting," Irene said, "he'll use the same arguments he used forty years ago—that he's clearly not good enough for me."

"Don't listen to him," Pepper said, hoping against hope that for once in her life, the feeling she had was dead wrong. But with each step she took toward the elevator, the queasiness in her stomach grew stronger. "Besides, he didn't steal it. You did. So his record is still clean."

"Right."

Pepper's cell phone vibrated in her pocket and her heart sank. It couldn't be good news. Cole was only supposed to call if there was a problem. She released her grip on Irene and dug out her phone. "Yeah?"

"Atwell and LeBlanc are on their way up. Get out on the balcony and hide until we can get there."

Not going to happen, Pepper thought as the elevator doors slid open and Evan and Le Blanc stepped out. For a moment they all froze, but Pepper's mind was racing. The hallway behind her was a dead end. Their only chance was to get to the suite and bolt the door.

She managed one step back before LeBlanc pulled out a gun. "Go back to the suite, ladies. And if you're thinking of trying something, make no mistake, I'll kill you."

COLE FELT A WAVE of cold fear wash over him as he heard LeBlanc's words.

"LeBlanc's got them and I think he has a gun." Even as

he relayed the information to his two companions, Cole was making his way out of the cluster of palms. Then he broke into a run. "He's taking them back to the suite." He kept the cell phone pressed to his ear, but Pepper didn't speak again.

By the time he reached the lobby, he'd pushed the swirl of emotions down and managed to get to that cold place that he'd always been able to find when he had his rifle in hand, waiting. H was holding an elevator for them.

"H has a gun," Butch said as they moved into the waiting car.

"So do I," Cole said. But he didn't have what he wanted—a rifle with a telescopic sight. "We can't rush in. It's too dangerous. But I think we have a little time. From what my colleague Luke was able to gather, this guy's a planner. He's got two hostages, three if he decides to use Atwell, so he'll take a little time to figure out how to play that to his advantage. I wouldn't be surprised if he has an escape plan in place. My guess is that he planned to leave the island with the money and the painting."

"Bold son of a bitch," Butch muttered.

"We'll split into two teams," Cole continued. "Butch and I will come down from the roof the way the women did. H, you and Happy will wait outside the door of the suite until I give a signal. Got that?"

The men nodded, and no one spoke for the rest of the ride. When the elevator door slid open on the top floor, Butch led the way to the roof. The sun beat down, and in the distance, the sea was the color of a turquoise gemstone. They walked together to the ropes that Irene had tied to the pipe.

"Go for a soft landing," Cole said.

"Got it. You got any plan once we land on the balcony?" Butch picked up one of the ropes and they moved toward the edge of the roof.

"It all depends on what's going on inside. Those women are both smart, and Pepper can think on her feet." It helped to remind himself of that.

"I watched some tapes of Irene's show. She's pretty inventive."

Cole met Butch's eyes as they each threw one leg over the abutment. "One way or another, we're going to get them out safely."

Butch nodded. "Yeah. Let's do it."

Together, they lowered themselves hand under hand until they were on the balcony.

The shutters were still closed, but as yet, no one had thought to close the door that Irene and Pepper had left ajar. Cole felt a little trickle of relief as he moved closer and peered through a crack in the slats of the shutter. The interior of the room was dim, and he could hear voices before he could make out exactly where the four people were.

"…understand what's going on," Evan Atwell was saying.

"I have to say that some of this puzzles me too," LeBlanc said. "Would one of you ladies like to explain the body in the entranceway?"

"Another thief," Pepper said. "The Monet is very popular, Leblanc."

"Why do you keep calling him LeBlanc?" Evan asked. "His name is Jean Claude Rambeau."

"His real name is Maurice LeBlanc," Pepper corrected.

"No," Evan said. "You're mistaken. Tell her, Jean Claude."

"I'm afraid I can't do that, Evan. She's right, you see."

A little sliver of fear worked its way up Cole's spine as he registered the coolness in LeBlanc's tone. It told him that the Frenchman was in control and thinking, weighing his options.

"What are you saying?" Evan asked.

"Your ex-girlfriend has ruined everything," LeBlanc said without emotion. "Now I think we should move farther into the suite until we can sort this all out."

Cole felt the cold knot in his stomach tighten. LeBlanc might have been inviting friends in for a drink. He studied the scene as the group moved down the stairs into the living room. The two women seated themselves on one of the sofas facing the balcony. Evan took a chair to the left of them and LeBlanc settled on the arm of the sofa to their right. For the moment, neither of the men was thinking about the balcony doors.

But Pepper was. He'd seen the way she'd walked deliberately to that sofa. That meant she was keeping her cool and thinking. She would expect him to come in through the balcony.

The bad news was the Frenchman had a gun pointed directly at Pepper. Even with a rifle, Cole would have had to push the shutters aside first to get off a shot. The noise would have given LeBlanc too much warning.

Cole pulled his revolver out, and did what he was trained to do. He waited.

"I STILL DON'T UNDERSTAND." Evan ran a hand through his hair. "She hasn't ruined everything. We still have the painting. Castellano wants it. He's moved closer to what we're asking."

"He's dragging his heels. But thanks to the ladies, I think we've got something that will motivate him."

Pepper swallowed hard and struggled against the fear that was threatening to numb her. Luke's description of LeBlanc was swirling around in her mind. Not only a master thief but a sociopath too. As her mind raced, one chilling thought kept rising to the surface. Whatever scenario LeBlanc was hatching to get off the island, he didn't need three hostages. They would only slow him down.

There was no time to try to figure out how a super sleuth like Veronica Mars would handle this. She had no one to rely on but herself and her aunt. She remembered what Cole had told her about trusting her instincts. Instinct told her she had to keep the two men talking. If she could succeed in rattling one of them into doing something stupid, they might have a chance. She edged her foot slowly sideways until it rested against Irene's. It was some comfort when her aunt nudged her back.

"What are you talking about? Castellano wants that painting," Evan said. "If you hadn't walked out of the meeting, he would have met our price. And you said this morning that the plane is gassed up and waiting."

"It's a little more complicated than that," Pepper said.

"Damn right," Irene said. "Once Butch finds out that LeBlanc stole the Monet, he won't buy it."

"And then there's the fact that LeBlanc has lied about more than his name," Pepper added. "He's a professional con man and a master thief."

"And he's a killer," Irene put in.

Evan stared at them. "You're lying."

Pepper shook her head. "Look at him. He isn't denying it, is he?"

Evan glanced at LeBlanc, but still the man said nothing. Pepper was sure that he was listening with one part of his mind, but in another part, he was planning his escape.

Keep the conversation going, Pepper told herself. Hopefully it would distract him. Turning to Evan, she said, "I understand why LeBlanc wanted to steal the Monet. But I haven't figured out why you're helping him. Why in the world did you steal your mother's painting?"

"Jean Claude and I are in love," Evan explained. "And we need the money. My mother expects certain things of me. And I can't give them to her. I've never been able to tell her that I'm gay. She's expecting me to marry properly and produce children to carry on the name. If she knew the truth, it would destroy her. You understand. I know you do."

Pepper did understand. But while she'd listened to his tale of star-crossed lovers, she'd also been trying to think of something she could do. So far she was drawing a blank, and it was LeBlanc that she needed to get talking.

"The painting will be mine someday anyway," Evan said. "So it's not really stealing."

"That's what we all say," Irene muttered under her breath.

Something—a flicker of light—from the glass doors that led to the balcony caught Pepper's eye. Cole, she thought. The knowledge that he was close by boosted her confidence.

She remembered something then. Something that Evan had said earlier about Butch coming closer to the price they were asking. Turning, she met LeBlanc's eyes dead on. The coldness she saw nearly made her shiver. "Why did you leave the meeting before you finalized the deal with Mr. Castellano?"

He seemed to consider the question for a minute. Then he answered. "When he was called out of the meeting, I had a feeling that something was going wrong. Now, it's my turn for a question." He shifted his gaze to Irene. "You've given me a great deal of trouble. Why do you want the Monet?"

"It's a long story," Pepper said.

"About another pair of star-crossed lovers," Irene added.

Pepper nudged her aunt's foot. It was LeBlanc they wanted to keep talking. "Speaking of star-crossed lovers, isn't it about time that you told Evan that you don't intend to run away with him and the Monet and live happily ever after?"

Pepper hadn't thought that it was possible for LeBlanc's eyes to turn colder. But they did.

"Jean Claude?" Evan asked.

"She's right, I'm afraid, Evan. I'm not going to be able to take you with me. That doesn't mean that I haven't enjoyed our relationship. But it's time for both of us to move on. I'm going to take one of the ladies with me instead."

"You'll never get off this island. Butch Castellano won't let you," Irene said.

"Oh, I think he will. Once I make my point."

Pepper realized with a sinking heart that LeBlanc had finalized his plan. Time was running out. Even though she knew she wasn't going to like the answer, she asked, "Point?"

"You're going to get hold of Mr. Castellano on the hotel phone, and he's going to listen while I shoot one of you ladies. Then he'll know that I mean what I say—that the hostage will only stay alive if I get off the island safely with the Monet and the money. Now let me see, which one will it be?"

Pepper watched in horror as he handed her his cell phone and then aimed his gun at Irene. "You, I think. Since you've given me the most trouble, I don't want to risk taking you with me. Pass the painting to Evan. I don't want it to be damaged."

Irene clutched the painting even closer to her.

"Shooting her would be a big mistake," Pepper said. "Butch Castellano loves her. She stole the painting to give to him for Valentine's Day. If you kill her, he'll hunt you down."

"Really."

Pepper held her breath. He hadn't seen that one coming, but he was far from rattled.

"It'll be bad enough for you if you steal his money," she added.

"Then I'll just shoot you," LeBlanc said in a pleasant voice, shifting the muzzle of the gun so that it was inches from her head. "Make the call."

"She's my niece," Irene said. "Butch won't like it if you kill her. Plus, she's got a boyfriend who's ex-CIA and very resourceful. You shoot her, and you won't get off the island."

Out of the corner of her eye, Pepper saw LeBlanc's hand tighten on the gun. Two thoughts raced through her mind. The good news—he was finally getting a little rattled. The bad news—it might cause him to pull that trigger just a tad early.

For a few seconds there was absolute silence in the room except for the steady tick of the grandfather clock.

Then LeBlanc shifted the barrel of the gun until it was pointed at Evan. "I guess it will have to be you. Make the call."

Irene moved like lightning then, springing from the couch and landing on Evan's lap. She'd managed to unfurl the painting and she was holding it in front of her like a shield. "Shoot us and you'll have blood all over the Monet."

It was the moment that Pepper had been waiting for. Once again, she went with instinct. Planting her hands firmly on the sofa, she kicked up with both feet at Le-Blanc's hand. When she connected with his wrist, everything happened in a series of freeze-framed flashes.

Her ears rang from the explosion, and she saw the flash of light as the gun sailed into the air. She also saw Cole and Butch burst through the shutters.

"Freeze or you're a dead man, LeBlanc," Cole said.

"Give him a reason to kill you," Butch said as he walked toward him. "Nothing would make me happier than seeing you dead. Threaten my woman, will you?"

"Don't kill him," Irene cried out just as Butch's fist connected with LeBlanc's face.

17

"MORE CHAMPAGNE?" Gari asked.

Pepper held out her glass. Butch had whisked all of them off to his private residence as soon as LeBlanc had been handcuffed and taken into custody. To make sure that the thief would stay put while authorities battled over jurisdiction, Butch had assigned two of his men, Angelo and Armando, to assist the local police.

The hotel staff, headed by Gari, had served up heaping plates of eggs, sausages and croissants while everyone had told their stories.

It wasn't until an overflowing plate had been in her hands that Pepper had realized she was starved. And from the looks of the empty plates that the staff was gathering up, she hadn't been the only one. Her regard for Butch Castellano went up just a bit. He reminded her of her father, who felt that the solution to every crisis in life was food. Even though her brothers had explained to her that it was an Italian thing, she'd never understood it before. But as she glanced around the room, she could see that it was working. Irene's color had improved and even Evan was looking less devastated than he had when they'd left the penthouse suite.

Evan had been the last to tell his story, and he'd given a shortened version. Of all of them, he had the most to recover from. Irene was currently holding his hand and no doubt offering some motherly advice.

Pepper glanced to where Happy and H were engaged in a heated debate over the proper lures to use for sail fishing. Happy was—well, happy. She'd never met a more unflappable man in her life. And as far as H went—she wasn't sure that anyone ever knew what he was feeling.

Taking a sip of her champagne, she glanced around the large airy room they'd all gathered in. Butch had given them a brief tour of his residence when they'd arrived, explaining that he'd renovated the original plantation mansion. There was a wide veranda that looked out over formal gardens. Inside, the decorator had followed the same theme that had been so prevalent in the bungalow and the hotel, but three walls had been knocked out and replaced with glass, so that the eye was always drawn to the turquoise sea. Butch had built his paradise, all right. As she looked at the water and felt the pull, she realized that she didn't want to leave.

Her gaze moved last to Cole. He'd stepped onto the veranda to place a call to Luke and Matt. He'd be giving them an edited version of the events of the past twenty-four hours. He hadn't given her all the details, but they'd all agreed that Evan's and Irene's roles would be deleted from the official version of the theft and recovery of the Monet. After all, if LeBlanc gave a different version, who would believe a sociopathic thief?

Butch cleared his throat and raised his glass in a toast. "All's well that ends well."

Irene dropped Evan's hand and set her flute down on a

nearby table with an audible click. "I'm not drinking to that until I know exactly what the ending is going to be between you and me, Butch."

Butch stared at her. "Well, I thought—"

"Hmph," Irene snorted. "You *thought* the last time, too, as I recall. You *thought* exactly what my parents thought. No one consulted me. Then there's all that *thinking* you did while you were in jail. I think it's high time I told you what I *think*. 'Cause I think you're a very stupid man."

For a moment no one said a word. The exchange had even caught Cole's attention. There was shock on Butch's face. Pepper figured that he wasn't much used to people talking to him in that tone. Or calling him stupid.

"Renie..." Butch began as he rose from his chair.

Irene pointed a finger at him. "Don't Renie me. I'm not that naïve teenager anymore."

Butch pulled out a cigar, and then glanced down at it as if he wondered how it had gotten into his hand.

He was speechless, Pepper realized and shifted her gaze to her aunt. *You go, girl,* she thought.

Butch glanced around the room and discovered that everyone was staring at him, except for the staff. But they were listening. His face flushed a deep red.

"My office," he barked at Irene. Then he whirled and strode out of the room.

Irene sent Pepper one quick wink as she followed.

Pepper's stomach lurched. Not a good sign, she thought as she tried to will away the queasy sensation. She should be thinking positive thoughts. In a moment, her aunt would know her fate. She stole a quick glance at Cole, but he'd turned and was intent on his phone conversation again. She admired her aunt's courage in forcing the issue. She was about to rise from the sofa and do the same thing with Cole when she remembered the Rossi curse and the fact that she was sitting in the living room of Adam's plantation—not the optimal setting for star-crossed lovers. It didn't bode well for her or her aunt.

She was still debating what to do when H sat down next to her.

"You look worried," he said.

"Yeah." Pepper glanced back at the closed study door. "My aunt has a lot riding on this."

"If I were a betting man, I'd put my money on her."

"Me, too—if it weren't for the fact that Aunt Irene and I come from a long line of star-crossed lovers." She waved a hand. "This plantation house isn't exactly the best setting for happy endings. There's got to be a lot of bad vibes here because of the way things ended up for Adam and Elena." She glanced toward Cole again.

"You know about their story then?" H asked.

"Not all of it. I couldn't read the ending. I figured it would be too depressing. A slave and a plantation owner— I mean you can't get much more star-crossed than that."

"They were married in the gardens at the back of this house. There's a gazebo on the spot."

Pepper turned to stare at him. "They got married?"

H nodded. "His parents tried to stop it. They even tried to send Elena away, but Adam prevented them and told them if they sent her away, he'd go with her. According to the stories, they had several children, and the plantation flourished for several generations. In fact, Butch bought this island from a woman who swears she's a great-great-great-granddaughter of Adam and Elena."

The story ended happily. They got married, Pepper thought, and the queasiness in her stomach eased.

BUTCH MOVED BEHIND his desk and waved at one of the chairs. "Sit down."

"Thanks, but I'll stand."

Butch grunted and did the same. For a moment the silence stretched between them. Butch found for the first time in his life, he wasn't sure what to say, where to begin. Worse, he wasn't even sure who this woman was. H had been right. She wasn't his sweet little Renie. She was the woman on the tapes he'd seen rappelling down from rooftops in front of a viewing audience that comprised more than half of San Francisco.

He lifted the hand that still held the cigar, intending to light it and gain a few minutes to think. His hand was shaking. That fact stunned him. No one had ever made his hand shake.

Irene planted her hands on her hips and though he couldn't see it, he was pretty sure her foot was tapping.

"Well?" she asked.

He stared at her. In the past twenty-four hours, she'd not only made his hand shake, she'd made his heart stutter. He didn't want to think yet about those endless minutes when he'd stood on that balcony—waiting.

Her eyes narrowed and flashed as she moved toward the desk. She wasn't the old Renie, but she was magnificent.

"I stole that damn Monet twice for you."

He narrowed his eyes. "You didn't get away with it the second time."

She planted her hands flat on his desk and leaned toward him. "It was in my hands when you and Cole busted in. Possession is nine-tenths of the law. Therefore, I stole it twice. Plus, Pepper and I took out the amateur you sent up. You did send that guy, didn't you?"

Butch shrugged. "H had just figured out who LeBlanc really was. I thought the painting would be safer in my hands until we sorted everything out. So I sent in my man Tony."

Irene gave him a curt nod. "You gave me a few bad moments. When I first figured out that you must have sent him, I wondered if your taste for French Impressionists had overcome your resolve to stay straight."

"No. I'm still resolved to do that." He planted his hands flat on the desk and leaned forward until they were nearly nose to nose. "And if we're going to talk about handing out bad moments, you're winning. Thanks to Cole, I witnessed your descent from the roof to Atwell's balcony. And I never want to relive those moments I spent waiting on the balcony outside that room."

IRENE DIDN'T BLINK, but her heart was not steady. It never had been when she was in Butch Castellano's presence. This was a man she hadn't seen for almost forty years. She knew she loved him, but she hadn't been sure that the chemistry would still be there. The fact that it was—at least for her—had her heart beating faster and her body heating.

She pushed the realization away so that it wouldn't distract her. He was going to try to send her away again. She felt it in her bones. Otherwise, why the big invite back to his house for the group party? He hadn't touched her, hadn't made a move to talk to her until she'd called him stupid in front of his guests and his staff.

Even now he wasn't making any move to get close to

her. He'd even put his desk between them. Nor had he tried to bring up the topic that they'd come in here to discuss.

Men. Irene mentally shook her head. They always had so much damn *trouble* talking about their feelings. Why couldn't a man be more like a woman?

Well, she knew quite a bit about unlocking doors and safes. She would just unlock him too.

"Renie..." he began.

She slammed a hand down on the desk. "That's just the way you started out forty years ago. Whatever else happens here, history is not going to repeat itself, Butch Castellano. I am not going to listen to you tell me again that you are going to send me away for my own good." When he opened his mouth, she held up a hand to stop him. "Let me finish. I'm sixty years old. I know what's good for me. And I've decided that it's you. I still love you. I've never stopped. Oh, I've dated. I've even taken some lovers. But none of them ever compared to you. And I never loved them. The one thing I have to know before I go any further is how you feel about me. Do you still love me?"

There, she thought. Let him wiggle out of that one. And then she held her breath.

He said nothing, and as the silence stretched, Irene felt her heart sink.

Finally, he cleared his throat. "I was going to tell you tonight. In the moonlight. After all, it's Valentine's Day. I thought you might like some romance."

"To hell with romance," Irene said. "I've waited too long for you." But as Butch circled the desk, she held up a hand. "One more thing. Do I still turn you on? I mean, my heart has been doing little tap dances and my nerve endings have been zinging ever since you crashed into Evan's suite."

Butch took her hand, raised it to his lips and pressed a kiss into the palm.

Irene felt pleasure streak right down to her toes. It took her a moment to get her breath and then she managed, "Well?"

"I'm not sure," Butch said as he drew her into his arms. "Let's try this."

Irene looked into his eyes, and she saw what she'd dreamed about seeing.

Then Butch lowered his mouth to hers.

Irene had one moment of coherent thought before her mind went blank and filled with Butch. Here were all the sensations that she'd dreamed of—the heat, the incredible melting sensation—and more. Could it be that passion bottled up for forty years could improve with age?

Butch drew away and as if he'd read her thoughts said, "It's like a fine wine."

She smiled at him. "Or a French Impressionist painting?"

"Yeah," he said with a grin. "I'd say the zing is definitely still there."

PEPPER SAT DOWN next to Evan. "Did my aunt give you some good advice?"

Evan glanced at her, then back at his untouched champagne before he placed the glass on the table. "She thinks I should tell my mother."

Pepper covered his hand with hers. "I think you should, too."

Evan shook his head. "She'll be so hurt. She has these expectations."

Pepper nodded. "I know. I've spent my whole life trying to be what others have expected of me. We're a lot alike,

Evan. I think that's why our relationship lasted as long as it did."

"You're not gay. How can you know what it's like?" Evan asked.

"You're right. I don't know what it's like to be gay in a world that's still afraid of and uncomfortable with the idea of same-sex couples. I have no idea what that's like. But I do know about trying to change what you are to win your family's approval. I tried with the Pendletons in Philadelphia. No matter how hard I tried, I never quite measured up to what they wanted. And I've been trying to do the same thing with the Rossis. But I made a mistake."

"What?" Evan asked.

"I always imagined myself to be someone else." Her lips curved. "With my grandmother, I always tried to be my mother. With my father, I tried to be the perfect daughter. I thought dating you would please him, so I did. With my brothers, I've tried to be a super sleuth like the ones on TV and in movies." She glanced over to where Cole was still standing on the porch. "But a good friend told me that I'd have more luck fitting in if I was myself, and I think he's right. I didn't give my grandmother the opportunity to really know me for myself. I'm not sure it would have done any good. She still might not have liked me. But I would have liked myself better, I think."

Evan said nothing, but she could see that he was thinking about what she'd said.

"When I get back to San Francisco, I'm going to give the Rossis a chance to see me for what I am. And I'm going to see what kind of a contribution I can make to Rossi Investigations. They may not like me any more than my grandmother did, but I'm going to give them a chance to get to know the real me."

Evan turned his hand and gripped her fingers hard. "What if they can't accept you for what you are?"

"What if they can? I don't want to miss out on that. And you don't want to either."

Evan drew in a deep breath. "You make it sound so easy."

She shook her head. "Believe me, it's not. But there's one thing that we both have if things get rocky."

"What?"

She smiled at him. "We've got a good friend to talk to about it."

"NOW WHY DO I GET the feeling that I'm not getting the whole story?" Luke asked.

Cole bit back a grin and sat down on one of the lounge chairs that dotted Butch's veranda. Stretching out his legs and crossing his ankles, he let the silence stretch for a minute. He could picture his old friend sitting behind his desk, his blond hair tousled from running his hand through it, his fingers working magic on his computer. Cole wasn't a bit surprised that Luke Rossi wasn't completely buying the story they'd manufactured.

"This is the Caribbean," Cole finally said. "The criminal justice system works a little differently down here."

"Bullshit." Luke's tone was amiable, and this time Cole did grin as his friend continued. "The thing I'm still trying to figure out is how my sister beat you down there, and why you didn't mention her before."

"She swore me to secrecy," Cole said easily. Leave it to Luke to zero in on the weakest part of the story. "But she was the one who had a line on LeBlanc. She didn't know his name, of course, but she found out the name he was using when he crashed Evan's party." Of course, LeBlanc hadn't crashed the party. He'd been on the roof waiting to steal the painting. But Luke wouldn't have any way of knowing that. "She was the one who swiped the glass and lifted his fingerprints. I don't think that you have a Pepper Problem anymore. She's going to be a real asset to the firm."

"Really? And you say she rappelled down from the roof, broke into LeBlanc's suite and stole the painting right out from under his nose—while you sat around twiddling your thumbs?"

"There are witnesses," Cole said. "You can talk to Butch Castellano. He owns the place and he saw everything."

"Okay, I give up. But one day I'll figure out the true story."

Cole laughed then. He had no doubt Luke would do just that. There was no one who was better at tracking down the truth than Luke Rossi.

"So when are you going to be back here with the painting?"

Cole let his glance stray to the living room of the mansion where Pepper was holding Evan's hand. He hadn't had a chance to talk to her since they'd sorted things out in Atwell's suite. Their time on the island had just about run out. He could hear each minute slipping away in his mind.

"Cole?"

Luke's voice drew him back to the conversation.

"I'll be leaving here within the hour. I've already called the airport and told them to gas up the plane I chartered. Tell Mrs. Atwell her painting will be back in plenty of time for the auction."

"I'll do that."

"And tell her that she has Pepper Rossi to thank for it."

"I'll do that, too."

As he hung up his phone, Happy joined him on the veranda.

"Looks like we're the odd men out," Happy said.

"Yes, it does." On the outside looking in, Cole thought and he remembered Pepper's reference to Jane Eyre and Heathcliff.

"I don't think I ever had a chance with Irene," Happy said. "But I'd say you have an excellent chance with Pepper."

Did he? Cole said nothing. The time for their island "deal" had almost run out. And part of the agreement had been that when they got back to San Francisco they'd go back to the way things had been between them. The one thing he knew for certain was that he couldn't allow that to happen. Ever since LeBlanc had been carted off, he'd been trying to come up with the right strategy. Everything depended on the right plan. And so far his mind was a blank.

"A man like you, I bet you've got a plan."

He'd always had one before. "I thought I might give her some time. I've rushed her and pushed her into something that she might be having second thoughts about."

"You're in love with her, aren't you?"

"Yes." Later, he would think how odd it was that it was there on the veranda, talking to Happy and watching Pepper take Evan's hand in hers that he finally was able to say it out loud. Yes, he was in love with Pepper Rossi. He'd probably fallen in love with her the first time he'd seen that picture that Luke carried around in his wallet. What in hell was he going to do about it?

Happy patted his hand. "Life's short. It gets even shorter when you get to be my age. Don't wait too long to tell her."

"She's going to need some time with her aunt. And I have to get the Monet back to San Francisco." Maybe he could think of a plan on the long flight across the continent. And then he'd approach her in San Francisco. With his head still spinning, Cole turned to the man beside him. "What are you going to do?"

Happy grinned at him. "Butch is gassing up his private launch, and I understand that one of his men is going to give me a personal escort. He's not taking any chances where Irene is concerned. Can't say I blame him. I have five days left of my vacation package on Eden. I still might find someone, not that she'd hold a candle to Irene."

As Happy spoke, Irene came into the room, her hand in Butch's. Cole didn't hear what she said, but it caused Pepper to leap up from the couch and throw her arms around her aunt in a fierce hug.

They'd have a lot to talk about, he mused. And he had a job to do. Turning, he walked off the veranda and headed toward the car he'd driven from the hotel.

18

"TO HAPPY ENDINGS," Irene said as she raised her champagne flute in a toast.

As Pepper raised hers, she realized that Cole wasn't in the room. The last time she'd seen him he'd been on the veranda talking to Luke on the phone.

"If you're looking for Cole, he told me that he was going to take the Monet back to San Francisco," Happy said.

A mix of panic and anger streamed through her. "Thanks," she murmured to Happy as she moved toward H.

"I need to get to the airport," she said. "Cole's on his way there. He's on his way back to San Francisco."

"If you want, I can make sure he doesn't take off," H said.

She glanced at him. "You'd take him on? He's ex-CIA."

For the first time since she'd met him, H smiled at her. "I wasn't thinking of anything quite that dramatic. I'll just call the control tower and make sure his charter isn't cleared for takeoff."

"Thanks." When they stepped out the door, Pepper stopped short and stared as Cole's sporty red convertible pulled into a parking space at the end of the long driveway.

"Looks like he's changed his mind," H murmured, then moved back into the house.

Pepper watched as Cole climbed out of the car and started toward her. Relief and anxiety slammed into her as she tried to gather her thoughts. Their time on the island was up, and they were going to have to talk about what came next.

Panic bubbled up. On the surface, he seemed all wrong for her. That much hadn't changed. He was patient; she wasn't. He was a planner; she almost always relied on instinct. She wished, oh how hard she wished, that she was a better planner right now. But she was going to handle this. Because she knew. She started walking toward him.

She recalled the conversation she'd had with Irene on the night that her aunt had stolen the Monet for the first time. "I knew the first time I looked at Butch that he was the only man for me."

Out of the corner of her eye, she saw the gazebo in the garden that H had mentioned. Elena had probably known that about Adam, too.

Cole Buchanan was the only man for her. She'd known it the first time she'd seen him, and it had scared her to death. Wasn't that part of the reason that she'd tried so hard to compete with him? Why she'd tried to avoid him? And why she'd agreed so readily to the twenty-four-hour deal he'd offered her?

She was only about ten feet away from him when she realized that not only didn't she have a plan, she couldn't even think of anyone to pretend to be. And she had no idea what was going to come out of her mouth.

THE MOMENT COLE reached her, every coherent thought emptied from his mind. He caught her scent—something he would always associate with the island and with the time they'd spent together. He'd thought he'd had a plan. He'd get away while she was involved with her aunt. Then back in San Francisco, he'd approach her again and propose a new deal. But he hadn't been able to leave her. He never wanted to leave her. He curled his hands into fists to keep them from reaching out to her.

"I thought you'd left," she said.

"I changed my mind. I promised you it would be your case. That was our deal. You should be the one to take the Monet back."

"You came back because of our deal?"

"Yes, I—"

She cut him off, saying, "Seems to me you already broke our deal when you burst into that room with Butch. Irene and I were handling it."

His eyes narrowed and he felt a surprising surge of anger. "I won't apologize for doing that. Do you have any idea what it was like for me to wait on that balcony while that psychopath was pointing a gun at your head?" All the emotions that he'd had to shove down during those endless minutes erupted. "All I had was a revolver, and those damn shutters were in the way. It seemed like hours went by, and all I could think of was it was my fault. You wouldn't have been in that position if I hadn't proposed that damn twenty-four-hour deal. I'll regret that for as long as I live."

"You regret it?" She poked a finger into his chest. "You regret our deal?"

"Yes!" He grabbed her by the shoulders. "Dammit, I love you! I never should have agreed to any part of it. And it's not going to end. Not in twenty-four hours. Not in—!"

The sudden realization that he was shaking her made him stop, and he abruptly set her away from him.

For a moment neither of them said a word. He was shocked at his behavior, shocked at what had come out of his mouth. He wasn't sure what his next move should be. Even worse, she was looking at him as if she'd never seen him before. He felt a little like he was a smear on a microscope slide.

"Well," she finally said reasonably. "You're scared."

"Yes," he admitted.

"Me, too," she said. "But I know that's not as big a news flash since I live with fear pretty much on a twenty-four-seven basis." She paused for a moment to draw in a deep breath. "I love you, too."

He stared at her, but the words were already sinking in. His mind might still be trying to absorb it, but his heart had softened and swelled.

"Pepper." He reached for her then and pulled her to him. "That *is* scary."

"Yeah." She drew in another deep breath. "And there's more. I want a new deal."

"You do?"

"Yeah, and I want more than the twenty-four hours we've had here."

"So do I."

"Good." She swallowed. "I figure we'll need it. I've got the Rossi curse to contend with, and we're as different as night and day, and we'll probably always be in competition at Rossi Investigations. So we're going to need a lot of time."

He drew back and looked down at her. "Yes, I can see that. How much time do you figure we'll need?"

"Quite a bit. I don't have any experience in long-term relationships."

"I'm a little short on that kind of experience myself."

She nodded. "One thing in our favor is that we both like to learn."

The gleam of humor that had come into her eyes had his lips curving. "We'll just have to give each other lessons." Taking her hands, he began to walk toward the gardens at the back of Butch's house. "We could start right now."

"Of course, you're a quick study. You'll probably get the hang of it right away. But I'm a slow learner."

"Thank God," he said as he drew her to a secluded part of the garden.

"Good thing you're patient," she said as they reached a spot that was out of sight of the house. The moment he stopped, she began to unbutton his shirt.

"As a saint," he promised as he pulled her T-shirt off. Then he enfolded her in his arms.

"Say it again," she said. "And this time, don't shout it."

"I love you."

She rose to her toes and brushed her lips against his. "I love you, too." Then with a laugh, she glanced at her watch. "But I don't think patience is what's called for right now. We only have fifteen minutes left of our first twenty-four hours together."

They were both laughing as Cole drew her to the ground.

Epilogue

One month later...

"I'M TOO OLD TO GET MARRIED." Irene frowned at her image in the mirror. "A woman my age should have more sense."

Pepper tugged on the hem of the antique lace jacket her aunt was wearing. "You're not too old." She knew enough about panic attacks to recognize one when she saw one, and she had to nip this one before it grew.

With a snort, Irene whirled away from the mirror and began to pace. "I should know better."

Through the glass wall, Pepper could see that the guests had all been seated in rows of chairs around the gazebo. Many of Irene's friends and co-workers had flown in from San Francisco, excited to be invited to a destination wedding. Irene was going to continue her TV show. She and Butch would visit San Francisco two months each year so that she could film the episodes. Many of the hotel staff members had also come to the wedding: Gari and Reynaldo, Marlene and Henry, and Tommy the concierge. Pepper had even spotted Tony, the poor man that Butch had sent to steal the Monet.

And they'd all been waiting patiently for almost ten minutes.

Flowers were everywhere, all over the gazebo and along

the path the bride should have walked down a full five minutes ago. The small band was starting on their fourth love song, "I Love You Truly."

The bride-to-be continued to pace. To the right of the gazebo, Pepper could see Butch pacing, with Cole and her father nearby. Now and then, Butch would shoot a glance at the house. Behind him, she could just make out her two brothers and H.

Pepper turned her attention back to Irene and sent up a short prayer that she could figure out the right thing to say. "What you have to remember is that you love Butch."

Irene whirled on her. "What does that have to do with anything? I love him and he loves me. Why does that mean we have to get married? Why can't we just go on as we are? Why mess with a good thing? That's what I say."

Pepper tried another tack. "Maybe after the wedding, things will be even better."

"Hah! Fat chance of that with the Rossi curse hanging over your head."

"I don't think you need to worry about that. You and Butch spent all those years apart and now you're together. I think you've broken the curse."

Irene pointed a finger at her. "That's exactly what Butch said when he talked me into agreeing to all this."

"He was right." Pepper could see Butch was now in a heated discussion with her father. Here and there, guests glanced curiously toward the house.

"Yeah, well, if Butch and I have broken the Rossi curse, then why aren't you and Cole setting a date?" Irene asked. "If I've got to do this, then so do you."

"Well, I—we're—still getting to know each other."

"And that's going well?"

"Yes." The truth was she and Cole hadn't talked about anything like marriage. They'd just been busy with work and being together and enjoying each other. Cole was even teaching her to cook.

"Good. Then why screw it all up by getting married? That's what I say."

Footsteps pounded on the veranda steps, and a moment later Butch burst into the room followed by Cole.

"Oh, shit," Irene muttered.

"What the hell is going on?" Butch asked.

Irene advanced on him pointing a finger. "You shouldn't be here. The groom shouldn't see the bride before the wedding. It's against the rules."

"I couldn't stop him," Cole murmured softly as he took Pepper's hand.

"I'm not having any luck with her either," she whispered.

Butch fisted his hands on his hips. "Do I look like a man who cares about the rules? I want to know why you're still in here."

"I'm in here because I don't want to do anything to ruin things between us, Butch Castellano." Taking his arm, Irene dragged him across the room and out onto the patio. "Look at all those people out there. You see the ones who are crying?"

"So? A few people are crying. People cry at weddings."

"Exactly." Irene spoke in a triumphant tone. "There has to be a reason for that."

Butch turned to study her for a minute. "You're scared, aren't you?"

Irene's chin lifted. "I'm not scared. I'm just trying to be smart."

Pepper tugged on Cole's hand. "We've got to do something."

"Maybe we won't have to. Don't look now but the troops are coming."

Sure enough, Pepper could see her father, Peter Rossi, a fit gray-haired man in a summer-weight suit, striding toward the veranda. To his right was Matt, a younger-looking version of her father, looking as if he'd just stepped out of the pages of *GQ*. And Luke, wearing chinos and a linen jacket, looked like he'd just pulled himself together after a day of surfing. A funny but warm feeling stirred in her stomach as she watched them climb the steps.

She turned to look at Cole and found that he was smiling at her. "Family," he murmured. "Riding to the rescue."

They *were* a family, Pepper thought. Her father, her brothers, and Cole. And for the first time she felt like she belonged.

"Irene, you want out of this?" her father was asking.

"No," Butch said, taking Irene's hand in his. "She doesn't."

"You want us to beat him up for you?" Matt asked.

"No," Irene said.

Butch turned to Irene then. "I knew from the first time I saw you that you were the one woman I wanted to marry. And I let you go. But I still had part of you in those letters. Then I got scared and stupid and I pushed you away. I was afraid if I let you come to the island and we got together, it would mess up what we had together. But it didn't, did it?"

"No," Irene said.

"Right." Butch nodded at her. "I'm not going to lose you again, Renie. I want more than a living arrangement. I want my ring on your finger, and I want to say the vows."

Pepper felt tears sting her cheeks as her aunt sighed, stepped into Butch's arms and laid her head on his shoulder.

After a moment, Butch spoke to Peter. "You can go out there and tell them we're coming."

Once Peter, Matt and Luke had left, Butch took Irene's hand in his. "You ready for this?"

She met his eyes steadily. "Yes. Let's do it."

Pepper felt the tears on her cheeks.

As they followed the bride and groom out, Cole turned to her. "*You* ready for this?"

Pepper stumbled as her heart stuttered and her throat dried. "You mean…?"

He glanced out at the garden as Butch and Irene walked through the flowers, hand in hand. "Yeah."

She looked into Cole's eyes, and suddenly, every part of her steadied. "Well. I think with a little time, I could be persuaded."

He went absolutely still, his eyes narrowing as he studied her. "How much time do you have in mind?"

She smiled slowly. "I thought that after the wedding we might sneak away to this place I know. How does twenty-four hours of persuading sound?"

He threw back his head and laughed. Several heads turned their way. Then he lifted her off her feet and kissed her hard. "You've got a deal."

UNCUT

Even more passion for your reading pleasure!

Escape into a world of passion and romance!

You'll find the drama, the emotion, the international settings and happy endings that you love in Presents. But we've turned up the thermostat a little, so that the relationships really sizzle.... Careful, they're almost too hot to handle!

Check out the first book in this brand-new miniseries....

Cameron Knight is on a dangerous mission when he rescues Leanna.

THE DESERT VIRGIN,
by Sandra Marton

on sale this March.

"*The Desert Virgin* has it all from thrills to danger to romance to passion."
—Shannon Short, *Romantic Times BOOKclub* reviewer

Look out for two more thrilling Knight Brothers stories, coming in May and July!

#243 OBSESSION Tori Carrington
Dangerous Liaisons, Bk. 2

Anything can happen in the Quarter.... Hotel owner Josie Villefranche knows that better than most. Ever since a woman was murdered in her establishment, business has drastically declined. She's very tempted to allow sexy Drew Morrison to help her take her mind off her troubles—until she learns he wants much more than just a night in her bed....

#244 WHAT HAVE I DONE FOR ME LATELY? Isabel Sharpe
It's All About Attitude

Jenny Hartmann's sizzling bestseller *What Have I Done for Me Lately?* is causing an uproar across the country. And now Jenny's about to take her own advice—by having a sexual fling with Ryan Masterson. What Jenny isn't prepared for is that the former bad boy is good in bed—and even better at reading between the lines!

#245 SHARE THE DARKNESS Jill Monroe

FBI agent Ward Cassidy thinks Hannah Garret is a criminal. And Hannah suspects Ward is working for her ex-fiancé, the man who now wants her dead. But when Hannah and Ward get caught for hours in a hot, darkened elevator, the sensual pull of their bodies tells them all they *really* need to know....

#246 MIDNIGHT OIL Karen Kendall
After Hours, Bk. 1

It's the trendiest salon in Miami...and landlord Troy Barrington is determined to shut it down. As part owner and massage therapist, Peggy Underwood can't let him—and his ego—win. So she'll use all of the sensual, er, *spa* tools at her disposal to change his mind.

#247 AFTERNOON DELIGHT Mia Zachary

Rei Davis is a tough-minded judge who wishes someone could see her softer side. Chris London is a lighthearted matchmaker who wishes someone would take him seriously. When Rei walks into Lunch Meetings, the dating service Chris owns, and the computer determines that they're a perfect match, sparks fly! But will all their wishes come true?

#248 INTO TEMPTATION Jeanie London
The White Star, Bk. 4

It's the sexiest game of cat and mouse she's ever played. MI6 agent Lindy Gardner is determined to capture Joshua Benedict—and the stolen amulet in his possession. The man is leading her on a sensual chase across two continents that will only make his surrender oh, so satisfying.

www.eHarlequin.com